# FATE OF AN ANGEL

The Dark Prophecy Series - Book Two
A Blood Prophecy Novel

BARB JONES

The Blood Prophecy Saga

The Blood Prophecy Trilogy

Queen's Destiny

Queen's Enemy

Queen's Ascension

The Blood Prophecy Novellas

Marcus: Origins

Chloe: Visions of the Future

Amber: The Birth of a Queen

Machiel: Stone of the Damned

Zaraquel: Moral Compass

The Dark Prophecy

Rise of the Hunter

Fate of an Angel

Published by Immortal Cravings Publishing, LLC
Venice, Florida
Paperback ISBN: 979-8-9922349-8-5
eBook ISBN: 979-8-9922349-9-2
First Edition
Library of Congress Control Number: 2026905994
Edited by Paige Lawson
Cover Design by Brandi Kae Designs

Acknowledgments

Fate of An Angel carries the weight of the world in this one book. This amazing journey would not be possible without the people who continue to support me, both in life and in the worlds I create with my writing.

Arianna & Kaiden: You are my everything. Every story, every character, every word comes from my feelings for you. You both have always been the best creations.

Mom: You have always been my best friend. I don't know how many more books I will write with you by my side, but each day is a treasured one to me. I finally got you to watch the reruns of Supernatural with me!

To my readers: Thank you for your ongoing support and messages. Your ideas come, sometimes at the right times, when I need them most. And like always, they find a way into the stories I create.

To my amazing team: editors, designers, formatters, personal assistants and more—I could not be where I am today without you. Your dedication allows me to write and create the worlds and characters for my readers.

The world of Blood Prophecy would not be where it is today without everyone. It has grown from a dream to a massive world, one in which the final book has yet to be written.

Barb Jones

Previously In The Blood Prophecy

The prophecy was never whole. It was spoken in fragments, carried across time by imperfect hands. Diana was never marked for protection, but for revelation. What began in Seattle did not end. Instead, it followed them to Hawaii, where the war did not die, only changed form.

The Tall Dark Man now moves within the Dark Prophecy itself. He does not question the cost, nor does he doubt its necessity. The blood spilled has only strengthened his belief.

The conflict is no longer distant. And it is not slowing down. He rules with intelligence and authority, making his mark on the angel, the one destined for the world. She will either fall or she will rise to save it.

PROLOGUE

THE SHADOW COVENANT

*Hawaii Island, 1795 — The
Battle of Nuʻuanu Pali*

Every kingdom is born from an agreement with the dark.

At the edge of the cliff, Kamehameha stood and watched the sea devour the last of his warriors. Below him, the valley steamed. The rain smelled of iron and men who had fought too long. Mud streaked the slopes, where crushed ferns and broken spears lay scattered like prayers gone unanswered. The wind bent the palms until they shuddered, carrying chants of mourning from Waiʻanae to Kāneʻohe. Victory had come, yet it tasted hollow.

The king looked at his hands, calloused and trembling. Though the rain rinsed the blood from his skin, it could not wash away the weight that settled in his chest. Behind him, his remaining warriors waited, their torches hissing in the downpour, eyes lowered, unsure whether to celebrate or grieve. Kamehameha lifted his gaze toward the dark line of the ocean, where lightning split the night sky.

"E Kū, e akua o ke kaua," he said quietly, his voice nearly lost to the storm. "The islands are one. The blood you asked for stains every stone. Give my people peace."

Thunder rolled, low and unkind. The mist thickened and glowed red beneath the firelight. From the heart of the storm, a figure emerged with skin black as basalt, eyes burning like veins of fresh lava. Kū stepped out of the rain, and each of his steps cracked the earth.

"Peace?" His voice was the sound of surf breaking against rock. "You feed me slaughter and now beg for quiet? Blood keeps the world alive. Peace feeds nothing."

The king bowed. Around him, his men fell to their knees, unsure whether they knelt before a blessing or a curse. A softer glow followed the storm's red haze, golden and steady. Kāne appeared first, carrying the scent of freshwater and breadfruit bloom. Lono came next, the sweetness of harvest in his breath. Kanaloa arrived last, his eyes deep as the tide. Lightning flared, stitching their forms together. Kamehameha sank to the earth, trembling beneath the weight of what he had called forth.

Kāne's voice was calm but edged with sorrow. "Enough, brother. The world is weary of thunder. Balance asks for life now, not more death."

Kanaloa's gaze drifted toward the sea. "The balance was broken long ago," he said softly. "Something stirs beneath the waves."

Even Kū fell silent when the ocean began to climb. It did not rise as a tide should; it clawed upward, as though pulled by something unseen. From that churning water came a figure, tall and lean, smoke curling from his shoulders. His eyes glowed with ancient fire, and the air turned heavy with the scent of burning earth.

"Who walks unbidden among the gods?" Kū demanded.

The stranger smiled. "I have worn many names," he said. "In your tongue, perhaps, Ka Kāne 'Ele 'ele Loa, *the Tall Dark Man*. I was born before your heavens found speech."

The mist thickened until breath itself became a struggle. Kamehameha clutched his fist to his chest as pain staggered his breathing.

"I do not seek worship," the stranger continued. "I came for the dead. Their souls rot beneath your feet. Give them to me, and I will give you peace."

Lono tightened his grip on his gourd of rain. "Peace bought with death is corruption."

The Tall Dark Man's smile faltered, though his eyes burned brighter. "Peace is the lie the living tell themselves to endure death."

Kāne's light dimmed. "You would unmake what we guard."

Kū took a step forward, hunger stirring again behind his eyes. "If I give you the fallen, what do you offer me in return?"

The stranger bowed slightly. "For every soul I take, your name will live in blood and memory. You will never fade."

Lightning tore across the ridge. The pact sealed itself without chant or ink.

Kamehameha watched in horror as the bodies below began to stir. Warriors rose from the mud, eyes glowing red, voices hollow. They turned toward the sea and marched into the storm, the first huaka'i pō, the Night Marchers.

Kanaloa whispered, "You have broken the balance, Kū. The sea remembers."

The Tall Dark Man tilted his head, his voice soft and certain. "Balance is a story told to frighten children. There is only will, and those strong enough to wield it."

He raised his hand, and the sea obeyed. Waves climbed the cliff and washed the blood away. When the water fell back, the beach was clean, the dawn pale and new.

The gods turned from him, and in the silence that followed, the rain ceased. Kāne lifted his hand and spoke no blessing. Lono let the harvest rot where it stood. Kanaloa drew the clouds across the sky to hide the stars, as if night itself could forget what had been seen. They agreed only on this: his name would never again be spoken upon the islands. But silence is not a weapon against memory. The covenant lingered in the blood of men who had heard him, in their chants, in the children they sired. The Tall Dark Man did not vanish. He waited.

And when the time came, when the descendants of those warriors called to their gods once more, he would answer—not as a stranger, but as a promise fulfilled.

CHAPTER I

MAGIC THAT BINDS

Zaraquel, The Witch's Cottage,
Present Day

Zaraquel had not slept properly in days, at least that was what it felt like when her eyes kept opening to the same ceiling beams and the same smell of wet roots and herbs hanging on strings that never dried. Sometimes the cottage hummed at night. The floors throbbed as if the ground remembered footsteps that were not hers and did not welcome her. She kept counting the creaks in the hallway because it helped her keep track of time since Nimue left through the hole and did not come back. Five days, or six. Maybe more. She couldn't tell anymore. The kettle hissed on its own now, and the mirrors fogged even when there was no fire lit.

She sat by the table Witch Anne called the heart, the one with the jars nobody should open and the picture she refused to look at because the eyes seemed to warm when the candles guttered. Her hands shook when she held the chalk. She had tried to sketch the sigil that would call Garnet Rose back to her hand, not to her mind, because her mind felt like a window with a broken latch. The chalk kept snapping. The sigil looked wrong each time. She wanted to blame the chalk, then the tea, then herself for taking anything that witch bitch offered when her belly pinched with hunger and her magic felt like a thread that could not hold a button anymore.

She pressed her palm to the floorboards and tried the small side spell again, the one she whispered under the old ritual when Witch Anne made her speak to shadows. Not to call Garnet Rose back. To send her. Find my father. Find Marcus. Take my light to him because he will not betray it.

The floor warmed beneath her feet. Something answered from far away. It made her breath catch. It also made her choke, because something else came right after, a voice that did not belong to her father, not to Rae, and not to Nimue.

Hello, little flame.

He always sounded tired of other people's prayers, even when he pretended to be soft.

She moved to the basin and threw water on her face and tried to think of nothing. That was impossible, because thinking of nothing is another way of calling the dark thing that waits for the empty places. She didn't want to hear his voice. Not now. Not ever.

She hated the mirror because it did not lie. The skin under her eyes carried a deeper shadow, and the lines at the corners of her mouth felt like someone had drawn them with a fine needle while she slept. The quick aging Uncle Mac promised would quiet had crept back in like a burglar who knew the latch. But this time, Zaraquel hadn't made any justified kills lately. She shouldn't be growing right now.

She pressed her fingers into her cheeks and lifted them and laughed under her breath. Then she stopped herself, because she heard Witch Anne's footsteps in the hall. There were only two kinds of footsteps here. Nimue's careful ones had been gone for days. Witch Anne's were patient. It is worse when patient people want something from you.

The witch appeared in the doorway without knocking, as usual, and the air bent toward her. It always did. The old witch carried a cup, and Zaraquel did not move toward it. She watched the steam curl and told herself not to drink anything she did not brew. It did not matter, because her hands were already reaching, polite hands raised by two people who taught her that good women say thank you when elders bring tea.

She took a sip and wanted to spit it back because something bitter lived at the bottom. She swallowed anyway. Maybe it was only bark. Maybe it was only fear.

"You need to practice the last binding," Anne said. "Your body will answer if your words are steady." Her voice took the edge off the room without softening anything. "You are close. Your balance will decide it."

Zaraquel wanted to tell her that balance meant both feet on the ground and a sky that did not hum and a friend in the next bed who made jokes when the dark pressed in. Instead, she nodded and followed her back to the room with the jars, the picture, and the words cut into the wood along the baseboard that looked like a prayer but tasted like a chain when spoken out loud.

She spoke them again. Her mouth knew them now. They scraped going down and left her throat sore. The candles burned low and then high, and she could feel something tug at her from the inside, the way a wave pulls at your ankles when the tide turns. She felt Rae nearby the way you feel a hand touch your shoulder from behind when the room is full and you know exactly who it is. She wanted to turn. She held the line like she had been taught.

It hit her then, the weakness that comes when a door opens but clears only enough space for a hand, not a body. She sat before she fell. The witch bitch brought her another cup and called it tea. The room leaned. The edges of the jars went soft. The picture on the wall brightened, and the Tall Dark Man's eyes shifted from black to ember.

Witch Anne touched her hair as if she were a child and told her to sleep. The hand was gentle, soothing. Zaraquel nodded. She did not mean to. She closed her eyes anyway. Her mouth moved on its own, and she breathed one word into her palm and pushed it down through the floor.

Daddy.

Marcus — The Order, Present
Day

The Order did not look like anything from the outside if you were not invited to see it. A single tower rose out of the empty like a trick of fog. The door showed itself when it was ready and not one second sooner.

Marcus kept his hand inside his coat, his palm against cold stone that made a humming sound only he could hear. The Totem of Death. He did not like the totem, and the totem did not like him, yet he was the only one who could touch it. He trusted Mac with the other one, because life in Mac's hands had always been the reason any of them were still breathing, an obvious choice.

Sabre moved ahead and then behind and then beside them, a shadow with a heart that could break stone when it needed to. Rowe and Kabos kept to the corners of the hall to avoid the light. Nimue lay quiet because they did not give her any choice. Marcus did not enjoy seeing a woman bound and blindfolded and carried like cargo, yet there was no other option until he felt they could trust her.

The door at the end of the hall breathed open. Marcus did not see the floor change, but he felt it. Mac spoke softly to the tower, and as he did, the stones brightened. A new corridor revealed itself.

Marcus did not get to take a step.

Pain drove a nail through his temple and shoved him sideways. He did not mean to show his fangs. He did not mean to climb the wall. He did not mean to growl. It was embarrassing, and it was familiar.

He heard her before he came back to himself.

Rae used his mouth to speak, and he would have cried if there had been time, because the feeling of her in his bones made him twenty years younger for one breath.

It broke like a wave and left him on his knees. He tasted iron and old smoke and remembered the first time he held his daughter and promised her that monsters would only ever see his back.

He stood because he still could. Mac steadied him with a hand that understood too much and not enough. The others asked questions he could not answer. He told them what mattered.

The Tall Dark Man had found a way to claim his daughter. Zara's light had already begun to dwindle, and her heart, though pure, was turning toward evil. He could hear Chloe's voice in his head, amused and angry, calling him stubborn. He held on to that too.

"Finish what we started," Mac said after the room quieted.

He spoke to Marcus as if he could hear him, but Marcus couldn't. The pain was unbelievably strong and distracted him. "Then we go to her."

Marcus nodded and did not trust his voice. He closed his eyes and bent his head and spoke to his little girl as if she could hear him. He told her the truth. He would come, or he would die trying. He told her the other truth. She had to hold her own light until he arrived.

Her answer was simple.

Hurry, Daddy.

He put his hand back on the totem. He hated the way it sounded to him.

*The Tall Dark Man — The
Underground, Present Day*

The Tall Dark Man did not worry when his witches walked by him with fear in their eyes. In fact, he loved it, and it only made the intimacy more intense when he was with them.

He walked through the halls with the new weight in his arms and smiled, because a child does not know he is a weapon until someone gives him a target. He had not needed to keep Tituba after all. The boy had taken one breath, and the child had learned a new master.

He handed the swaddled body to a nearby witch waiting at the nursery door and continued walking.

He paused in the corridor because a familiar scent still lingered. The vampire Michael. He stood in it for a moment and let himself feel the old irritation of his ally, his enemy, his servant, all in one.

They *never learn. They keep making kings and then crying when the crown burns.*

He opened a door without touching it, and the room was quiet. The wolf chained to the post snarled when he smelled him, then made a softer sound, because pain does that when one begins to submit.

The Tall Dark Man crouched. Animals understand height. He looked into eyes that were still Malakai's under all that fury. He did not touch him. He wanted to, but instead he let the wanting sit in his chest, because the wanting was part of the pleasure of bringing the animal to submission.

"You are going to be useful," he said. "You always wanted to be. The difference now is that I will not pretend your usefulness is a choice."

The wolf lifted his lips and showed him white. He admired the teeth.

He turned and left the room because there was time.

He returned to the nursery to watch his son.

Sabre, The Order Balcony,
Present Day

Sabre stood on the outer ledge where the tower met the dark. The air was colder than it should have been for that hour, and the moon looked too thin to offer light. He had not slept since they brought the witch back bound, and he doubted he would until Marcus gave the word to move.

The wind carried nothing but silence until it changed.

He caught it first, the shift that came before weather or magic. His claws scraped the stone when he leaned forward and tested the air again. Something was moving toward them that did not walk on the ground. It smelled like burnt sage and iron, the kind of scent that did not belong to death or to life but to something made from both.

Black Wind joined him without a sound. They did not speak at first because words were useless between them. Sabre felt the tension ripple through the other wolf's shoulders, the same pull that told him the pack bond still worked even when everything else was falling apart. They had been trained to scent the Tall Dark Man's reach, but this was not his. This was smaller, sharper, like a spark trying to rise in the middle of ash.

Sabre knew that smell could only mean one thing.

Demon.

"You feel it too," Black Wind said, his voice rough from disuse.

Sabre nodded. "It's close. But it doesn't carry his mark."

They waited.

The sky broke open above the valley without thunder or lightning, only a pulse that made the hairs rise along their spines. Sabre crouched low. The pulse came again, and within it he heard a girl's whisper. It was not Zara's voice, yet her name lived inside it.

Find my father.

A shape began to form in the air below the balcony, half smoke, half flame. It wavered like heat above stone and then solidified. The wolves backed away. When the smoke cleared, a woman knelt on the ground with her head bowed. Her skin carried a faint red shimmer, as if light moved beneath it.

She lifted her eyes, and for one moment Sabre forgot how to breathe.

The creature looked like no demon he had ever seen. There was pain in her, but no hunger. There was a sense of purity in her, something that reminded him of Zaraquel.

Black Wind's low growl broke the silence. "What is she?"

Sabre answered because he knew even before the demon spoke. "She's Zara's."

The woman raised her hand, palm open, showing a flicker of light that trembled like a heartbeat. "My name is Garnet Rose," she said. "I was sent to find Marcus. I have a message meant for him. It's urgent."

Sabre exhaled slowly and glanced toward the door that led to the inner hall. "Then you found him," he said. "Now we just have to make sure nothing else finds you first."

Marcus — The Order Hall,
Present Day

The door opened on its own before Sabre could knock.

The air filled with smoke as the door swung wide, a gust of wind and a hint of magic rushing in. Marcus stepped into the hall from the inner room because he felt it before he saw it. The hum in his pocket changed pitch. The Totem of Death had begun to shake against his hand as if it recognized what waited on the other side of the stone.

He pulled it free, and the moment the air touched it, the walls of the tower trembled.

Sabre stood in the doorway with Black Wind at his shoulder. Between them, the creature knelt. Her head was still lowered, and her skin carried that dull red shimmer that made the light bend.

For a moment Marcus thought she was one of the master's creations and reached for his knife. Then she lifted her face, and everything in the room shifted.

Her eyes were bright, not with fire but with something he had not seen in years. He recognized it too quickly.

His daughter's light.

It reminded him of the glow beneath the Blood Moon on the night Zaraquel was born.

"Mac," Marcus said, "you feel that?"

McPherson had already crossed the floor. He stood beside Marcus, close enough that their shoulders brushed. "Yes," he said, then paused. "It's her. Zaraquel sent this one."

Garnet Rose turned her palms upward. The air above them glowed white, and a soft hum filled the hall. It wasn't sound exactly; it was pressure, like a force pushing against them. McPherson began muttering words Marcus did not understand, his hands tracing invisible lines through the air.

The totem in Marcus's hand pulsed once in answer, and the tower lights flared.

Marcus took one step forward. "If you were sent by my daughter," he said, "say her name."

Garnet Rose looked up. "Zaraquel," she whispered.

The word rang like a bell struck underwater. The glow in her hands flickered, and a thin line of light ran from her palms to the totem, connecting them for a moment before vanishing.

Sabre and Black Wind both stepped back. Sabre's hand went to his chest. "That isn't just a name," he said quietly. "That was her calling him."

McPherson looked from the wolves to Marcus. "It's a binding," he said. "She poured part of her magic into this demon to keep it alive long enough to find you. But the link cuts both ways."

Marcus frowned. "Meaning?"

"Meaning she'll feel whatever happens to this creature," Mac said. "If it dies, the light dies with it. And if she loses too much of that light, she becomes what she's trying to fight."

Garnet Rose stood. The red light along her skin dimmed to the color of old wine. "I came with a message," she said. "He has her. The witch keeps her weak, and the master waits for her to break. The light is fading."

Marcus closed his hand around the totem. It went cold again, as if it understood.

He looked at Mac. "Then we go. No more waiting."

McPherson nodded once. "We go," he said. "But we take her with us. She's part of the spell now. And we bring Nimue. We need to know which side she has really chosen."

CHAPTER 2

THE BLOOD THAT CALLS

*The Tall Dark Man, The
Underground, Present Day*

The room was colder than it had been when he left. The fire had gone out long ago, yet the parchments still burned with their own light. The Tall Dark Man stood before the long table where the ink glimmered like oil.

He did not sleep anymore, though his body sometimes pretended.

The witches whispered when they thought he could not hear them. They said the child had not cried again since the birth, that he only stared at the ceiling and watched something they could not see. He liked that. It meant the boy already knew to listen for what most would never hear.

He reached for the parchment he had read a hundred times before. Tonight, it was different. The words that once refused him began to change shape, sliding across the page like small creatures that had been waiting to move.

He pressed a finger to the surface and spoke the names one by one until he came to the one he did not know.

The letters burned through the skin of his fingertip, leaving no mark, though the sting remained.

Illyris.

Flesh. Blood. Bone.

He understood then what had been missing. The last of the stones. The one that bound his dominion to the realm of the living and sealed his loss centuries ago.

The Queen's line had hidden it. The vampire's house had guarded it. The witch's hand had touched it. He had always known the heart of his defeat was buried where their lives met, but the parchment gave him more now. It told him who held the key and what words would open the spell.

"Flesh, Blood, and Bone."

He said them aloud, and the flames in the room turned blue.

He turned when he felt a presence at the edge of the chamber. The mirror in the corner clouded and then cleared. A woman appeared in the reflection, her face pale and her eyes darker than the last time he had looked upon her.

Mary.

The voice that had once trembled when she spoke to her betters now sounded calm. He admired that. Power always changed the way people spoke. He had given her a dangling carrot, and she had taken it. Her baby was the carrot, and she was his little white rabbit.

"Master," she said. "You called for me."

"I did." His voice was steady, unhurried. "You took a witch's gift and made it your own. You were clever enough not to die from it. You will prove yourself again. You tried to betray me, yet you lived. Now you will serve me in another way."

Her reflection did not move, though her hands tightened around something he could not see. "What do you ask of me?"

"There is a stone buried in the Queen's ground, under the estate where your mortal self once walked. You will go there. The guardian will not yield it easily. You will use what remains of Tabitha's power and take what is mine. Bring it to me intact. Do not fail me, Mary."

He watched her swallow, slow and deliberate. "And if the guardian resists?"

He smiled. "Then you will make him understand what obedience costs."

The mirror went dark before she could answer. He did not need to hear the words. The obedience was already written in her body.

He looked back at the parchment and the fire and thought of the girl whose light had flickered across his kingdom only hours ago. He would let her burn a little longer before he touched her again.

First the stone.

Then the father.

Then the angel.

Chloe — Honolulu, Present Day

The room was too quiet for her liking. Amber slept in her coffin while Chloe sat alone by the open window, the ocean pressed close enough to hear it breathe.

She had been reading through the old book Kawika lent her, a record of chants and burial rites that made her hands prickle when she traced the ink. Somewhere between one page and the next, the parchment darkened beneath her palm. The letters shifted into words she had not seen before.

Her throat went dry.

She had seen that writing once before in a dream she thought belonged to another life. A woman's hand had guided hers across a table rough with splinters. The candlelight had been uneven. The stench in the air unbearable.

When Chloe blinked, she was no longer in Honolulu.

She was back in the old room with low beams and a window nailed shut. The woman in front of her looked up and smiled without warmth.

"Blood remembers, even when it wants to forget," she said.

Chloe knew her name before the woman spoke it.

Sarah Good.

The ancestor she had studied, pitied, even defended for years. But now the woman stood alive before her, eyes too calm, voice clear as water.

"You have opened the book again," Sarah said. "That means it begins."

Chloe's mouth felt dry and heavy. "What begins?"

"The calling. It wakes what has been quiet too long. Our line was broken but not erased. You will need the blood to stand when the light falters."

The candle went out.

Chloe felt a breath against her ear that was not hers.

"Find the stone," Sarah whispered. "Before he does."

Chloe gasped and her eyes flew open. The room was bright again, the book on her lap blank and old as before. Amber still slept and would not wake until night. Outside, the wind had shifted.

She wiped her palms and stared at the sea until her breathing slowed.

Then she whispered the words Sarah had left her.

"Blood remembers."

Jerome — The Estate, Present Day

The halls of the estate had been silent for so long without the others around, especially Zaraquel. Jerome preferred it that way. The night held its own company: the refrigerator making ice, the clocks in the hall chiming, the distant sounds from outside.

He had finished polishing the brass handles of the main doors and locked everything twice before allowing himself the small mercy of his own room. He still set the kettle, though he no longer drank tea. Habit was a kind of prayer for him. It meant everyone was safe. And prayers, he had learned, were needed in times like this.

The room smelled of cedar and old books. On the low table by the window sat a wooden box no larger than his two hands. He had never opened it.

Michael had given it to him the year the estate was rebuilt, placing it in his care without ceremony.

You'll know when it's time.

Jerome had known him long enough to trust that tone. It was never a question, always an order.

Tonight felt like that time.

Something had felt off since the others departed in separate directions to save the little angel. That mischievous yet pure child he had grown to love as if she were his own granddaughter.

He sat, brushed the dust away, and undid the latch. The hinges groaned softly.

Inside, wrapped in linen, lay a small leather folio and a piece of jewelry. The folio held only a few lines written in Michael's sharp hand.

If the wards fail or the queen's power dims, the estate will call you first. The stone is not only earth and magic. It is blood. Protect it through her blood, not her crown. The words remain the same. Flesh, Blood, and Bone. Tell her to wear this when the sky burns.

Beneath the page lay the necklace. It was simple, a pendant of black coral bound in silver, faintly warm to the touch.

He felt the magic inside the pendant the way Chloe had taught him. She had once told him that each enchanted item awakens when its true owner has need. It was one of the many laws of magic she had shared with him.

Jerome exhaled through his nose and looked toward the dark window. He did not know what danger was coming, only that it was already moving.

He wrapped the necklace in fresh cloth and sealed it in a courier box. The address was simple:

Honolulu

c/o Ms. C. Tudor

He hesitated before writing *urgent* across the top.

When he finished, he sat again and looked at the open box. Michael's scent was long gone, but his presence still lived in the careful folds.

Jerome closed the lid and spoke softly to the empty air.

"Message received, old friend."

The Hunter — The Underground, Present Day

The child did not cry. He did not sleep.

His eyes stayed open, fixed on the ceiling above him, as if he could see through the stone walls. His body was still, but the air around him felt different somehow.

The witches avoided the nursery now. They said the master's son watched them even when his eyes were closed.

The Tall Dark Man stood in the doorway and said nothing. He did not like the smell of the room. It was too warm, too human. But he stayed.

The boy's chest rose, fell, and then stopped for a long moment. The silence deepened until it became a sound. Then the breath returned, and with it, something else.

Blood called blood.

Far away, Tituba stirred in her sleep and turned her face toward the wall. Her body still lived, though her spirit was bound, and through that thin tether the child reached for her.

The Tall Dark Man felt it too, a faint pull in his chest like a thread winding around his ribs. He clenched his hand.

The pull remained.

He stepped closer to the cradle. The child's eyes turned toward him, not red, not black, but a pale gray that looked almost silver in the light. He was smiling, though his mouth barely moved.

"You feel her," the Tall Dark Man said.

The air between them trembled. A faint sound, more thought than voice, passed through his mind.

She feeds me still.

He should have been pleased, but what he felt instead was the unfamiliar edge of caution. The bond had formed without his command.

He looked down at the small face and saw no fear there, only recognition.

"You will need her blood to live," he said. "That is the price of birth. But remember who named you."

The child blinked once.

The Tall Dark Man turned away from the cradle, his expression unreadable.

"Then she lives," he said to the empty room. "I will not end her. Not yet."

He left the nursery in silence.

Behind him, the child's eyes followed until the door closed.

CHAPTER 3

THE SERPENT'S BLADE

Nostradamus,

Salon-de-Provence, France, 1559

The candles burned low, and the air in the chamber smelled of crushed herbs. Nostradamus sat alone, bent over a table worn down by years of ink and prophecy. He had spent the night transcribing letters for the king's physicians, but the page before him was not medicine.

It was a warning.

The words had come unbidden, not from dream or divination, but from something older that slipped through his quill without his knowing. He had tried to stop and steady his hand, but the ink kept spilling into symbols he did not recognize. They moved like webs across the parchment.

He was still studying the lines when the door opened without a knock.

A tall man stepped inside, his cloak carrying the smell of death. Nostradamus knew at once this was no ordinary visitor. The man's presence filled the room like a sickness waiting to be named.

His voice came soft but deliberate. "Michel de Nostredame. I come for what you have written."

Nostradamus did not ask who he was. He already knew. Every seer who had lived long enough learned to fear the shadow that walked between names.

"You cannot take it," he said quietly. "The prophecy is not meant for you."

The stranger smiled. "Everything written for light belongs to me in the end. Your quill was only a tool. You wrote what I seek."

Nostradamus glanced at the parchment. The ink had begun to shimmer. In the center of the page, the words shifted again, forming the mark of a serpent coiled around a blade.

The stranger reached for it, but Nostradamus pressed his palm over the paper.

"If you take it, the world will lose its balance," he said. "Even you need the balance."

The man's eyes burned with quiet amusement. "The balance was broken long before your birth. Do not pretend your rhymes can mend it."

Nostradamus turned away and crossed the room to a chest against the wall. From it, he drew a narrow bundle wrapped in linen. When he unwrapped it, the steel inside caught the candlelight and shone black as obsidian.

"You will not have the verse," he said. "But I will give you the vessel."

He lifted the sword and cut his own palm, letting his blood trace the serpent carved along the hilt.

"This will hold what you seek until another hand calls it back."

The stranger's expression shifted, interest replacing mockery. "You would seal your own words in steel?"

"I would bury them where only blood may find them," Nostradamus said. "And one day, the blood of the serpent will return to claim it. Not before."

The Tall Dark Man's smile widened, thin and patient. "Then we agree."

He reached out and laid his hand over the blade. The candle flames turned white. The room filled with the whispering sound of steel awakening. Nostradamus felt his knees weaken.

The symbols on the page vanished, leaving only the words he had written before the possession began, his own, clear and human.

The stranger took the sword and held it as if it already belonged to him.

"The world will remember this as your prophecy," he said. "But it will serve mine."

He dissolved into the air, leaving only the faint scent of corruption behind.

Nostradamus fell to his knees. His blood still marked the serpent on a blade that was no longer there. He pressed his shaking hand to his heart and whispered,

"Then let it return in a time of reckoning, when those born of blood and light will stand together or burn apart."

Kawika Kekahuna — Honolulu,
Present Day

The rain had eased by the time Kawika reached the museum. City lights reflected off the wet pavement, and the air felt clean after the storm. Inside, the lights were low, the night security crew gone. The silence made the old building feel more like a chapel than a place of learning.

He liked it that way.

The museum had been in his family's care for three generations, filled with relics that carried stories older than most remembered to ask about. His heart always felt heavy when locals stopped asking about their own Hawaiian history.

Tonight, however, one relic called louder than the rest.

Malia met him near the back hall, barefoot as usual, her long dark hair tied in a knot. She held the keys to the restricted room, the one he kept locked even from some donors.

"Eh, Kawika," she said softly. "Why you like come so late? You look all bus' up. You okay or what?"

"Can," he said, but his tone told her no. "Something stay wrong. I felt um since da queen left. Like da air get heavy."

She nodded and opened the door.

Inside, the temperature dropped.

The case lights flickered once and steadied, casting a soft glow over the glass display at the center. Within it lay a sword unlike any of the others, dark steel bound with old filigree. It had arrived a month ago, labeled only: *French, sixteenth century, origin uncertain.*

Kawika had not been able to look at it long the day it came. The serpent carved into the hilt seemed to move when the light hit it just right. His heart had begun racing whenever he stood near it.

He reached for the case key but stopped when he heard a voice behind him.

"You feel it too, my friend," Philip said.

Kawika turned.

Philip stood near the doorway, rain still clinging to his coat, his presence making the room feel smaller. There was no mistaking what he was. The serpent mark on his wrist glowed faintly in the dim light.

"I told you before, this place not for outsiders at night," Kawika said quietly.

"I'm no outsider," Philip replied. "My blood built this curse, and now it has found its way back here."

He stepped closer, eyes fixed on the glass case.

"This blade belonged to a prophet who thought he could bind me. He failed. The seal still breathes, and now it calls to me."

Malia edged closer to Kawika. "What he talking about? Da sword?"

"Eh, Malia," Kawika said softly, "go wait outside."

"No way, Uncle," she said, stubborn but scared. "If this da kine trouble from before, I stay."

Philip smiled faintly. "Let her stay. The bloodline in this land will matter soon enough."

He lifted his hand, and the glass fogged from the inside. The sword began to hum, a low vibration that traveled through the floor and into their bones.

Kawika instinctively reached for his rosary, the one his grandmother had given him. It burned hot against his skin.

"Stop," Kawika said. "You bringing darkness in here. This blade stay under kapu. My kupuna say no touch."

Philip turned his gaze on him, calm but firm. "Your ancestors placed their faith in gods that fled the moment this island bled. My family's oath has no such mercy. This sword is not your burden to keep."

Kawika stepped forward, heart pounding. "Then why it here? Why the gods let um come to my island?"

Philip studied him for a long moment before answering.

"Because the serpent always finds the hand strong enough to lift it. You, Kahuna Kekahuna, are the guardian of balance whether you wished it or not."

The lights flickered again. Malia whispered a prayer under her breath. The hum grew louder until the carvings on the hilt glowed faintly red.

Philip reached toward it, but Kawika caught his wrist.

"You no take um," he said.

Philip's voice softened. "I don't intend to. Not yet. The queen will need it before the end, and you will give it to her when the time comes. Until then, keep it buried beneath your prayers. The moment you stop believing in them, it will answer to me instead."

Kawika's hand loosened. He did not know whether faith or fear made him step back.

Philip lowered his arm. The mark on his wrist faded.

"Eh," Malia whispered, "you mean Amber? The queen?"

Philip nodded once. "Her blood and mine have met before, long before her birth. When the serpent rises again, it will be her fire and the witch's light that decide which way it turns."

He looked at the sword one last time.

"Keep it safe, Kahuna. The blade remembers its maker, and the one who forged it is already watching."

When the door closed behind him, the light steadied.

Kawika let out a slow breath. Malia touched his arm, eyes wide.

"Kawika," she whispered, "what he mean by da serpent's blood?"

He looked back at the glass case. The blade was silent again, but in the reflection he thought he saw movement, a faint coil of smoke along the hilt like a sleeping snake.

"I dunno yet," he said. "But I tink we going find out soon."

Amber and Chloe, Honolulu,
Present Day

The wind off the ocean changed long before dawn. Amber felt it first.

She had moved her coffin to the room that faced the sea; something about the sound made it easier to rest. But when she opened the lid that morning, it was not the ocean she heard.

It was a low, pulsing sound.

Chloe stood by the window, her black hair loose, holding the small parcel that had arrived just before sunrise.

"It's from Jerome," she said. "No note. Just the necklace."

Amber rose, still weak from sleep and lack of feeding. The pendant caught the light. Black coral wrapped in silver. She could feel the power in it before she even touched it.

"Michael's work," she said softly. "He must have left it for me before he died."

Chloe nodded. "Jerome must have waited for a sign before sending it. You should wear it. He wouldn't risk that kind of magic unless he felt something coming."

Amber took the pendant and clasped it around her neck. The metal felt cold, then suddenly warmed against her skin. Her crescent-shaped birthmark began to heat beneath her touch. When her fingers brushed it, the warmth deepened, rising from both the mark and the necklace at the same time.

She closed her eyes and whispered her old name.

"Illyris."

At the sound of it, the necklace and her birthmark began to glow in unison.

Realizing the connection between the pendant, her mark, and her past life, she smiled at the thought of Michael.

Then she turned toward the window and frowned.

"It's quiet," she said. "Too quiet."

Chloe followed her gaze. The horizon had darkened though the sun was already high. The ocean was no longer blue but the color of steel.

"It's the same pull I felt last night," Chloe said. "I dreamed of Sarah again. She said something about the blood waking."

Amber did not like the sound of that. "Whose blood?"

"Maybe all of ours," Chloe said. "There's something on the island now that wasn't here before."

They did not have to wait long to find out.

The ground shook hard enough to rattle the glass on the table. The sky split open with a sound like thunder, though no clouds gathered overhead. Outside, the wind bent the palms backward, and a column of light flared in the distance over the museum district.

Amber was out the door before Chloe could stop her.

By the time they reached the street, the light had faded, leaving behind the sharp scent of metal and salt.

Amber's phone buzzed. Kawika's name flashed across the screen. She answered breathlessly.

"David?"

His voice came through, tense but steady. "Eh, Queen, you gotta come museum side. Somethin' wake up inside da old room. The sword one. Philip was here. He gone now, but he left somethin' behind. I no like the feel of um."

Amber met Chloe's eyes.

"The Serpent's Blade," she said. "It's awake."

Chloe pressed her lips together. "That means whatever bound it has weakened. Nostradamus warned the balance would bleed when the blade stirred."

Amber turned toward the road, the pendant at her throat glowing faintly.

"Then let's make sure it bleeds the right way," she said.

They started toward the museum. Behind them, the air already carried the scent of rain though the sky remained clear.

Elizabeth — The Underground,
Present Day

The chamber had cooled since the Hunter's birth, though no one dared say why.

Elizabeth sat alone beneath the stone vault where water ran thin across the floor, as it always did when something ancient stirred. The torches hissed and bowed, but she did not move. Her hands rested on her lap, still pale after centuries, veins faintly dark as if her blood remembered fire.

Above her, the Underground hummed with restless energy. She could hear the whisper of the master's witches, the shuffle of bare feet, the small sounds of fear pretending to be devotion.

She did not fear him. She had not feared him for a very long time.

The pool before her rippled though there was no wind. Her reflection wavered. Her own eyes looked back at her, but something behind them had changed.

She felt it then.

A pulse deep in the marrow of the world.

The serpent she had carried in her womb had turned in its sleep.

Her fingers trembled once. "It wakes," she said.

The sound of her own voice startled her. She had not spoken aloud in days.

The water darkened, then cleared again. Within it came another image: the ocean, distant but familiar, and a blade half buried in shadow. Its hilt burned red, and around it she could almost hear the murmur of the old tongue.

A name rose to her lips.

"Illyris."

She tasted it, and for the first time in centuries, she understood what it meant.

The Queen's blood, awakened by her lover's line.

Her eyes closed, and she whispered another name.

"Charlotte."

The first daughter of her darkness. The one who carried both light and shadow and forged a balance Elizabeth herself had never found.

"Your charm has been found, child," she murmured. "Your descendants will rise before the end."

The reflection shifted again.

This time she saw him. Not his face, but the shape of him, the weight of his shadow stretching across the wall.

He had not summoned her.

That alone made her uneasy.

"I felt it," his voice said, though he did not appear. "The serpent's heart stirs."

Elizabeth bowed her head. "The blade," she said. "It calls to its maker. Philip's blood still walks the earth, and through it, my line answers. You cannot stop what you began."

Silence filled the chamber.

Then the air grew warmer, and the torches flared until smoke gathered at the ceiling. His laughter came low and soft, the kind that made her bones remember the first time he had spoken her name.

"Do you think I wish to stop it?" he asked. "Let it wake. Let it cut. The world is ready to bleed again."

His presence faded, leaving the echo of his words behind.

Elizabeth stared into the pool until her reflection steadied. Beneath her calm, she felt something she had not felt since the days of her mortal heart.

Pity.

Not for herself.

Not for him.

But for the children who would soon carry both their sins.

She rose slowly, joints stiff from centuries of kneeling.

"So be it," she whispered. "Let the serpent rise. But remember, my love, its first bite was mine."

CHAPTER 4

THE LIGHT UNMADE

Zaraquel, The Witch's Cottage,
Present Day

She woke to the smell of smoke and salt.

The walls were whispering again, though she could not make out the words this time. Either she was imagining it, or the witch bitch had done something to her. The sound came from the cracks that had begun creeping across the ceiling.

Her arms felt heavy. Her body was colder than it should have been.

Witch Anne stood near the hearth, bent over a bowl that steamed with something darker than water. In the shifting light, the old woman's hair looked different. The gray was gone. The strands were black again, as if the years had decided to run backward.

"You slept too long," Witch Anne said without turning. "The world does not wait for those who dream."

Zaraquel pushed herself upright. The motion made her head swim. She caught her reflection in the nearest jar: the faint shimmer of wings behind her, one pale, one dark, both only half formed.

"What did you do?" she asked.

Witch Anne smiled at the fire. "You should thank me. You were breaking apart. I took the sickness from your light before it killed you. I put it where it belongs."

She lifted the bowl.

Inside it, a crystal glowed faintly, the same deep red her wings had once been. It pulsed like a heart, though dimmer than before.

Zaraquel felt it instantly. The tug in her chest matched the rhythm of the crystal's glow.

"Give it back."

Anne turned then, eyes bright. "You still think it belongs to you. It never did. That light was given to you to cherish, but you chose to learn the dark. You must stand without it if you are to balance both. Otherwise, one will consume you."

Zaraquel swayed but stayed upright. "You're lying. You want to feed him. You're going to give it to him."

"The master will take what is his when the time is right. You will help him, whether you want to or not."

The floor shifted beneath her feet. She reached for the table to steady herself. The jars on the shelves began to tremble. The runes carved into the walls glowed red, then white, as if the house itself could no longer bear the strain of the magic.

Something deep inside Zaraquel cracked open.

"You can't keep me here," she said, her voice breaking. "I want to go home. Now."

The wind outside rose. The door slammed shut on its own. The jars shattered one by one, spilling smoke that smelled of herbs and blood.

The crystal in Witch Anne's hand flared brighter.

Zaraquel raised her palms and focused on her father's face, on Rae's voice, on anything that was not fear.

The light came.

It was not much, but it was enough to split the air between them.

Witch Anne shouted a word that made the walls shake. The light twisted and snapped back into Zaraquel's chest, throwing her to the floor.

She could not move.

Her mouth filled with the taste of metal.

The witch crossed the room and crouched beside her. "You're stronger than I thought," she said softly. "But you're still mine until he says otherwise."

Zaraquel forced her head to lift.

She saw the crystal flicker and then shatter in Witch Anne's hand. The light escaped in a thin stream that rushed toward the chimney and vanished.

Witch Anne cursed under her breath. "Foolish girl. You sent it to him."

Zaraquel smiled through the blood on her lip. "Not him," she whispered.

Her vision blurred. She heard the witch moving, the kettle being set back on the fire.

The witch's voice came closer.

"Drink. You need to sleep again. The master will be here soon."

The cup touched her mouth. She swallowed because she could not stop herself.

The world tilted sideways.

The last thing she heard before darkness took her was the witch's voice, low and certain.

"Almost ready. The bride will rise in shadow."

Marcus — The Order
Courtyard, Present Day

The tower shook hard enough to rattle stone from its foundation.

Marcus was on his feet before the second tremor struck. The totem in his coat pulsed against his chest as if something inside it had awakened in anger.

Across the courtyard, McPherson was already tracing symbols in the air, eyes tracking the streak of light that had sliced through the ceiling wards like a blade.

"Zara," Marcus said, his voice rough. "She sent it."

McPherson nodded once. "I felt it too. That wasn't a cry for help. That was power. The kind that snaps every seal between here and wherever she is."

Sabre had his hand on the hilt of his blade, claws half drawn. "If she's still alive, we go now. The witch won't wait for a second chance."

Before Marcus could answer, metal struck stone behind them. Nimue had woken.

The bindings around her wrists smoked where they touched her skin, but she was not fighting. She sat very still, her eyes clearer than before. Garnet Rose crouched a few steps away, her glow flickering like a dying ember.

"Easy," Marcus said, moving closer. "You've been out for days."

Nimue lifted her head. "I know. I felt her."

"You felt Zaraquel?"

She nodded. "She's still fighting, but Witch Anne is draining her. You won't reach her in time unless you trust me."

Sabre gave a low growl. "Trust is hard to earn after you sold your soul to the Tall Dark Man."

Nimue did not flinch. She looked directly at Marcus.

"I gave him power once. I won't give him her. You think I stayed alive all these years for his sake? He forgot what he made me. I remember."

McPherson stepped beside Marcus. "If you're lying, we end you before we reach the forest."

"Then kill me now," she said calmly. "Because the longer you wait, the more she forgets who she is. He wants her memory gone before he touches her."

Marcus saw Rae's face behind his eyes. Heard Zara's voice saying *not him.*

He made his decision before his next breath.

"Unbind her."

Sabre hesitated, but McPherson lifted his hand. The ropes fell loose.

Nimue rubbed her wrists once and stood, steady.

"Now what?" Sabre asked.

McPherson opened the Totem of Life.

A cold wind swept through the courtyard, carrying the scent of rain and smoke.

"Now we move," he said. "The bond between them is strong enough to guide us."

Garnet Rose rose to her feet. Her skin flared bright red, her eyes burning like coals.

"She's calling," she said. "I can follow it."

The ground split open in a line of light. McPherson's spell turned the air to water, and the tower's wards screamed as they bent.

Marcus took one last look at the stones that had sheltered them for centuries.

Then he stepped forward.

The rift widened. Lightning crawled across the courtyard floor. Nimue raised her hand, weaving protection over them as the magic buckled. Sabre shifted, the wolf in him rising to meet the scent of war.

"Let's bring her home," Marcus said.

They vanished into the light, leaving the courtyard empty but for the echo of Zaraquel's name ringing through the tower.

Kawika Kekahuna —
Hōnaunau, Present Day

The sky over the bay turned gray without clouds.

Kawika stood on the old lava shelf where his family had fished for generations, his feet sinking slightly into wet stone. The ocean should have been loud this close to the reef, but it was quiet now, the kind of quiet that made even the birds stop flying.

He did not need to look at the horizon to know something sacred had shifted.

The air smelled wrong. Salt, yes, but also something sweeter, sharp like burnt sugar.

Malia came running down the path. "Eh, Kawika. You feel dat?" Her voice shook.

He nodded. "Not da ocean. Da mana. She pulling back."

The tide had reversed itself. The waves crawled outward instead of in, dragging sand and coral with them. Out where the deep water began, a light flickered once and then vanished.

For a moment, the sea looked like glass.

Behind them, the wind rose through the palms with a sound almost like chanting. Old voices. The kind his grandfather used to hear before a storm.

Kawika dropped to one knee and pressed both hands to the lava.

The rock was cold.

Lava had formed their land. It should have carried life. But he felt nothing now.

He looked up at Malia. "Get da kupuna on da line. Call everybody. Somethin' happen to da light. Not da sun. Da one inside."

She ran toward the house.

He stayed kneeling until the first bird cried out again.

Only then did he whisper the old prayer for protection, the one his tūtū had taught him when he was a boy. The words trembled on his tongue.

Far offshore, a single wave began to rise against the others.

Kawika stood and backed away from the edge.

He did not know what the wave would bring.

Only that it was not water alone.

CHAPTER 5

WHEN THE ISLAND BREATHES WRONG

Chloe, Honolulu, Present Day

The first thing she noticed was the light. It had gone dull, the color of old brass instead of gold, as if the morning sun had lost its will. The air pressed heavily against the glass. Out past the hotel balcony, the palms leaned toward the sea, not from wind but from something beneath the ground. Amber slept below, the coffin sealed tight in the corner of the room. Chloe could hear the faint sound of her heartbeat, slower than usual. Even in sleep, the queen responded to the balance.

She reached for the book that lay open on the table. Its pages fluttered though the windows were closed. The ink bled across the paper, forming a single word she hadn't written.

Illyris.

Her stomach tightened. She could feel the same vibration running through her own blood. "Zaraquel," she whispered. The name made her heart ache for her daughter. A mother's love knew no bounds.

The ocean shifted. From her vantage point, she could see the line of white break just offshore, a perfect circle forming on the surface, a whirlpool without current. Then the birds began to scream.

She ran to the coffin and pressed her hand against the lid. "Amber, wake up," she said. "Something's wrong. The island's mana, it's turning inside out."

The lid shuddered. A muffled voice came through, slow, thick with the weight of day. "How long till nightfall?"

"Too long," Chloe said. "Kawika will feel it. We need to warn him."

The lights flickered, every bulb in the suite blinking once, twice, then steadying at half their brightness. From the street below came the sound of car alarms and the sudden chorus of dogs howling.

Amber's voice came again, clearer now. "He'll know before we reach him. The land always calls its own first."

Chloe turned back to the window. The whirlpool had vanished, leaving only flat gray water.

"Then the call has already gone out."

Kawika Kekahuna, Hōnaunau,
Present Day

By the time Chloe and Amber felt the disturbance, the kupuna were already gathering at the old compound. Kawika stood in the center of the courtyard, ringed by torches that refused to burn steadily. Malia stood beside him, her phone lighting up with messages from across the island, fishermen, priests, cousins on other shores, all saying the same thing: something was wrong with the land and the sea.

His uncle Jonah arrived last, leaning on his stick carved with shark teeth. "Da ground no hum today," he said. "I feel um go still since da night."

Kawika nodded. "Da light break somewhere. Da mana pull back."

Jonah spit into the dirt, an old gesture to ward off evil. "If da light unmade, da dark go fill um fast. You call da queen?"

"She know already," Kawika said. "But we no can wait on haole time. We got our own way. Da queen needs to sleep till dark."

He motioned for Malia to bring the bowl of salt water from the altar. When she set it before him, the surface was smooth as a mirror. Kawika held his hands above it and began the chant his grandmother taught him, a prayer to wake the sleeping gods. The others joined, their voices weaving with the rhythm of the surf.

The water darkened, rippling with light from beneath. For a moment, faces moved across the surface, ancestors, guardians, maybe even gods. Then the image cleared.

What they saw made the elders fall silent.

A young woman lay on a stone floor, her skin pale, wings flickering like broken light.

Malia's hand flew to her mouth. "Da angel Zaraquel. Chloe's daughter," she whispered.

Kawika closed his eyes. "She broke da balance," he said. "Now da island go bleed till she make um right."

The torches flared blue, then steadied. Somewhere beyond the reef, thunder rolled where there were no clouds.

Kawika looked to the sea and whispered, "Hold fast, girl. We coming."

Mary, Seattle, Present Day

The storm rolled over the city, heavy and low, the kind that made the glass rattle in the windowpanes and people panic on the road. Mary moved through the narrow house the Tall Dark Man had given her, barefoot, careful not to wake the child in the next room.

Elijah slept with one hand curled beside his face, the faint glow under his skin pulsing slowly. She had learned not to question it. The light wasn't human. It came from the spell that had pulled him back.

She stood at the crib and brushed his hair away from his forehead. "My sweet boy," she whispered. "Sleep."

The candle on the dresser flared blue. The floorboards shuddered once. Elijah's eyes flew open, bright silver for a second, and every candle in the room went out.

"Not now," she whispered. "Please, not now."

Her wrists burned. The markings that had been quiet for months blazed like hot iron, Tabitha's power roaring awake. The magic inside her turned against its master. The child began to cry, not with fear but with pain.

Mary lifted him into her arms. "Shh, baby, mama's got you."

But the voice that answered wasn't his.

It came from everywhere at once, layered and low.

The light is undone. The bond frays.

The air grew cold. The scent of brimstone slid into the room. Then came the Tall Dark Man's voice, soft and terrible.

"Do you feel it, my sweet Mary? Even resurrection bends when the heavens break. Keep the child still. His blood must not awaken before I command it."

She turned toward the corner where his shadow gathered. "You said he'd live," she said, her voice trembling.

"He does. But light calls to light, even from the grave. When the angel's heart broke, the world remembered what it lost."

Mary clutched Elijah tighter. The glow beneath his skin dimmed, then steadied. She looked down and whispered, "I won't let you take him again."

The Tall Dark Man laughed softly, the sound spreading through the walls. "You already did."

When the air stilled, the room smelled of death. The child slept again, but his pulse beat in time with a rhythm Mary didn't recognize, not death, not life, something caught between.

Raven, Romania, Present Day

The storm hadn't stopped for days, but tonight the thunder felt closer. The manor's walls creaked, old mortar shifting with each roll of wind. Raven stood at the high window watching the trees bend, her reflection cut through by lightning.

The mark on her throat burned again. She pressed her fingers to it, willing it quiet.

Behind her, Arioch stirred. The sound was not words at first, just a low rumble deep in his chest, the kind that meant danger. His arms flexed once, shaking dust from the rafters.

"What is it?" she asked without turning.

He made the sound again, this time shaped just enough to form words. "Bright. Burn." He clawed at the air as if trying to hold something that wasn't there. "Hurts."

Her pulse jumped. "You feel him?"

Arioch nodded, heavy and slow. "Master...scream."

Raven turned. His eyes glowed a dull red, and for a moment she thought she saw cracks running through the stone of his skin. "He never screams," she said.

The demon crouched, panting like a beast in pain. "Light. Cut him."

She moved to his side, tracing a sigil in the air that should have soothed him. It didn't. The mark at her throat pulsed again, weaker this time.

"Something broke," she murmured. "Not him, not yet, but something close."

Arioch's head tilted, his nostrils flaring. "Smell witch," he said. "Tudor."

Her hand froze. "Chloe?"

He gave a slow, uncertain nod, then looked at her as if waiting for orders. The bond between them, the same one Chloe had touched months ago, quivered with faint light before dimming again.

Raven looked back toward the storm. "No," she whispered. "Not now. Not her."

Arioch let out a low growl. "Master call. Go?"

She hesitated. The mark on her throat had stopped burning. For the first time since she had taken it, she couldn't hear the Tall Dark Man's voice in her head.

Only the wind.

"No," she said softly. "Not this time."

Arioch blinked at her, confused. "No go?"

She met his eyes. "We wait."

He didn't understand the words, but he understood her tone.

The storm outside cracked again, lightning flashing against his stone skin. Raven looked at him and felt the faintest sting of something she hadn't allowed herself in centuries.

Doubt.

Chapter 6

The Rift Between Worlds

Marcus, Between Realms,
Present Day

Marcus barely had time to draw breath before the ground vanished. The world turned inside out, and everything that held weight became smoke. McPherson's voice reached him from somewhere ahead, low and steady, chanting in the old tongue to keep the crossing stable.

It didn't work.

The rift pulled harder than anything Marcus had ever felt. The colors around him twisted, black bleeding into gold, red into silver, until nothing looked real anymore. Sabre fell first, half-shifting, claws scraping the air as if he could catch hold of it. Black Wind tried to grab him, missed, and vanished into the same whirl of light. Garnet Rose burned brighter than all of them, her body a torch of red flame cutting through the storm.

"Hold the line!" McPherson shouted.

Marcus reached for anything solid and found Nimue's wrist. Her skin was cold, almost stone, but her eyes were alive. "You said you could guide us," he said. "Do it."

She didn't answer right away. Her lips moved soundlessly. The markings on her arms began to glow, spreading up her neck like veins of fire. The magic in her blood had been sealed by the Tall Dark Man, and now she was breaking it.

McPherson saw it and started forward. "Stop! You'll tear the rift open wider!"

"I already did," Nimue said. Her voice was calm, but the air crackled around her. "It's the only way through."

The rift screamed. It sounded like metal dragged across stone, like a thousand voices crying out at once. Marcus felt the pull in his chest, the familiar spark that told him his daughter was on the other side.

"Zara..." he whispered.

The light answered.

Shapes formed in the air, her face, her eyes, her voice calling for him. For a moment, he thought he could reach her, but then the vision shifted. Her face went pale, her mouth opening with a scream he couldn't hear. Behind her stood Witch Anne, holding the broken crystal in her hand.

Marcus shouted her name, and the vision shattered.

Garnet Rose moved between them, spreading her arms wide. The red fire of her body turned white, bright enough to blind. The rift buckled, then snapped shut around them.

They hit the ground hard.

The air returned all at once, thick and wet with the smell of rain. Trees surrounded them, black bark slick with mist. The sky above was the wrong color, too green, too low.

Sabre landed next to Marcus and shook himself back into his human form, blood running down his arm. "Next time," he said, "we take a damn door."

McPherson was already scanning the treeline. "This isn't Earth," he said. "It's a reflection of it. The Witch's Forest."

Marcus pushed to his feet. "Then she's close."

Garnet Rose knelt in the dirt, her hands pressed to the ground. "I feel her. She's weak, but she's fighting."

Nimue staggered forward, her skin gray, eyes dim. "You see now why I broke the seal," she said. "He built this place from her fear. It feeds on the light she lost."

Marcus moved toward her. "If you ever betray her again, I'll kill you myself."

Nimue's smile was tired. "If I do, you won't have to."

Thunder rolled somewhere beyond the trees. The sound wasn't from the sky. It came from the ground. The forest shifted, roots twisting like snakes. McPherson drew a circle in the air, a ward of containment. It held for a second before the earth split open beneath their feet.

From the crack rose a figure made of ash and smoke, its face wearing Zaraquel's.

It whispered, "Daddy," and reached for him.

Marcus didn't hesitate. He drove his blade through the illusion's chest. The figure screamed once and vanished in a burst of light. The forest went silent again.

McPherson exhaled. "He's testing you. Every step closer, he'll use her image to break you."

Marcus wiped the ash from his blade. "Then we walk through hell until she's real again."

They started forward, the path lighting itself one stone at a time beneath Garnet Rose's glow.

Kawika, Hōnaunau, Present
Day

Kawika stood on the black rock at the edge of the sacred bay, the Serpent's Blade resting across his palms. The metal, dulled for months, pulsed with a faint red glow.

Behind him, the kupuna gathered in a half circle, wrapped in shawls the color of dark gray. None of them spoke. They didn't need to. The island had spoken to them in ways only they could understand.

The air felt wrong. It was heavy, not with heat or dryness but with weight, the kind that pressed on the chest and made one's lungs feel vulnerable to pain.

Malia approached from the stone path, carrying a calabash of saltwater and ti leaves. "Uncle," she said quietly. "The sharks moved close to shore again."

He nodded without turning. "They know what's coming."

When he raised the Blade, the sun's glow glistened against the metal as it began to come alive in his hand. Deep inside, the old prophecies murmured.

Blood of kings and witches shall reforge the blade, and through the serpent's blood, balance is remade.

Kawika could feel that blood calling now, not from Hawai'i, but from somewhere beyond the veil, where the living and the dead no longer obeyed their boundaries.

A rumble shuddered through the stone under his feet. Not an earthquake, not wind, but something deeper, as if the island itself had been struck.

He heard his grandmother's voice from long ago, the first lesson she ever gave him about mana.

When the island breathes wrong, child, it is not the weather. It is the world remembering a promise.

"The veil opened," Malia whispered.

He looked up. Above the western horizon, the clouds twisted inward, forming a dark spiral that pulsed with gold at its center.

"Not opened," he said. "Torn."

The kupuna began to chant, low and rough, a sound older than language. Kawika joined them. The rhythm steadied the ground, but it could not calm the Blade. It burned in his hands now, and he saw the reflection of a forest he did not know, trees black with mist, a sky too green, a girl's voice crying for her father.

He stumbled backward.

Malia caught his arm. "What did you see?"

"The other side," he said. "They crossed over."

She frowned. "Who?"

He wiped the sweat from his brow and looked at the sea again. The horizon was bleeding into the water, a thin line of light like a wound that refused to close.

"The ones tied to prophecy. The witch, the vampire, the wolves. The angel's father. They are walking through hell to bring her back."

The chant behind him faltered. One of the elders, a woman whose eyes had gone milk-white decades ago, reached for him.

"If they walk there, then the Tall Dark Man walks here."

Kawika swallowed hard. "Then we prepare."

He pressed the Blade point-first into the rock until it rang.

"Wake the guardian," he said. "Before the world forgets how."

As the kupuna's chant rose again, the surf began to move backward, pulled out to sea. The wind smelled of salt and old blood. Beneath the surface, something vast stirred, not evil, not good, only ancient.

Kawika lowered his head. "E mālama ke ao." Protect the light.

Far offshore, a glow beneath the waves brightened in answer to the call, and the people saw it.

Zaraquel, The Witch's Forest,
Present Day

The light came from nowhere and everywhere. It hung in the air above her like a thought that would not fade.

Zaraquel lifted her head and, for a moment, believed she was back at The Order. The bed beneath her was soft. A breeze moved through the curtains. Somewhere nearby, water dripped in a slow rhythm.

Then she smelled it.

It wasn't rain but something like burned earth and spoiled roses. The sound of the drip was not water at all, but blood falling in the distance from where the trees began.

She sat up.

The room changed as she moved. Curtains melted into vines, the bed into roots that slithered back into the ground. She was standing now, surrounded by slick trunks shrouded in mist. Every surface pulsed faintly, breathing in the rhythm of her heartbeat.

"Rae?" she whispered.

The forest answered with a young woman's laugh, thin and soft, carried from everywhere at once.

She turned toward the sound and saw her.

Rae stood at the edge of the clearing, hair in that same pixie cut, eyes bright, smile alive.

Zaraquel's knees went weak.

"You came back," Zaraquel said.

Rae tilted her head, the motion too sharp, the smile too still. "Did you miss me?"

Zaraquel took a step closer. The ground was wet, not with water but with something thicker. It clung to her boots. When she looked down, she saw her reflection in the black surface, but her eyes were wrong. The light in them flickered red.

"Where am I?" she asked.

"You never left," Rae said. "You've always been here."

The girl's skin began to pale. Her lips turned the color of ash. Zaraquel reached out to touch her, and her hand passed through smoke. Rae's face wavered, dissolving into the form of another woman, older, sharp-eyed, hair the color of bone.

Witch Anne smiled.

"Your heart makes such beautiful cages," Anne said. "All I had to do was build around it."

Zaraquel stepped back, her wings twitching with panic. "Let me out."

The witch moved closer. "Out? There is no out. You wanted Rae, and I gave her to you. You wanted love, and I showed you how easily it breaks. You wanted power." She touched Zaraquel's chest, and cold slid beneath her skin. "That is still mine."

Zaraquel felt the pull, the draining warmth that always followed the witch's touch. She tried to fight it, to summon light, but her palms glowed only faintly before the forest swallowed the glow.

"You think your father will save you," Anne said. "He walks the edges of my world now. Every step he takes, I see through his eyes. Every breath he draws, I taste his fear."

Zaraquel's throat tightened. "He's coming."

Anne's smile widened. "Then I will be ready."

The light above flickered again. For a heartbeat, Zaraquel saw another world, her father's hand reaching through mist, a flash of the Serpent's Blade glowing red across distant water.

Then it was gone, and the forest was dark once more.

She sank to her knees, palms pressed to the ground, whispering her mother's words like a prayer.

"Light endures."

The soil trembled beneath her, and something below the roots whispered her name.

"Hold on," it said. "I'm coming."

She closed her eyes. The voice was faint, but she knew it as clearly as day. It was her father's deep, steady voice.

The forest howled in answer.

The Tall Dark Man, The Underground, Present Day

He stood where no light belonged. The walls around him breathed like lungs made of smoke. Every sound in creation reached him there, every heartbeat that still feared the dark.

The forest's cry was the first thing he felt, a tremor that moved the world around him and made him think of his little angel. The girl had broken the silence of his realm. Her light had touched its roots.

He could taste it and feel its purity, yet he knew she was suffering. This was the moment before her final break into submission. The only thing he wondered was how much longer she would last before she fell to her knees.

He raised his hand and saw the burn across his palm. It was not blood, but something worse.

It was memory.

"So, the child remembers," he murmured. His voice filled the chamber and came back to him like thunder.

A shape moved in the dark beside him, the witch who bore his mark. Tituba knelt, her forehead touching the black floor.

"Master," she said. "The rift trembles. The forest bends but does not break."

He watched her for a long moment before speaking. "The vampire crossed."

"Yes."

"And is a certain witch with him?"

"Yes. She has broken your seal," Tituba whispered.

He smiled without warmth. "Good. Let her. The seal was meant to hold only until the forest learned her name."

He turned toward the far wall, where a cradle of bone and crystal stood waiting. Inside it, a child slept, breath shallow, eyes moving behind closed lids.

The Hunter.

His creation. His weapon.

The Tall Dark Man laid a hand over the cradle. Shadows rippled across its surface like black water.

"He grows too slowly," he said. "The world shifts faster than time allowed. I will not wait for prophecy to choose its moment."

Tituba lifted her head. "You would break the law of death."

"I wrote it," he said.

He reached into the cradle and touched the boy's chest. A spark leapt from his fingers. The child gasped and opened his eyes, pupils glowing white, mouth forming a word that demanded to be spoken.

The Tall Dark Man listened and smiled.

"Father."

The word echoed through the shadow realm and out into every world that still dreamed. The walls trembled. The air thickened. In the Witch's Forest, a thousand roots twisted in pain.

The Tall Dark Man lowered his hand and straightened.

"The veil is open," he said. "Let them come. The end has already begun."

He walked back into the dark as the light in the cradle grew, not golden, not pure, but the color of fire seen through smoke.

CHAPTER 7

THE SERPENT CRIES

Amber, Hōnaunau, Nightfall

The compound had gone silent after sundown. Even the waves appeared calm at first sight. Amber sat in the open chamber with the Serpent's Blade across her knees. The metal no longer felt cold; it pulsed with a slow rhythm, like a living heart. She ran her thumb along its edge and watched a line of light travel the length of the blade until it reached the carved serpent on the hilt.

The serpent began to move.

She whispered the old prayer Chloe had taught her to calm relics, but it was no use. The blade reacted as if it remembered something while she held it.

A noise sounded from outside, and the room shuddered. The oil lamps dimmed. In the blade's reflection, she saw not her own face, but that of another woman—Elizabeth Hexham. The scent of iron and ash filled the hall, and the vision pulled her under.

England, 1564

Elizabeth knelt in the road, skirts heavy with mud, eyes locked on the boy who was not a boy. Sammael's smile was too wide, his voice too smooth.

"From thy womb and my seed will arise the world's most ruthless witches of all time. The Alchemy of Three will lead to the opening of a new world, my world."

Amber felt Elizabeth's terror, her hunger, the touch at her throat, the first serpent mark burning into skin.

The vision shifted to Philip of Macedon writing in blood, a crown falling, the same sigil searing into his wrist. His voice followed:

Blood of kings and witches shall reforge the blade.

Amber gasped, and the blade dropped to the mat. Blood ran down her palm, where the serpent mark now glowed faintly.

Chloe and Kawika rushed in, Malia at their heels.

"What did you see?" Chloe asked.

Amber looked at her palm. "The blade showed me their covenants. Elizabeth Hexham and Philip of Macedon. Both gave themselves to the same darkness."

Kawika studied the blade. "Philip spoke of this mark, the serpent blood. He said a charm was passed from king to witch until light and dark met again. You've called it forward."

"The Hexham line," Chloe whispered. "My line. Yours, too."

Amber nodded. "They built the prophecy together. Flesh and throne, light and shadow. And now the blade remembers both."

Outside, the night burned red above the sea. The wind carried the low chant of the *kupuna* beginning their vigil.

Kawika lifted the blade. "The island hears it. The serpent stirs. We prepare."

Amber pressed her bleeding hand to her heart. "Then we find Zaraquel before he claims her."

The serpent hissed once and went still, the metal cooling. The mark on Amber's palm faded to a pale scar, the prophecy writing itself on living flesh once more.

Nimue, The Witch's Forest,
Present Night

The ground trembled. Not the quiet she had grown used to in the forest, but something sharp and violent snapping through the roots beneath her feet.

Nimue froze where she stood.

The trees whispered, every leaf murmuring the same word in a hundred voices. She remembered this feeling from long ago in Camelot.

Serpent.

She turned slowly. The mist folded and pulled like waves of black silk. Somewhere above the canopy, lightning flashed red, not white, and thunder cracked from beneath the earth.

"Marcus," she called softly. "Did you feel that?"

He appeared out of the fog, eyes bright, the scent of rain clinging to him. Behind him came Sabre and Black Wind in half-wolf form, hackles raised. Garnet Rose glowed faintly at his side, the ember at her core flaring with each heartbeat.

"The air changed," Marcus said. "Something's moving under us."

"It's older than this forest," Nimue replied. "From before I was bound. I know the pattern, but not this kind of evil."

She knelt, pressing her hand to the dirt. The pulse struck through her skin, a rhythm too deliberate to be random. A sigil formed in the soil beneath her palm, a serpent biting its own tail, drawn in glowing red lines.

Sabre growled. "What does it mean?"

Nimue's voice was hollow. "A covenant has awakened. The serpent of kings and witches rises again. Someone on the other side has broken through, awakened it, and now it seeks its master."

Marcus turned to Garnet Rose. "Can you trace it?"

She closed her eyes. Her body brightened until her skin turned almost white. "It's coming from the sea. From the west. From the island."

"Hawaii. Where the girls are," Marcus said.

Nimue looked up sharply. "Then Amber has touched the blade. She must have awakened it."

The serpent sigil quivered and sank back into the ground. A hiss echoed through the trees, followed by a low laugh that did not belong to any living thing.

Witch Anne's voice spilled from the mist.

"Little witch, little angel's friend, do you really think you can outlast what you helped create? The blood you fear now answers me. You ran away, but you came back, dearie."

Marcus drew the Totem of Death from his belt. "Show yourself."

The fog thickened until the shape of a woman formed, her hair white as bone, her eyes endless black. Anne smiled.

"You walk my forest and call my name. Brave, but foolish vampire."

Nimue stepped forward. "You built this place from Zaraquel's pain. You fed on her light. I'll tear it from your roots."

Anne tilted her head. "Then let the serpent judge which of us he will serve."

The ground split.

From the fissure rose a column of fire in the shape of a coiling serpent, its scales molten, its eyes like the moon seen through blood. The heat forced them back, but Nimue held her ground, her palms blazing with silver light.

Garnet Rose reached for her. "You can't hold that alone!"

"I can," Nimue said. "It's my sin to burn."

The serpent reared its head, hissed, and struck, but the moment its fire touched her, Nimue's light burst outward. The serpent convulsed, screamed, and dissolved into ash.

The ground sealed itself.

When silence returned, the forest seemed smaller, afraid of its own shadow.

Marcus caught her before she fell. "You'll kill yourself fighting every demon in this world."

Her lips curved into a tired smile. "Then at least I'll die facing the right direction."

The glow on the horizon shifted again, faint but visible through the trees, a shimmer of gold breaking through the green mist.

Zaraquel's light, fighting to return.

Marcus looked toward it. "We're close."

Nimue nodded, breath shallow. "Closer than we should be."

The forest answered with a sound like thunder rolling backward toward them.

*The Tall Dark Man, The
Underground, Present Day*

The stone beneath him moved like flesh, shivering under the weight of what had been broken. The serpent's death tore through his kingdom like a vein split open, and the Underground bled for it.

The walls wept ash. The air thickened with the scent of blood and death.

He did not speak at first. He let the tremor roll through him, eyes half-closed, as the realm around him howled. Every sound found him, the shriek of dying fire, the whisper of fading souls.

The roots hanging from the ceiling writhed like serpents trying to flee the light now burning somewhere far above.

The angel's light.

He felt it searing through the cracks, thin but steady, defying the weight of his dominion.

He moved through the cavern slowly and deliberately. The smoke that followed him curled around his feet like dogs waiting for command.

"You bleed for her," he said to the darkness. "You forget who shaped you."

The walls groaned in answer. Black stone split, and from within came the sound of wind through hollow bone.

He smiled. "So even you remember pain."

At the center, the regeneration chamber glowed faintly. A figure floated within, neither child nor man.

The Hunter.

His skin shimmered as if made of glass, veins of white fire mapping his body. The serpent's death had reached him, twisting through his bloodline. The mark on his chest, once dormant, now burned crimson.

The Tall Dark Man placed his hand against the chamber wall. The black stone beneath his palm cracked and bled light.

"You feel it too," he whispered. "The loss of the serpent. The breaking of the circle. All that fire wasted."

A whisper rose through the darkness.

Not wasted.

His gloved hand tightened. "Who speaks in my house?"

The whisper grew stronger. It came from the walls, the earth, the dead.

The serpent lives. Not in flame but in flesh.

He rose, his head brushing the low ceiling. Darkness rippled away from him, bowing.

"Find her and bind her," he said. "The one who dares to wear my light. Let her see what becomes of stolen breath."

He walked deeper into the dark. Each step sent ripples through the stone, and every ripple birthed another whisper. They followed him, repeating the words he had spoken.

The light walks.

The light burns.

The light remembers.

He turned once more toward the chamber.

The Hunter's eyes opened, white as salt. His lips moved, and the first sound that left his mouth was neither cry nor breath, but a hiss, the echo of the serpent itself.

The Tall Dark Man smiled.

"Good. The world remembers fear."

The cavern roof shook, dust falling like black snow. Above, the sea churned, and the island groaned.

The serpent was not gone.

It had only changed form.

The Tall Dark Man stepped into deeper shadows, leaving behind the echo of a single heartbeat, the pulse of the world realigning itself to his will.

CHAPTER 8

FIRE AND BLOOD

Zaraquel, The Witch's Forest,
Present Night

The thunder reached her first as a vibration, not a sound, trembling through the roots beneath her feet until the vines that bound her began to shrivel. The forest moved in time with her, as if trying to remember what it once was, a fertile land.

She pressed her hand to the ground.

The pulse beneath her skin was not the forest's. It was older, heavier, darker, as if it had come from elsewhere.

When she closed her eyes, she saw fire. Not the cold flame of witchcraft that surrounded her prison, but true fire, red and alive. It moved beneath black stone, beneath water, beneath the bones of the island. She could smell salt and smoke and hear chanting carried on the wind.

"Who calls to me?" she whispered.

The forest answered with silence.

Then the roots beneath her palm grew warm. The air thickened until it shimmered like heat on glass. A single word formed against her skin, not written, not spoken, but simply *felt*.

Hōnaunau.

The name filled her mouth with the familiarity of her mother and Amber. She whispered it once, and the forest shuddered. Light flickered behind her eyes, and when she opened them, she was no longer in the forest.

She stood on black stone on another night, watching a man and woman kneel before the sea as it swallowed the moon.

Kupaʻaikeʻe and Kalamau,
Hōnaunau, 1850s

Kupaʻaikeʻe stood at the edge of Hōnaunau, where lava met tide, and watched the horizon. The sky was bruised red. Even the wind moved strangely, carrying no salt, no birdsong, only the taste of stone.

Behind him, the pu'uhonua stood silent. The old priests were gone, the temples stripped bare by the new faith, yet the bones of the place still hummed with mana. He felt it under his heels, deep and restless.

Kalamau came down the path with a torch in her hand. Her white kapa skirt whispered against the stone, and her dark, certain eyes found him without surprise. "You feel it too," she said.

He nodded. "The sea does not breathe with the island."

She placed the torch in the sand. The flame shuddered as if hiding from the wind. "The moon is wrong tonight. It turns away from Hōnaunau."

He looked up. The moon was a thin slit, half eaten by shadow. Around it, the stars swirled as though caught in a net.

"An omen."

She touched his arm. "Not an omen. A memory."

He understood. The island remembered what men tried to forget. "Pele stirs," he said. "She calls her children."

Kalamau's gaze shifted toward the cliffs. In the distance, faint lights moved down the ridge, a long file of shadows carrying torches that gave no smoke. The air trembled with chanting too far away to understand.

"Huaka'i pō," she whispered. "The night marchers."

Kupaʻaikeʻe gripped the stone charm around his neck. "They do not walk without reason."

The marchers reached the shoreline but did not cross. Their leader, a tall figure crowned with red feathers, lifted his hand.

The ocean behind him peeled back, drawing into itself until the seabed glistened bare. Fish flopped helplessly in the sand.

Kalamau fell to her knees. "Kū is angry. The covenant between men and gods is breaking."

Kupaʻaikeʻe raised his hands and began to chant in the old tongue, words passed down through generations of kahuna. The chant rose like smoke, and the marchers answered.

The leader's eyes flared gold, then red, and the wind struck them both to the ground.

When they looked up, the sea was gone, drawn far beyond the horizon.

From the black trench that remained, something began to rise.

Scales shimmered under moonlight, long and slick, glistening like wet stone. A serpent of fire uncoiled from the depths, its body half smoke, half light, its eyes twin mirrors of the sun.

Kupaʻaikeʻe did not run.

He drew a circle in the sand with the end of his spear and cut his palm above it, letting his blood fall into the salt.

"I am of Pele," he said, voice trembling but strong. "If the covenant is broken, let the island speak through me."

The serpent lowered its head until its heat scorched his skin.

Its voice was not sound but thunder in his chest.

Blood for blood. Fire for fire. The balance sleeps but shall not die.

Kalamau rose behind him, her hair whipping in the hot wind. "If you take his blood, you take mine. We are one body, one spirit."

The serpent's eyes narrowed. It opened its jaws, and a single tongue of fire struck between them, curling like a brand. Both cried out as the mark seared into their skin, a spiral coiling down to the wrist.

The serpent withdrew, its voice sinking into the returning tide.

When foreign blood and island blood meet again, I will rise. The serpent will breathe anew, and the fire of the gods will walk in flesh.

The ocean rushed back all at once, crashing against the rocks, throwing salt and foam high into the air.

The serpent was gone.

The marchers faded with the tide, leaving only the torch still burning beside them.

Kalamau touched the new mark on his arm. "We have bound our blood to the gods."

He took her hand and pressed it to his heart. "Then our children will guard this place until the sea forgets our names."

She looked toward the horizon where dawn bled through the clouds. "It will not forget. The sea never forgets."

Kupaʻaikeʻe lifted the torch, still burning though soaked in saltwater, and held it over the stone until the lava beneath glowed faintly red. He carved the serpent's spiral into the earth and whispered, "E mālama ke ao. Protect the light."

The sea answered with a wave that bowed before the shore.

Then all was still.

*Amber, Chloe, Kawika, and
Malia, Hōnaunau, Present Day*

The night was too calm. Even the ocean seemed to wait.

Kawika stood knee-deep in the surf, the Serpent's Blade raised above his head, its metal catching what little moonlight remained. Behind him, the women formed a circle in the sand, torches planted at their feet, shadows dancing across their faces.

Amber watched the water pull away from the shore, retreating farther than the tide ever should.

"Is that supposed to happen?"

Kawika's expression was grave. "It happened before. Once."

Malia lifted a calabash filled with saltwater and ti leaves. She sprinkled it around the circle, whispering prayers her grandmother had taught her. "Pele watches. I can feel her."

Chloe knelt and pressed her palm to the ground. The earth answered with a faint hum. "Something beneath us remembers," she said. "It's old. Very old."

The sand rippled.

A dull glow spread outward in a perfect spiral. Kawika lowered the Blade until its point touched the center of the pattern. The mark on his wrist burned through his skin, the same spiral the serpent had carved into Kupaʻaikeʻe generations ago.

Amber felt it before she saw it.

A presence. Vast. Patient. Waiting.

The air grew heavy with heat. The sea began to steam. Beneath the surf, light flickered like veins of molten gold.

Chloe whispered, "It's the same fire Nimue fought in the forest."

Kawika's voice cut through the rising wind. "The covenant is awake. The serpent answers the bloodline."

The glow brightened until it turned white. The sand cracked, revealing a slab of stone buried beneath their feet. Symbols glowed along its surface, carved deep in a language older than time.

Malia traced the carvings with trembling fingers. "These are my ancestors' words. They speak of balance, of keeping fire and shadow apart."

Amber bent closer, her pendant flaring against her chest. The stone responded, pulsing rapidly.

"It's connected to Zaraquel," she said. "I can feel her through it."

The sea surged forward, swallowing the beach, but the circle held. Steam rose in sheets, blurring the horizon.

A voice rolled from the deep, ancient and smooth as obsidian.

When the child of fire meets the child of blood, the sea will choose its heir.

The words sank into their bones.

Amber's eyes widened. Her hand tightened around the pendant. "Zara."

Lightning split the sky without thunder. The spiral on the stone shattered, releasing a hiss that shot across the water like smoke through glass.

Far below, in the heart of the Underground, the Tall Dark Man raised his head and smiled.

"Found you," he whispered.

The ocean roared once more, then fell silent.

Only the sound of the waves remained and the slow, steady pulse of the island's heart beneath their feet.

CHAPTER 9

THE FIRE THAT BETRAYS

Eve, Hōnaunau, Present Night

The sea had not moved in an hour. The waves hung at the edge of the reef as if the world had forgotten how to breathe.

Amber and Chloe stood within the circle of torches, their faces lit by red flame and reflected in the wet black sand. Kawika and Malia remained at the waterline, murmuring chants meant to keep the veil steady.

The island felt alive beneath them, too alive.

Chloe's skin prickled. Her pendant, long silent, began to pulse against her throat. The glow was not gold this time, but the deep red of magma, a color drawn from the core of the world. The heat built until it burned through the chain. She gasped and pressed it into her palm.

The stone cracked, bleeding light.

Amber stepped toward her. "Chloe, what is that?"

Before Chloe could answer, the ground opened beneath their feet. Steam rose in columns. The smell of iron and rainless fire rolled through the air.

From the pool of molten water forming in the fissure, something began to take shape. First the outline of a woman. Then the shimmer of glass skin and eyes like polished obsidian.

The sea withdrew in fear.

Eve stepped from the heat as if she had been walking there all along. Her hair flowed behind her, black streaked with gold. When she spoke, her voice was soft, the tone of someone who had not used it in centuries.

"You called me back."

Chloe staggered backward. "No. You were sealed. I—"

Eve smiled faintly. "You created me to guard your queen. You gave me your strength, your grief, your blood. Did you think a lock made of mortal words could hold that?"

The torches flared one by one. The circle no longer looked human. It looked like an altar.

Kawika lowered the Serpent's Blade, eyes wide. "Eh, that one no spirit," he muttered.

Amber moved between them. "She isn't here to fight."

"I am always here to fight," Eve replied. "That is why I was made."

She looked toward the ocean where the serpent's spiral still glowed faintly beneath the tide.

"The covenant broke. The fire you woke burns through every realm now. I felt it tear through me before I rose. He felt it too."

Chloe whispered, "The Tall Dark Man."

Eve turned her gaze on her creator. "He knows your name again. He knows your blood still breathes."

The wind shifted. The flames bent inward. Amber's pendant flared, matching the rhythm of Chloe's broken one.

"Then he's found the angel."

Eve nodded once. "The angel's light reached his throne. He cannot see her face yet, but he can feel her heartbeat. He is moving."

The surf behind them pulled back again, exposing the reef. Far along the cliffs came the slow thrum of pahu drums. No feet followed the sound. The sea began to shimmer as if something enormous was turning beneath it.

Kawika raised the Blade. "We bettah get ready now. No mo' time fo' wait."

Malia tightened her grip on the calabash. "Eh, Uncle, you feel dat? The 'āina get scared. The mana no stay still."

Eve's gaze softened, almost human. "You cannot prepare for him. You can only delay him. The fire in his world is already spreading through yours. Every creature he ever touched is waking."

She stepped into the circle, the glow of her body dimming.

"He will cross through the angel's light because it burns with his mark."

Chloe steadied her breath. "Then we stop him at the crossing."

Eve tilted her head. "You made me for this. I will stand at the gate. But understand what that means."

"What does it mean?" Amber asked.

Eve's eyes lifted toward the horizon where thunder rolled beneath the sea.

"When the Tall Dark Man steps onto this island, every barrier will fall. Heaven, hell, earth—they will bleed together. Your prophecy will end or begin again. You will not know which until it is done."

The torches went out all at once.

Only Eve remained visible, lit from within.

"He is coming," she said quietly. "And he is not coming alone."

From far out in the dark water came the sound of chains breaking, followed by a single roar that shook the island to its roots.

Marcus, The Witch's Forest,
Present Night

The roar reached them before the light. It rolled through the Witch's Forest like thunder dragged across bone, flattening the mist and bending the trees.

Marcus lifted his head sharply, every nerve alive. The forest pulsed with heat. It was unnatural. It was the same sound he had heard in past wars, when worlds bled into each other and the intensity of the fight became unimaginable.

Garnet Rose flared at his side, her body trembling with light. "Something is coming," she said. "Not from here. From the sea."

McPherson's wards flickered around them, sigils cracking in the air. Nimue steadied herself against a tree, her hair plastered to her face.

"The serpent is dead," she whispered. "He felt it. Now he wants retribution."

Marcus tasted metal on his tongue. "Then let him come."

The forest opened.

Roots shot from the ground, writhing like living chains. A column of black fire rose from the center, not smoke but shadow made solid.

From within it stepped shapes that carried the scent of rot. They had once been human. Faces stretched thin, skin peeled back to reveal eyes burning with borrowed light. The forest had given them form.

McPherson drew a circle in the air, words of protection falling from his lips.

"Hold position!"

The first wraith lunged. Marcus met it before it reached the line. His blade sang once, silver cutting through rot. The body split in two but still moved, crawling with hands that burned like tar.

He drove his fangs into the wraith's throat, tasting rot and shadow.

"Not enough," he muttered.

A second wraith dropped from the branches above, claws extended. Marcus caught it midair and tore it apart. The blood that poured from it burned his skin, but he did not stop.

The old hunger rose in him, the pulse of the predator he had buried for centuries. He felt his teeth lengthen, the veins in his neck flood with cold fire.

Sabre and Black Wind had shifted fully now, their forms massive and sleek, fur slick with ash. They tore through the dark like storm clouds.

Nimue called lightning from her palms, white and sharp, searing holes through the shadows. Each bolt tore another rift in the forest, and through those rifts Marcus glimpsed other worlds bleeding in, cities burning, oceans boiling, angels turning to ash.

"Stop tearing it open!" McPherson shouted.

"I can't!" she screamed back. "He's pulling me through!"

Garnet Rose grabbed Nimue's wrist. "Then burn him instead."

When her fire joined Nimue's light, the air itself screamed. The sky split.

Marcus drove forward through the chaos. Every movement was instinct, centuries of war in his bones. He moved faster than sight, faster than breath. His claws tore through one wraith, then another, until the clearing was littered with bodies that refused to die.

They crawled still, whispering his daughter's name in voices not their own.

He turned on them, fangs bared, eyes red as furnace glass.

"You do not get to speak her name."

The forest answered.

The mist drew together, forming a single figure.

Witch Anne stepped from the dark, her smile too calm for the storm raging around her.

"You should not have come, vampire. This is her sanctuary."

Marcus's voice dropped to a growl. "You built it from her pain."

"I built it from her truth," Anne replied. "She will be mine soon, and you will thank me for saving her from what you made her."

Marcus moved without thinking. One blink, and he was upon her. His claws cut the air where she had stood.

The witch dissolved into smoke. Her laughter echoed above him.

"You cannot kill me in her dream."

"Then I'll wake her," he said.

He plunged his hand into the soil. The ground burned his flesh, but he did not stop. He felt Zaraquel's pulse deep beneath the roots, faint but alive.

The moment his blood touched the soil, the forest convulsed. Trees bent away. Light flashed through the mist—her light.

Anne screamed.

The wraiths turned to ash.

Nimue fell to her knees, gasping.

"You broke the link."

Marcus's hand still smoked, but his grip on his blade never loosened. "Then we move before it seals again."

McPherson looked toward the horizon, where gold light rippled through the green sky. "He's coming. The roar you heard was the gate opening. The Tall Dark Man walks again."

Marcus sheathed his blade, blood running down his arm. "Then we walk faster."

The ground trembled once more, not from their magic, but from something larger. A shadow moved across the treetops, tall enough to scrape the sky. The sound of chains dragging through earth followed. Garnet Rose's light dimmed.

"He's already here," she said.

Marcus turned toward the sound, fangs bared, hands still bleeding. "Then this forest burns tonight. I will save my daughter. I will bring her back to her mother."

The Tall Dark Man, The
Underground, Present Night

The realm answered him before he moved.

Every wall in the Underground trembled, black veins glowing red through the stone as the balance between worlds broke again. He felt it burn through his bones like molten glass. Marcus had touched her light. His angel's pulse was awake.

The darkness recoiled from its rage.

Chains lining the chamber walls tightened, links shrieking like a chorus of blades. Across the hall, the obsidian gates sealing the Hunter's chamber began to bleed light from their hinges. The air turned wet, heavy with the scent of burning blood.

He stood at the center of it all, head bowed, every line of his body still except his hands. The veins beneath his skin crawled with red fire. The shadows that served him drew back in silence.

They knew what was coming.

"She bleeds through my house," he said. "The light dares my dominion. The vampire thinks himself a savior. He will learn the price of waking my bride."

His voice struck the air like thunder. The chamber bowed. Stone cracked. From the walls, black liquid poured, thick and slow, shaping itself into bodies. Demons born from the marrow of the realm crawled into being, eyeless, scaled things moving on four limbs, their spines arched like drawn bows.

"Go," he said. "Find the intruders. Feed on the wolves. Leave the vampire for me."

They scattered, vanishing into fissures that split the floor. The scrape of claws against stone faded into the distance.

He turned toward a shadowed cell at the edge of the hall.

A low growl came from within.

Malakai.

The wolf was enormous even bound in chains. His fur was matted with ash and blood. The links holding him were forged from spells, glowing faintly where they bit into his skin.

His eyes opened when the Tall Dark Man stepped closer.

Gold. Alive with fury.

"You fight me even now," the dark one said. "You should have learned by now that defiance is wasted breath."

Malakai's growl deepened. The floor beneath him cracked.

The Tall Dark Man smiled.

"Your queen calls to you even now. She bleeds for her child. Tell me, wolf, when I take her, will she scream your name or mine?"

Malakai lunged. The chains snapped taut, shattering rock and tearing blood from his throat. The sound that came from him was not a roar but a scream of pure rage. It shook the cell, bending the bars outward.

The Tall Dark Man did not move.

"That's it," he said softly. "Break yourself for her. Every drop of blood you lose, every breath you waste, feeds my fire."

A soft rustle came from behind the throne.

Raven stepped into view, hood shadowing her face. Arioch lumbered behind her, stone arms dragging along the ground.

"You summoned me, my lord," she said.

Her voice was steady, but her pulse betrayed her. Even through smoke, he could smell doubt on her skin, sharp as blood in rain. She glanced once toward the chained wolf. Too long. Too human.

He almost laughed.

"You will take the demon band lead him to the breach," he said. "Marcus Tudor has entered my forest. The wolves stand with him. Bring me his head and the witch who walks beside him."

Raven bowed. "And the angel?"

"She will come to me. She always does."

Her hesitation rippled the air. The wolf's growl deepened, answering her silence.

He stepped close enough to feel her shiver.

"Do not disappoint me again, little witch. I can smell your pity. It is a weak perfume."

His hand brushed her face. She flinched as the burn seared her skin.

"You will obey."

"I will," she said.

The lie tasted sweet enough for him to let it pass.

When she turned away, he spoke again, not to her but to the realm itself.

"Let the forest burn. Let the vampire bleed. If the serpent's fire wishes to walk again, it will do so in my image."

The Underground shook.

The floor split open beneath the chamber where the Hunter had been forged, spilling molten light into the chasm below. The stone shell cracked, and from its heart the grown form emerged, no longer a child but not yet a man, skin veined with fire, eyes white and blind.

The sound that left his throat was not a cry but the echo of every creature that had ever died in darkness.

The Tall Dark Man spread his hands, welcoming the storm tearing through his realm.

"Yes," he said softly. "Now the world will remember why it feared me."

Above, in the Witch's Forest, the trees burst into flame.

Raven, Between the Forest and the
Veil, Present Night

The forest opened before her like a wound that would not close.

Smoke rolled through the trees, thick and low, carrying the scent of blood and rainless fire. Arioch lumbered ahead, stone feet crushing roots that bled sap dark as oil. Each impact made the ground shudder, the forest's heartbeat gone wild.

Raven kept pace behind him, cloak streaked with ash, hands shaking from the spells she had cast to hold the paths open.

The master's voice lingered in her skull.

Bring me the vampire's head. Bring me the witch who walks beside him.

Each time he spoke, the mark on her wrist burned.

Each time it burned, she saw Malakai's face in the red light of his chains.

She bit her lip hard enough to taste blood.

Guilt was useless here, yet it followed her like scent follows prey. She had chained the wolf herself. She had whispered his name to the Tall Dark Man when she should have stayed silent. She had watched his eyes dull when the fire sealed his cage.

She had done nothing.

The wind shifted.

A hiss ran through the branches.

Arioch stopped.

"Mistress," he rumbled. "They come."

Raven lifted her head. The trees swayed, bark blackening as if scorched from within. Through the smoke she saw flashes of silver and white—Marcus's blade, Garnet Rose's fire.

He was close.

Too close.

She drew her staff and whispered an old Hexham charm she had not used in centuries. The air thickened. Shadows slid down the trunks and pooled at her feet. Arioch crouched, ready to leap.

"Wait," she said. "Not yet."

Her heart pounded.

In its rhythm, she heard another: the steady, heavy heartbeat of Malakai in the Underground. She could almost hear him growl.

Kill *me or die trying.*

The words twisted through her spine.

Arioch turned his head, stone grinding. "Mistress hurt?"

"No," she lied. "Just angry."

The ground shook.

Marcus's voice cut through the smoke, cold and clear.

"Show yourself, witch."

Raven stepped forward. The trees bent away from her. Her hair lifted in the heat. The mark on her wrist burned through her skin until light poured from it like a wound.

Arioch roared and charged, slamming into the first of the wolves. Sabre met him head-on, claws flashing, teeth tearing into stone. Sparks burst through the clearing.

Raven raised her staff. Lightning cracked around her, lashing through the mist.

Marcus moved through it, faster than sight.

His blade struck her shield. The impact drove her back.

He was fury and blood and purpose.

His eyes met hers.

She felt the weight of his hatred.

"Where is she?" he demanded.

"Alive," Raven said. "For now."

He lunged again.

Their clash split the air. Arioch screamed, stone shattering. Wolves howled. Trees broke. The smell of blood and sulfur filled her lungs.

She fought with everything left in her, every spell she had ever learned, every sin she had ever buried.

But when his blade cut through her guard and grazed her shoulder, warmth flooded down her arm.

Real blood.

The pain sharpened her thoughts.

Malakai's eyes again. His voice.

You're already dead.

She swung her staff with both hands, forcing Marcus back. The forest behind him rippled. Light poured through cracks in the world—gold and red and blinding.

The roar that followed came from below, deep enough to ache in her bones.

The Tall Dark Man was rising.

Raven fell to one knee.

The light washed over her face, and for a moment, she almost prayed.

Forgive me, Malakai. I tried.

Then the forest exploded.

CHAPTER 10

THE RETURN OF THE SERPENT KING

Philip II of Macedon,
Hōnaunau, Present Night

The sea struck the lava without sound, steam rising where they touched. Every wave rose and broke upon the black stone with the weight of uncertainty. Far along the shore, the old heiau still stood, its terraces veined with salt, its altars smoothed by centuries of forgotten prayer. The night carried no moon. Only the glow of Pele's restless heart beneath the island gave the air its dull red pulse.

Philip walked out of that light as if the sea had carved him from its own shadow. His body still bore the shape of a king, though centuries had stripped it of softness. The mark of the serpent wound from wrist to shoulder, scales of fire that brightened with each step he took upon the stone. He moved like a man who had risen too many times from too many graves.

In the distance, Kawika and Malia stood at the water's edge. The Serpent's Blade lay across their joined palms. The metal trembled, catching the island's breath.

Malia's lips parted. "Uncle," she whispered. "It knows him."

The sea pulled backward, leaving a path of wet sand between them and the approaching figure. Philip's eyes were fixed upon the Blade. The weight of its call bent his spine. When he spoke, his voice was raw, as though unused for ages.

"I was buried without it. I have walked the earth as half a man since that day."

Kawika's hands shook. The Blade's glow became unbearable, red and white tangled like blood in sunlight. He tried to hold on, but the relic tore free, flying from his grasp with a sound like thunder cracking across the sea. It crossed the air in an arc of light and struck Philip's waiting hand. The impact threw him to his knees.

The glow spread through his body, devouring the old wounds and replacing them with something fierce. His hair turned silver, his eyes burned gold. The serpent mark along his arm flared until it covered his chest. The Blade and its bearer were one again.

Malia covered her mouth, tears running down her cheeks. "Is he god or ghost?"

"Both," Kawika said. "And neither. He is the curse that learned to speak."

Philip rose slowly, the Blade balanced in his hand as if it weighed nothing. The sand around him hissed, turning to glass.

"I feel every death I caused," he said quietly. "Every bargain made. Every child born of my sin."

He turned toward them. "The serpent's blood burns again in the angel. Tell your gods to ready themselves for me."

Behind him, the water began to boil. Steam rose high into the sky, shaping itself into the outline of a coiling serpent. The roar that followed shook the cliffs. Philip did not turn to look. He pressed the flat of the Blade against his forehead and whispered in a tongue the world had forgotten. A forgotten language, the language of the serpents.

The sea calmed. The serpent vanished. Only his voice remained, low and certain.

"This time," he said, "I will not fail her. I will not abandon my promise."

He walked inland toward the sacred terraces, and every torch left by Kawika's people bent its flame toward him in recognition. The serpent king had come once more.

Eve, Hōnaunau, Present Night

Eve stepped from the smoke as if it had been her doorway. The sea had barely stilled, yet her body still burned with the color of fire left too long without air. The others turned as she approached, the witch's creation, born of light and blood, moving with the restraint of something that remembered damnation.

Philip watched her come, the Blade still in his hand. Its glow had dimmed to a slow pulse, like the beat of a buried heart.

"So, this is what crawls from the queen's circle," he said. "The daughter of craft and pity."

Eve stopped several paces away. "And you are the serpent they told me about. The man who bartered kingdoms for a soul he never kept."

Kawika tensed, but Philip only smiled. "I bartered for the world. Souls were a fair price."

She ignored the arrogance and looked to Kawika. "Why does he hold that weapon? You said it was meant for the guardian's line, not a dead king."

The Blade trembled as if her words reached it. Its edge flared, spilling red light across the sand. The sound that followed was not wind but a whispering chorus, thousands of voices layered together, each one calling a different name.

Malia covered her ears. "What's it saying?"

Philip lifted the weapon. The glow steadied. "It speaks to blood," he said. "Yours. Mine. Every drop that ever paid for its forging."

Eve stepped forward, unafraid. "Prove it, then. The gods here remember deceit. Show them whom you serve."

For a heartbeat, he hesitated. Then he turned the blade point down and drove it into the rock. The island answered with fire that erupted around them. A ring of flame rippled outward, climbing the terraces, tracing the old petroglyphs until every carving blazed like molten gold.

The ocean pulled back again in recognition of the king. From the reef, shapes rose, ghosts of warriors, their bodies formed from steam and salt. The Night Marchers bowed, not to Eve or Kawika, but to the man who had once been their king.

Eve's glow dimmed. "The serpent's curse was never only yours."

Philip's eyes were distant, his voice a whisper. "It was theirs too. Every man who dies in battle feeds it."

The ghosts began to chant, their voices rolling with the tide. The Blade pulsed in rhythm. Kawika took a cautious step closer while Malia spoke.

"Eh, uncle, he not lying. Look how da ʻāina listen."

Eve looked from the ghosts to the Blade. "And if that power turns again?"

"Then you will strike me down," Philip said, steady. "Until that moment, we fight the same enemy."

The sea hissed, as if in agreement. The torches along the shore rose higher. Eve's eyes narrowed, but she nodded once.

"Then let the island decide," she said. "If you speak truth, it will keep you. If not, it will swallow you whole."

Philip wrenched the Blade free. The flames along the terraces surged, then steadied. He looked toward the mountains, where thunder still carried the echo of the Tall Dark Man's roar.

"It seems," he said, "the island has chosen me."

CHAPTER II

BROKEN CHAINS

Malakai, The Underground,
Present Night

The chains trembled before the air did. It wasn't metal that spoke; it was the spell running through it, whispering with every beat of his heart. The sound rolled through the stone and found its way into Elizabeth's mind before she even realized she was listening.

A voice, low and raw, pressed against her thoughts.

You shouldn't be here.

She froze mid-step, the black glass vessel in her hand pulsing with dull light. "You've found your tongue, beast," she said, forcing steadiness into her tone.

Not tongue, the voice growled inside her skull. *Hunger.*

She steadied herself. "Then feed. Drink this, and he may even let you keep your soul."

The wolf's eyes opened fully now, burning amber through the smoke. His next thought came sharper, each word like teeth scraping metal.

You serve a coward who hides behind borrowed gods.

Elizabeth flinched. She hadn't expected the words to cut so cleanly. "Careful," she warned. "He can hear you."

Then he knows I'm coming.

The air thickened. The flames in the sconces stretched straight upward. From somewhere far below, a deep, rhythmic pulse began, one that didn't belong to the Underground. The serpent's call had reached even here.

Elizabeth turned toward the sound. "Impossible," she whispered. "No mortal power crosses the veil."

The wolf's laughter filled her mind, dark and hot as breath against glass.

Then maybe hell's tired of your master.

The floor split. Steam poured up, and the smell of salt flooded the chamber. The magic holding his chains dimmed, its color bleeding from red to gold. One by one, the links fell away, clattering against the stone.

From the next chamber, Malakai sensed that the Hunter stirred. His thoughts were faint at first, like echoes breaking through water.

The hunter wants his father. The father calls him.

Elizabeth's eyes widened. "No," she breathed. "He cannot call you."

But the wolf was already standing. His shape shimmered in the molten light, fur rippling, muscles tightening as the serpent mark burned along his chest. The roar that left him wasn't sound; it was thought made thunder.

Then I will answer.

By some unknown power, Malakai's curse broke at the call of the Serpent King. He was a man once more and let out a piercing scream, more wolf than man, that would let his brothers know he was returning to their side.

Tall Dark Man, The
Underground, Present Night

The light in the chamber dimmed as the prophecy parchment curled in on itself. Words that had been carved into the vellum for centuries lifted off the page like ash and hung in the air before vanishing.

The Tall Dark Man straightened from his desk. He felt it first in the walls, a shiver of pressure that traveled through the stone and split the nearest column. The chain had broken. The wolf had howled.

He did not speak. He simply drew one breath, and the torches guttered out. The only light came from the brands across his back, where the runes began to glow. Power hit the air in waves. The floor cracked.

The witches closest to him stumbled. One fell to her knees, clutching her head. The other tried to reach for the door. He moved his hand without turning, and she froze mid-step.

When he looked down again, the parchment had rewritten itself in fresh blood.

The Wolf Walks. The Bride Bleeds. The Fire Divides.

Tituba's chains rattled against the wall. "Master?" Her voice shook. "What did he do?"

He turned toward her. The brim of his hat cast his eyes in shadow, but the scar along his cheek caught the faint glow from the runes.

"He remembered what it is to be free." His voice filled the room like heat before a storm. "He remembers me."

The iron cuffs around Tituba's wrists smoked. She tried to pull away from the wall and could not. The younger witch screamed when the table at the center of the room split in half. Scrolls and crystal jars slid to the floor.

He raised his gloved hand. The tattoos across his shoulders moved, black fire spreading through them until it reached his wrist. The flames that answered weren't orange, but the color of coal just before it breaks. They ran down his arm and pooled at his feet.

He spoke the word that had forged Malakai's curse, the one Raven gave him to control the wolf. The sound cracked the ceiling. Fire wrapped around the broken parchments, fusing them into a single sheet of molten script that hung in the air.

He drew the sigil again, every stroke a knife through the dark. When the circle closed, the air folded inward, heavy and wet.

For a moment, he felt the wolf's heartbeat through the spell, the old bond sparking alive. He clenched his fist. The flames roared.

Then the pulse slipped away.

Malakai's freedom was complete.

The fire backlashed. It hit him hard enough to hurl him against the wall. Stone exploded behind him. The two free witches were thrown across the room. One did not rise. The other crawled to her knees, eyes wide as the heat blistered her skin.

He stood from the rubble, coat in tatters, hat still shadowing his face. The runes along his back blazed until they bled through the fabric. Every line of his body carried both fury and control.

He walked to Tituba's chains and placed one finger against the metal. The iron turned white-hot. She screamed.

"You failed me," he said quietly. "You let my wolf forget his leash."

She shook her head, sobbing. "It was Raven, my lord. She bound him. I only obeyed."

"Then you will remind her how obedience is measured."

He released the chain. The heat seared her wrists to the bone. She fell, trembling, smoke rising from her skin.

The Tall Dark Man crossed to the center of the chamber, raised both hands, and drew the broken sigil again. The flames gathered above his head like a storm.

"Malakai will crawl back to me," he said. "And if he does not, I will tear the world until his soul remembers the sound of my name."

The fire consumed the chamber, leaving only black glass where his desk had been. The witches did not move.

The prophecy pages re-formed out of the soot, blank now except for a single word carved deep into the parchment.

Return.

Raven, Between the Veil and the
Forest, Present Night

The word reached her as heat beneath the skin.

She had been walking the narrow path between worlds, the forest on one side, the black void of the Underground on the other, when the call tore through her chest.

Return.

It wasn't sound. It was a brand. Every mark the Tall Dark Man had ever left on her body flared at once. The smell of smoke filled her lungs.

Arioch froze ahead of her. The demon's skin cracked and hissed as his runes caught the same fire.

"Master," he groaned, the sound dragging stone through his throat.

She clenched her jaw. "Keep moving."

The forest rippled. Branches bent away from her as if the trees themselves recognized the summons. The mist thickened, carrying the metallic taste of blood and ash.

The air behind her folded inward, and she knew what waited beyond it, the chamber, the scorch, the ruin he had made when the wolf broke his chain.

She didn't want to go back. Every instinct screamed to keep walking until the veil closed behind her forever.

But his mark on her wrist bled light.

The command burned through every nerve until her knees buckled. She hit the ground, fingers clawing the wet soil.

"Raven," the voice said. Not from the air, not from the forest, but from inside her skull. "You failed me once. You will not fail me again."

Her mouth filled with blood. "He was never yours to keep," she said.

The answer came with pain. The mark on her skin split open, lines of red running up her arm toward her shoulder. Arioch reached for her and recoiled when the light touched him.

She bit down a scream. "Stop," she hissed. "I'm coming."

The forest darkened. Roots wrapped around her ankles and began to pull. She didn't resist. There was no point.

The earth swallowed her whole, dragging her down through layers of cold stone and into the heart of the world she had hoped to escape.

She fell for what felt like hours before landing hard on the black glass floor of the study. The smell of burned parchment hit her first.

The Tall Dark Man stood where the flames had died, coat torn, hat low, the runes along his back still glowing beneath the fabric. He looked at her and the room seemed to tilt toward him.

Raven pushed herself up, shaking. "You called."

He turned his hand palm up. The chains that bound Tituba lifted from the floor and hung in the air like a threat.

"The wolf is free. The leash you made broke. Tell me why."

She forced her voice steady. "Because you asked me to bind a heart, not a beast. Hearts remember."

He crossed the distance between them in two steps. The brim of his hat hid his eyes, but she could feel the heat of his breath.

"Then you will bind it again."

Her pulse hammered. "And if I refuse?"

He leaned close enough that she smelled the iron on his gloves. "Then I'll remind you what obedience feels like."

The air between them caught fire.

Raven held her ground.

Somewhere deep in the rock, the wolves howled, and the serpent's mark on those linked by the bloodline seared into their skin, including Raven's.

Far above the earth, others felt it too.

And the wolves howled uncontrollably.

Amber, Hōnaunau, Present
Night

The first tremor came through the soles of her feet. The sand turned hot.

Amber staggered and grabbed the edge of the altar. Every torch in the courtyard bent inward at once.

Chloe caught her arm. "Amber, what is it?"

Amber tried to speak, but the air thickened. Her mark burned through the skin of her neck until it glowed beneath her red hair. The heat rolled down her spine and into her chest. She doubled over as if something had struck her from within.

Kawika moved to the doorway. "Eh, da ʻāina get angry again. Look at da fire."

The torches flared blue, then red. Malia backed away from the wall as cracks spread through the plaster.

The sea answered with a single wave that climbed higher than the reef and fell again without a sound.

As Amber lifted her head, she could feel her eyes had changed. They were no longer red but gold. The pendant at her throat burned white.

"He's alive," she whispered. "He's human."

Philip stepped out from the shadows near the courtyard arch. The light from the torches caught the serpent mark coiled along his arm.

"Who?"

Amber's breath came in short bursts. "Malakai."

The name carried across the compound like a gust of wind. The ground shook again.

Kawika steadied a falling torch. "Da wolf king? Thought he stay trapped."

Chloe's expression shifted from fear to understanding. "No. Not trapped. Reborn. That bond between them, it's older than any curse."

Amber pressed her hand to her chest. Through the fire and the pain, she could feel him. Not the beast that had fought beside Marcus, but the man beneath, the same heartbeat that had once called her name in another age.

She saw flashes that weren't hers, moonlight over snow, the smell of iron, her own voice crying out as she died in his arms.

The memory broke her.

She fell to her knees. Flames rushed outward from her palms, bright enough to blind them all.

Malia shielded her eyes. Kawika muttered a prayer in Hawaiian under his breath.

Philip stepped forward, his voice low but sure.

"The serpent's blood remembers its pair. When one rises, the other burns."

Chloe crouched beside Amber, touching her shoulder. "Amber, listen to me. He's calling through the mark. You must control it before it consumes you."

Amber's head snapped up. The gold in her eyes burned brighter.

"I won't shut him out. I've already lost too much."

The air thickened again, charged and alive. The flames in the torches stretched higher, taking the shape of a wolf's head before bursting apart.

The sound that followed came from far away, deep under the sea, a howl so vast it shook the island.

Amber reached toward the horizon where the ocean glowed faintly red.

"He's coming," she said. "He's coming for me."

Philip's hand closed around the hilt of the Serpent's Blade.

"Then the island had better decide whose side it's on."

Malakai, The Underground,
Present Night

The chamber stank of smoke and salt. Steam rose from cracks in the floor where molten stone cooled in thin red lines.

Malakai lay at the center of it, naked, the last of the chains fused to his wrists.

Every breath scraped his lungs raw.

He rolled to his hands and knees, coughing black ash laced with blood, feeling the weight of a body that was finally his own again.

A sound moved through the haze, bare feet across glass. Elizabeth stood at the edge of the smoke, her white dress gray with soot. She watched him without moving. In her face he saw something that didn't belong in this place, a flicker of fear, but he didn't think she was afraid of him. If he didn't know any better, he would have seen her as a beautiful woman aging gracefully rather than the centuries-old witch standing near the tunnel.

"Malakai," she said in a whispered voice.

He looked up, eyeing her closely. She was anything but calm. "You shouldn't say my name. He'll hear you."

"He hears everything," she whispered.

"Then let him hear this." He stood. Every joint cracked like stone settling as his legs trembled from lack of use. His full height filled the chamber, shoulders broad, skin gleaming with sweat. His muscular frame showed his power, yet his feet were still unsteady. "I'm done being his dog."

The words hit her like a blow. He saw it in the tremor of her mouth. Once she must have been something other than the pale priestess before him. The scent of incense and old faith still clung to her. But as he stared at her, part of him felt pity. Her demeanor reminded him of the day Nikoli and Miriam left Amber at the orphanage. She wore the same sadness and guilt on her face as they had. Malakai let a tear fall before returning to his senses. The witch wasn't someone he could trust. Or was she? In wolf form, he had noticed the Tall Dark Man's witches beginning to question his judgment, but they still served him.

"You don't understand what he is," she said.

"I understand cages," he replied. "I've worn enough of them."

Her eyes dropped to the floor. "He was light once."

"Then you followed the wrong fire."

The air quivered as the Tall Dark Man's rage rolled through the deeper halls. Dust fell from the ceiling. Malakai turned toward the iron gate, wrapped his hands around the bars, and pulled until the metal screamed and broke. Elizabeth flinched at the sound. For an instant he thought she might reach for him, but her hands stayed at her sides, fists white. He stepped past her, close enough to feel her breath catch.

"You can still choose," he said.

She didn't answer.

He climbed through the breach and into the dark passage above. Behind him, the chamber shook again, and in the echo of the collapse he thought he heard her voice, soft and broken, ending in silence. In the end, he left her behind, though he wondered if he should take the chance to save her. After all, it was only her and Raven who had shown a sliver of compassion toward him. He turned once in the tunnel and looked back. The glow from the ruined chamber pulsed faintly against the rock, the kind of light that followed death instead of life. Somewhere deeper below, he heard the Tall Dark Man's voice rise through the stone, low and cold, promising the end of every creature that betrayed him. Malakai pressed his hand to the wall and felt the urge to find Amber. As his palm touched the stone, he let his heart call to her. He started toward the exit, step by step, until the air thinned and the first trace of moonlight touched his face. For the first time in a while, he breathed without chains.

CHAPTER 12

BROKEN BONDS

Marcus, The Witch's Forest,
Present Night

The forest closed in around them as they continued their journey. Marcus led the way, machete in hand, the blade useless against roots that shifted as if alive. The ground moved under his boots, and he slowed without meaning to. McPherson kept his rifle ready but low, eyes flicking from the ground to the canopy. Nimue held one hand in the air, fingers twitching as she murmured to the forest in the witch's language. Her voice was calm, yet Marcus sensed dread. Threads of light drifted from her fingertips, leaving a trail so they could find their way back.

"It knows we're here," she said. "The old magic has woken. It can smell the blood of the prophecy on us."

Garnet Rose moved last, the flame in her palm lighting their path. Her fire burned low and blue, the only thing the darkness seemed to respect. Every few minutes she paused to breathe it back to life, the glow catching in her crimson hair. "I hate this place," she muttered. "The ground makes a disturbing noise. It's like it feels us but doesn't want us getting closer."

Marcus stopped long enough to glance back. "Keep close. The path changes if you lose sight of me." He felt the vines travel up his legs, a throb that found his chest and settled against his ribs. It wasn't danger. It was a call. Malakai. The link between them hadn't been this strong in years. He forced his breathing to steady. Now wasn't the time, but his brother and friend was calling him. *Could it be that Malakai* had *returned to human form?*

McPherson noticed. "You all right, brother?"

"Fine," Marcus said. "Just move. We're heading toward Zaraquel." They pushed on until the mist thinned and the ground dipped into a shallow clearing. A ring of black stones marked the center, carved with runes that pulsed a dull red. Nimue's light touched one, and the air above it rippled like heat.

"This is where Zaraquel fell," she said quietly.

Marcus felt the hair on his arms rise. He could smell her magic, a sharp mix of silver and ash. "Is she alive?"

"For now," Nimue said. "But the forest feeds on her light. If we don't reach her soon, it will consume her completely."

Garnet Rose knelt beside one of the stones and pressed her hand to it. The mark flared, and for an instant an image bled through the surface, a winged figure sinking into darkness. The flame at her palm sputtered. "She's slipping," she said. "And something down there is pulling her. It might be him."

The ground shifted. Roots snapped like whips, curling around the stones. McPherson fired once into the dark, the sound swallowed by the mist. The forest fell still again, listening. Marcus raised his machete and stepped into the ring.

"Then we go after her," he said.

Nimue shook her head. "Not yet. The way isn't open. The forest guards her now, and it answers to a power older than ours."

Marcus looked toward the trees, toward the faint glow of a dying light beyond. "Then tell it we're coming anyway."

The wind moved through the branches, carrying a whisper that sounded almost human. Somewhere in that voice he thought he heard Zaraquel call his name, but there was only the low growl of a wolf.

Zaraquel, The Witch's Forest,
Present Night

Sound came first. It wasn't wind. It wasn't rain. It was a single breath, deep and slow, drawn by something huge hidden in the dark. The forest was breathing her in, or at least it felt that way. She lost count of the tea drinks the witch had given her. Zaraquel chuckled to herself, remembering when she and Nimue nicknamed Anne "witch bitch."

Cold followed. It pressed against her ribs from the inside, reaching for the place her light once shone bright. She tried to move, and the ground shifted under her palms, damp and warm like the skin of some great beast. The air smelled of iron and moss, mixed with something else. *Blood? Death? Him?* Every shadow twitched when she blinked.

Fragments of memory broke through the darkness. The cottage. The broken crystal. Witch Anne's hand on her chest. The voice that always sounded kind right before it turned violent.

She tried to speak, but the darkness closed in around her, leaving her breathless. She pressed her hand to the dirt. A faint light answered, weak and pale. Something brushed her cheek, warm and soft. For a second, she thought it was a hand. When she turned, she saw a feather tangled in spider silk, the tip burned red.

Rae.

The name hurt. She missed her best friend and cousin. The wind shifted. Her friend's voice came from nowhere and everywhere at once.

"Little flame. You keep falling toward the place you already are."

She tried to block it out, but the harder she fought, the clearer the voice became. It wasn't cruel. It sounded tired, like someone who had been waiting too long. But Zaraquel remembered how impatient Rae could be.

The ground softened beneath her. She sank an inch, then another. Roots flexed around her ankles, tightening their hold. The forest didn't want her to leave.

She forced herself upright. The trees leaned closer, hiding the thin gray slice of sky above. When she moved, the path curved and brought her back to the same clearing. It repeated with every step. She was trapped.

A ring of black stones waited there. Red symbols burned across them like embers. The glow hurt to look at. It was her light, fractured and bleeding into the ground.

Someone stepped from the fog. For a heartbeat it was Rae again, but then the shape hardened, and Witch Anne stood where the ghost had been. Her hair was white as salt, her eyes calm in that cruel, knowing way.

"You can't keep fighting both," the witch said. "Light and dark can't live in the same skin. Give him what's his, and the world will stop taking from you."

Zaraquel laughed, sharp and frightened. "You think I'll beg him?"

"No," Anne said. "I think you already are."

The air behind her shifted. The forest whispered something too low to hear, but she knew the voice before it spoke clearly. The Tall Dark Man didn't shout or roar. He murmured. The words slid through the ground like roots finding water.

All I want is balance. Your light keeps the world awake. Let me hold it so it can rest.

Her hands began to glow again, faint and uneven. The color had shifted, still white, but threaded with red. She stared at it, terrified.

She needed a way out. Any way out.

She whispered one of the old spells she'd learned in the cottage. A dangerous one. A blade of shadow formed between her palms, not metal, not light, something that hurt to hold. She hurled it into the fog. It tore a hole through the mist. A narrow path opened, twisting forward like a throat.

Witch Anne smiled, small and quiet. "There," she said. "Now you'll live long enough to learn."

Zaraquel ran.

The path writhed, trying to close around her, but she forced her way through. The trees leaned in, brushing her shoulders. Her wings flickered behind her, nearly black now, with only the faintest hint of red remaining. Weak.

The forest whispered her name, over and over, shaping it into something that sounded like bride.

She caught herself against a tree. Sap ran over her fingers, warm and red. The stain sank into her skin, sticky and hot. The warmth spread to her chest, to the birthmark near her heart. The mark that bound her to her mother and father. The mark that united the Tudor coven and the vampires.

Amber.

The name steadied her. As she focused on Amber, the ground shook, trying to break her concentration. It felt like the forest was trying to keep her from her family. She clung to the thought, and the corridor narrowed until she could barely breathe.

The whisper came again, softer this time.

"Little flame. Stop fighting what will keep you."

She kept going.

Somewhere ahead, through all the dark, she heard wolves. The sound came and went like breath, and within it she almost heard her father's voice.

The light at the end of the path wasn't daylight. It was cold. Colorless. Wrong.

She stepped through anyway.

Stone replaced soil. Carvings spread beneath her feet, glowing faintly. The air was thick with the scent of burned incense and salt. Her light rose from her chest in one final burst, bright enough to blind her. It fractured down the center, red fire spilling through the cracks.

When it broke, she didn't fall.

She sank.

The forest closed over her, quiet and complete. The last thing she saw was a tall figure in the glow, hat brim low, coat torn, standing perfectly still. He didn't reach for her. The forest delivered her to him, and she didn't even realize it. Her strength was nearly gone.

Tall Dark Man, The
Underground, Present Night

The chamber still smelled of scorched parchment and rain. What little light remained came from the lines carved into the floor, each rune pulsing faintly red where Zaraquel's essence had bled through. The Tall Dark Man stood in the center, coat torn, hat brim low, gloved hands streaked with ash. The glow from the brands across his back had not yet faded; the skin there was alive with heat, a map of old fire tracing the first language of creation.

Thessara was already waiting. She knelt near the edge of the light, head bowed, hair black and heavy over her shoulders. The silence wasn't obedience; it was habit, centuries worn smooth. She didn't look up until he moved. When she did, the faint sigil on her hip began to wake, a serpent biting its tail, first dull, then rimmed in red. The glow bled through the thin fabric of her dress.

"You felt it," he said. His voice filled the room in low ripples. "The forest gave her to me."

"Yes, my lord." Thessara's accent softened the word, almost into worship. "The little angel has fallen."

He removed his gloves and set them on the table. The air shifted with him. "Balance always returns. Even light must rest, and when it does, the darkness can become the light."

She nodded, eyes half-closed. "Your balance burns, Kyrios mou. It burns everything."

He crossed the distance between them in two strides. The scent of burnt myrrh rose from her skin, and the mark at her hip flared brighter, tracing her heartbeat. "You doubt me?"

Her lips curved in the smallest smile. "Never. I am the flame you left burning."

He reached down and touched her chin. His fingers were cool now, but when his skin met hers, the brand responded. The glow ran up her side in a thin line of red light, following the shape of his hand. She did not move.

"Then burn," he said.

She exhaled slowly. The heat from the mark spread through her body, soft light spilling into the runes on the floor. The circle that had been fading reignited, feeding on her energy. He watched her with something that almost resembled affection.

"You have served me well," he murmured. "When I walked among the kings of men, you read the fire for me. Do you remember what they called you?"

Her voice was barely audible. "The Oracle of Pella."

He smiled beneath the shadow of his hat. "The first to kneel, the last to break."

The red light reflected off the brim of his hat and cut across her face. For a moment, he saw what mortals had once seen in her, a woman, not a vessel. He didn't like that. He pressed his thumb to the serpent mark. The glow flared crimson. She gasped, sharp and real, then softened into a low hum as her eyes went glassy.

"You give me what I need," he said. "Through you, I am remembered."

The runes on the floor burned white-hot, then steadied to gold. The chamber grew warm again. The power he had spent trying to hold Malakai was returning. When he lifted his hand, the mark cooled but remained faintly red, a promise beneath the skin. Thessara's breathing slowed. She looked up at him as though seeing sunlight for the first time in centuries.

"What will you do with the girl?" she asked.

He turned toward the molten wall, the image of Zaraquel's fall still faintly visible in the glass. "She believes she's running from me," he said. "But she's only running deeper into my shadow."

He settled his hat back on his head, voice calm now, almost tender. "The world mistakes obedience for evil. I only bring it peace."

He looked down at her one last time. "Rest, Thessara. Tomorrow I will make a new bride."

The words echoed through the chamber. The sigil at her hip glowed once more, then dimmed, as if the serpent had swallowed its tail again. The torches along the walls flared back to life, and the Tall Dark Man stood in their light, still and satisfied, a hero in his own mind.

Jerome, The Order, Present Night

The house was quiet in that strange way it always was after a storm, too still, too clean, the air heavy with the smell of sage and salt, just as Chloe had instructed before they left. Jerome felt a small sadness with the house empty, though he preferred the quiet. It had been some time since they departed, and he thought of himself as an elderly grandfather waiting for his grandchildren to visit. Sometimes he wondered who would be next in his family to serve the estate.

Dusting, sweeping, polishing, it was routine, and routine had always been his way of making sense of magic.

He moved through the main hall with a rag over his shoulder and a brass oil lamp in his hand. The Queen's chambers were closed, her coffin removed, and the others' rooms stood empty and silent. He could hear the ocean breathing through the open archway; the tide carried a rhythm that matched his heart.

In the library, he straightened a shelf that had leaned since the last quake. The books were old. Rowe's handwriting filled their margins, notes written in ink so faded it resembled smoke. He set the lamp down and ran a finger along the back panel, wiping away the last soot from the battle weeks earlier.

That's when he felt it.

A tiny separation in the wall. Nothing more than a hairline crack between boards, but the wood shifted beneath his thumb. He pressed harder, and a section of the wall clicked forward with a sigh of trapped air. Behind it lay a small alcove no wider than his arm. The lamp light caught on something green.

Jerome reached in and pulled out a statue no taller than his hand. It was a horse, carved from jade so dark it looked black until touched by light. The workmanship was ancient, smooth, almost too detailed. The mane curled in spirals that caught and bent the lamp's glow. Its eyes were obsidian, polished to a deep shine. On the base, words had been engraved in a language Jerome couldn't read. One looked familiar.

Philipus.

He turned it over and found a symbol burned into the bottom, two serpents intertwined around a crown. He had seen it before, on Philip's arm.

"Lord have mercy," he whispered.

He set the horse carefully on the table and reached deeper into the hollow. There was more, a small bronze coin and a scroll wrapped in leather so dry it cracked beneath his fingers. The coin bore Alexander's face on one side, a serpent winding across the other. The scroll carried a single seal. It belonged to Rowe.

Jerome broke it gently. The parchment inside was thin and brittle, the ink still sharp.

The heir of the horse will open the gate of kings. Keep the relic until the Queen commands its return. The serpent will come for it. Do not let him claim the past; he will make it the world's end.

Jerome stood for a long moment, the words heavy in his hands. The lamp hissed, its flame leaning toward the jade horse as though drawn to it. He heard footsteps above. He thought of the mark coiled along the young man's arm, the same serpent now staring up from the relic.

The skin between Jerome's shoulders prickled.

Something shifted in the air, subtle enough to be imagined if not for the lamp flickering blue. The horse glowed faintly from within, a soft green light moving through the stone like breath.

A voice came, not loud, not human.

My history belongs to me.

Jerome stepped back, nearly dropping the relic. The light died. He set the horse down and crossed himself out of habit.

"You'll go to her, little thing," he said quietly. "But not tonight."

He wrapped the jade horse in cloth and hid it beneath his coat. Whatever this was, it wasn't meant to stay inside a wall. Outside, the wind picked up, rattling the glass. In the Queen's chambers, a faint tremor of light stirred the serpent mark on Philip's arm, tracing up to his shoulder where it burned like a warning.

Jerome paused at the door and glanced back at the open panel. The alcove seemed deeper than it should have been, black as a well.

"God help us," he murmured, and shut it.

Raven, The Deluxe, Broadway,
Present Night

The rain hadn't let up since dusk. It fell in sheets down Broadway, washing the streetlights into long amber streaks. Inside The Deluxe, the windows were fogged, casting the bar in a haze that made it feel like a photograph from another decade.

Raven sat in a back booth where the shadows met the jukebox glow. She didn't remove her coat. Her hair was damp and carried the faint scent of the Sound. The crowd was light for a Thursday, a few regulars, a couple of students stretching the night, a man in a construction jacket nursing a beer at the counter. No one paid her attention. That was how she liked it.

She traced the rim of her glass, the ice long melted.

The door opened, spilling headlights and wet air inside. Mary slipped in, hood up, scanning the room before spotting Raven. She crossed over and slid into the opposite side of the booth. The smell of cold rain clung to her.

"You picked the noisiest quiet place in the city," Mary said, pulling back her hood.

Raven gave a faint smile. "Noise is cover. You forget how to blend in, you don't last long."

Mary studied her. "You still running from him?"

"Who says I'm running?"

"You're hiding in a bar on Broadway at midnight. That's not running?"

Raven's smile thinned. "Maybe I'm waiting."

The waitress came and went, leaving two untouched bourbons. Neither woman reached for them.

"You felt it," Mary said.

Raven looked up. "The girl? Zaraquel?"

Mary nodded. "She fell. He's calling her *bride*."

The lights flickered once. Raven's hand tightened around her glass. "He doesn't get her. Not this one."

"You still believe there's a difference between what he wants and what he gets?" Mary asked.

"There's always a difference," Raven said. "The world just hasn't remembered it yet."

Mary stared into her drink. "He took my boy. I told myself it would save Elijah, that the Tall Dark Man would teach him control. All it did was teach him how to die slower."

Raven watched her. "You can hate him and still feel the pull. That's what makes it work."

The faded mark on her wrist began to warm, then burn. She knew Mary felt hers too. The silence tightened between them, charged. He was calling. Or listening.

Mary's gaze flicked upward. "He hears us."

"He always hears us."

The rain drummed against the windows. The hum of conversation blurred into white noise.

Finally, Mary leaned forward. "I have something he wants. Something Rowe hid before the Order burned."

Raven's eyes narrowed. "Then move it. If he's sent for the girl, he'll send for you next."

"You're going to help me," Mary whispered.

Raven tilted her head. "Why would I do that?"

"Because you still owe me for Rae."

The name landed heavy. Raven looked away, jaw tight. "You know I tried."

"I know you failed," Mary said gently. "And I know you hate yourself for it."

Raven stood abruptly, her glass trembling. "Careful, Mary. Guilt is a dangerous language. He taught it to both of us."

Mary held her gaze. "Then let's unlearn it."

The light above their table flickered again, brighter this time, and for a brief moment the reflection in the window behind them wasn't the two women. It was a tall figure in a wide-brimmed hat, the outline cut in static.

Both women froze.

The light snapped back.

Raven grabbed her coat. "We can't meet here again."

"Where then?"

"Somewhere he's never walked."

"Does that place exist?" Mary asked.

Raven gave a small, bitter smile. "We'll find out."

She left first, slipping into the rain, her coat vanishing into the dark. Mary sat for a long moment, staring at the space where she'd been. The bourbon glasses sat untouched, the ice melted to nothing.

When she finally rose, the window beside her fogged again. Written in the condensation were two words that hadn't been there before.

Little flame. Little angel.

She wiped them away with her sleeve and stepped into the night.

CHAPTER 13

THE FIRST VOW

Zaraquel, The Bride of Shadow,
Present Night

The first thing she saw was light.

Not daylight, not flame, but something softer, like dawn reflected in black water. She thought it was sky until it moved, and she realized it was alive, breathing with her heartbeat.

The floor beneath her wasn't stone. It was glass. Inside it flowed rivers of pale fire, moving in slow, endless circles. Every breath she took made the light rise. Every exhale dimmed it.

It was a perfect trap.

"You're awake."

The voice came from behind her, low and steady.

Zaraquel turned, muscles heavy as if she'd been asleep for years. Witch Anne stood a few steps away, hands folded neatly in front of her apron. Her face looked younger than Zaraquel remembered, smooth, calm, unburned. Only the eyes were the same, sharp enough to slice thought from memory.

"Where am I?" Zaraquel asked. Her throat ached.

Anne smiled. "In the place your heart built when it broke. He only gave it shape."

The answer made no sense, but the room felt familiar. The air smelled faintly of salt and roses, the same perfume Amber used when she brushed her hair. The scent twisted in her chest.

Anne reached into her apron and drew out a small vial. Inside, red dust shimmered.

"Drink this. It will steady the light that's left in you."

Zaraquel shook her head. "No more tea. No more tricks."

"This isn't a trick." Anne stepped closer, her voice softening. "You've been fighting too long, little flame. You're burning yourself out. He can't protect what's already ash."

Zaraquel flinched at the name. Little flame. Rae had called her that once.

"I don't need his protection."

"You already have it."

Anne's smile deepened. She reached out and touched Zaraquel's shoulder. The contact sent a tremor through her. Beneath the witch's skin, magic pulsed like a second heartbeat.

"He gave you a gift," Anne said. "You can let it consume you, or you can learn to command it. The first lesson is surrender."

Zaraquel wanted to step back but couldn't move. The light beneath the glass had risen around her ankles, warm and humming. It felt almost gentle. She could feel it reaching through her, rewriting her pulse.

"What happens if I refuse?" she asked.

Anne tilted her head. "You'll fade. Someone else will take your place. Maybe the Queen. Maybe your mother. He doesn't mind which."

The threat struck harder than any spell.

Amber. Mother.

She couldn't let that happen.

Anne pressed the vial into her hand. "Drink. Think of it as mercy."

Zaraquel hesitated, then lifted it to her lips. The dust wasn't bitter. It tasted like snow melting on metal.

For an instant, she saw her reflection in the glass floor. It wasn't herself, but someone older, dressed in black, the Tall Dark Man's mark faintly visible over her heart.

The light flared.

Anne stepped back, her smile calm and complete. "Good. You've taken your first vow."

Zaraquel dropped the empty vial. It shattered, the sound echoing through the room like a bell. The rivers beneath the glass turned red.

Somewhere in the distance, she heard his voice.

She screamed, hands clamped over her ears.

My bride learns quickly.

Amber, Hōnaunau, Present
Night

The sound came before the shake, a deep, splitting crack that tore through the cliffs as if the island itself were breaking apart. The floor beneath Amber's feet lurched. Glass shattered somewhere down the hall. Outside, the ocean roared, the waves violently out of control.

She was already running when Kawika burst through the door, bare-chested, skin streaked with ash and salt.

Kawika caught up to her, breathing hard. "Eh, da 'āina stay mad, yeah? Da cliff jus' wen drop like da island spit somethin' out."

Amber didn't answer at first. The wind pulled at her hair, carrying heat that stung her cheeks.

"It's not the island," she said finally. "It's her."

Philip stepped beside them, lava glow reflecting in his eyes. "Zara?"

"She's fighting something she can't win," Amber said. "And the island feels every heartbeat."

Malia came out behind them, holding Chloe close. "Then we better make the gods listen before the land breaks apart too."

Amber nodded, gaze fixed on the red horizon. "Call them. Tonight we make the pact."

The call went out without words. Kawika knelt in the sand and pressed his palms to the ground. The others followed.

For a moment, there was nothing, just the ocean, ash, and wind through the palms.

Then the sand began to tremble, small rhythmic pulses matching the beat of his heart. A low hum rose from beneath the surface. At first it was soft, like distant thunder. Then the rhythm split into many voices.

The shoreline shimmered. The air thickened into mist and color.

Amber stood at the center, bowed, and waited.

Malia whispered, "Da kaimoni coming."

They arrived first as light, then as shapes forming in steam, outlines glowing red and gold, skin of molten rock, eyes like sea glass. The guardians of the island.

Kawika lifted his face to them.

"Auwē, brothers, sisters. We call you 'cause da 'āina stay hurtin'. Da cliff fall. Da sea stay mad."

One figure stepped forward, towering and still. The glow around him dimmed until only his eyes burned bright. His voice rumbled like a tide over stone.

"We know. The balance breaks again. You call us too late."

Amber lifted her chin. "Then help us fix it."

Another voice joined, a woman's, smoky and deep, carrying the scent of rain on lava. "You ask for more than help, Queen. You ask for war."

"The war's already begun," Amber said. "You can hear it in the cliffs, smell it in the sea. He's reaching for the islands now."

The first guardian regarded her in silence. Behind him, the waves twisted higher, carrying faint shapes, fish glowing like embers, spirits rising and falling in the foam.

Malia's voice was small. "We get one god still listen, yeah?"

From the smoke, a new shape formed, taller than the others, his body black stone streaked with deep blue veins. The air around him turned cold.

Kawika swallowed hard. "Kanaloa."

The god of the deep tilted his head. "I listen, child. But I do not promise mercy. The sea remembers the one who first broke it. You bring me a Queen who carries foreign fire."

Amber met his gaze. "I carry life. If that offends you, then so does the world."

The surf hissed louder.

"Bold words," Kanaloa said. "But boldness burns fast."

Kawika stepped between them. "Eh, enough. We all stay part of da same 'āina. If we no stand together, da whole island go under."

Kanaloa's gaze shifted to him. Kawika flinched as cold washed over his skin.

"Maybe it should."

The sand rippled. The other kaimoni murmured uneasily, their voices like wind in coral.

Amber raised her hand. "Then I'll ask the others. Whoever still remembers what it means to protect, I ask you to stand with me against the Tall Dark Man. Against the evil spreading across this world."

Her pendant glowed white against her throat. The red horizon brightened in answer. The volcano released heat that all could feel.

One by one, the other guardians bowed their heads.

Kanaloa watched in silence, eyes narrowing to slits of light.

Amber did not look away. "The world is breaking. You can stand with us, or drown with him."

The sea swelled where his feet touched the water, forcing Amber to step back slowly.

Finally, Kanaloa said, "We will see whose fire lasts longer, Queen."

He vanished in a rush of foam, leaving the ocean black and still.

Kawika exhaled. "Ho, dat went better than I thought."

Amber looked toward the horizon, where the waves glowed faintly red.

"No," she said softly. "It went exactly the way he wanted."

Malakai, Blue Mountains,
Present Night

The scent of wolves filled the air, but it wasn't a new pack. It was old, mysterious, connected somehow. Malakai stood at the ridge where the trees thinned and the valley opened below him. Moonlight washed the peaks silver, but the snow never reached this far down anymore. The air had turned dry and bitter with smoke from the eastern fires.

He could feel the pack before he saw them, the family he had been missing for so long.

He stepped forward.

The soil smelled of cedar, gun oil, and the ghosts of brothers he had buried too long ago. His bare feet sank into mud still warm from an earlier hunt. Somewhere close, claws scuffed stone. Low growls rolled through the dark like a turning tide.

"Come out," he said quietly. "I know your scent."

The first shape appeared between the pines, a great black wolf with a streak of white down his muzzle, eyes gold and wary.

Kael.

Nikoli's blood, dominant now, scarred from too many winters without a leader. He padded into the clearing and shifted, bones cracking, fur pulling back until a man stood in his place, broad and bare, breath steaming in the cold.

"You were cursed and taken," Kael said.

"Yes," Malakai answered. "Didn't stay that way."

More shadows slipped from the tree line. Six, then ten. Males and females, all watching, half crouched, half ready. Their growls were a language older than speech. Malakai listened. Beneath the threat was confusion, and beneath that, recognition.

"You smell like the old world," one of the she-wolves said, awe roughening her voice.

He nodded once. "Because I am what your line was sworn to. You served the Queen before men had names for her. You guarded Illyris. You remember the oath, even if you forgot why."

Kael's eyes narrowed. "That's story, not blood."

Malakai let the change take him.

The shift was fast and brutal, bones splintering, skin tearing until the great gray wolf stood in his place. The earth bowed beneath his weight. Scars glowed faintly along his flank where the Tall Dark Man's chains had once burned.

The other wolves dropped low, instinct rippling through them. Kael fought it, teeth bared, but his knees bent before the howl came.

It began deep in Malakai's chest, low and resonant, carrying memory in its sound. Every wolf in the valley joined, voices threading through the pines until the night itself trembled.

When the sound faded, Kael rose again, eyes wide.

"Giorgos," he whispered.

Malakai lifted his gaze to the moon. "The same soul. A different cage. The Queen walks again. The world burns. We stand with her, or the darkness takes us all."

Kael started to nod, then stopped. His head tilted. The wind had shifted.

The wolves' ears flattened.

A new scent rolled in, thick with rot, iron, and fire.

The demon came on four legs. Its hide was half bone, half smoke, eyes like molten glass. It moved wrong, too fast, too quiet. When it hit the clearing, the ground cracked beneath it.

Malakai lunged first.

The impact was thunder. Teeth met flesh. Claws raked through shadow that screamed like tearing metal. Kael joined him, then the others, their howls turning savage. Blood, black not red, splattered the snow.

The creature threw them back with a pulse of fire that burned through fur and skin alike. Malakai hit the dirt, rolled, and came up half-shifted, human enough to grab Kael's fallen blade.

He drove it into the demon's chest and roared, "By blood and oath!"

The words carried power. The blade blazed white, then exploded.

Silence dropped.

The demon collapsed into smoke. Snow turned red where blood fell.

Malakai stood breathing hard, half naked, half wolf, eyes still wild.

Kael limped toward him. "Was that—"

"One of his," Malakai said. "The Tall Dark Man found our trail."

He looked east, toward the emptiness that tied him to Amber. "Then he'll find her next."

Kael followed his gaze. "What do we do?"

Malakai's mouth tightened into something between a snarl and a smile.

"We hunt."

The pack's answering howl rolled through the mountains, rising with the wind. It carried the weight of old vows and the promise of new blood.

A pack sworn to protect the Queen with loyalty and honor.

Marcus, Witch's Forest, Present
Night

The forest moved again, or at least it felt that way. Every step felt wrong and different at the same time.

Marcus froze mid-step as the ground shifted beneath him, vines tightening as if trying to hold him in place. The sound was low, deep, wet, as though the soil itself were alive.

McPherson's rifle came up out of habit. "Tell me that was an earthquake."

"Not this far north," Marcus said.

His eyes adjusted to the dark. The mist burned faintly green now, and the world seemed to tremble around them. That was when he understood.

The forest and Zaraquel were connected. And because she was of his blood, he could feel her more strongly than Chloe could.

Kabos' teachings surfaced in his memory. The blood prophecy. A child born whose bond to her father would be unlike any other. To sever that connection would be to destroy both the prophecy and the Queen.

"She's still here," Marcus said. "The forest is feeding on her."

Nimue closed her eyes, palms raised. Threads of light spilled between her fingers, drifting into the fog. "The forest is trying to keep her here, away from everyone she loves. I can feel its anger and its love at the same time."

Garnet Rose swore under her breath. "I can't keep my flame steady. Every breath makes it heavier to control. I can barely sense her anymore."

Behind them, Black Wind growled low and guttural, fur standing on end. Sabre circled him, tail stiff, hackles raised.

"They smell something," Marcus said.

McPherson turned slowly, flashlight sweeping across trees that hadn't been that close seconds ago. The trunks were twisted, bark slick like skin. "Bloody hell. Is this her magic?"

"No," Nimue said, her voice trembling. "It's his. I can feel him. He's close. And she's not alone down there."

Marcus crouched, brushing his fingers over the soil. It was warm, almost too hot. Sparks of light crawled up his wrist before fading.

"Then we dig her out before it's too late."

Garnet Rose shook her head. "You can't dig through this. It's not ground anymore. It's something else entirely. I don't know what."

The mist thickened. Shapes moved within it, not human, not animal.

Marcus stood. "Then we wake the dream."

He drew his machete. The blade caught the glow, reflecting sickly green light.

"McPherson, watch our backs. Nimue, keep that spell ready. Black Wind, Sabre, with me."

A low moan rippled through the forest.

It was terrifying. But not as terrifying as knowing Zaraquel was being tricked.

The trees leaned inward.

"Move," Marcus said.

They pushed forward, one step, then another, until the light in the mist began to shift. No longer green.

Red.

Pulsing like blood through a vein.

McPherson's voice came small behind him. "That's not her light, is it?"

"No," Marcus said. "That's the color of something taking her place."

Raven, Seattle Docks, Present
Night

The rain hadn't stopped since she left Broadway. It came harder by the hour, the kind that soaked through before you could blink.

Raven kept her hood up and her head down, walking the edge of the docks where orange lights flickered over the water. Every ripple fractured her reflection, breaking her face apart each time a drop hit.

The city smelled of diesel and grime. Beneath it was something else, burnt iron, faint and metallic.

His scent.

The Tall Dark Man's reach stretched even here, in the shadows beneath the cranes. He was everywhere.

She ducked between two shipping containers, boots splashing through a shallow puddle glowing faintly under a streetlight. The air buzzed.

Not electricity.

Memory.

The docks had seen more magic than most realized. Sailors once whispered about spirits in Elliott Bay, the ones that kept ships from burning when lightning struck. She had known one of them once. Fed it her blood.

It still owed her a favor.

Until now.

She stopped at the edge of the pier. The water churned though no wind touched it.

"Show me," she whispered. "Rowe's relic. Where is it?"

The surface flattened.

The rain slowed, each drop hanging for a heartbeat before falling again. A circle of stillness opened at her feet. The reflection in the water shifted.

Not her face.

An old study. Dust. Stone walls. A table. A single candle.

In the center sat a small bronze box etched with the serpent's sigil.

Raven leaned forward. "So Mary wasn't lying."

The circle snapped shut.

Footsteps sounded behind her. Slow. Deliberate.

She didn't turn at first.

"Still talking to ghosts, sister?"

Thessara's voice slid between the raindrops, smooth as smoke.

Raven turned.

The witch stood ten paces away, black hair plastered to her face, dress clinging like ink to her skin. The mark at her hip burned faint red through the wet fabric.

"Did he send you?" Raven asked.

Thessara smiled. "He doesn't have to. He feels every time you breathe. You think you can hide this from him?"

"I'm not hiding. I'm practicing."

"Practicing means you admit you are not powerful," Thessara said softly. "And if you are not powerful, he will not need you."

"Maybe I was," Raven said, stepping closer. "Maybe we both were."

The air between them felt stifling. Steam rose from the puddles, heat climbing around their legs. Thessara tilted her head, the faint red glow of her brand flaring brighter.

"He hears you, you know. Every word."

Raven's jaw tightened. "Then maybe it's time he started listening."

Lightning split the sky. For a heartbeat, Raven saw Thessara's expression falter, something like doubt, maybe even fear. Then thunder rolled overhead, and when Raven looked again, Thessara was gone. Only the scent of burnt myrrh remained.

Raven stood alone on the dock, breath fogging the air, the city stretching behind her. In the water below, ripples spread from a single point, widening until the surface broke. Something small and metallic floated up, a bronze coin stamped with a serpent wrapped around a crown.

She reached for it.

The moment her fingers touched the metal, a voice whispered from nowhere and everywhere at once.

"Bring it home."

Raven dropped the coin as if it burned, watching it sink back into the black water.

"Not this time," she said.

The rain intensified. Somewhere behind her, a shadow detached itself from the wall and began to follow.

Thessara, The Underground,
Present Night

The descent began with water.

Each step she took down the stone stairs sent rain dripping from her dress onto the slabs, darkening them one by one. By the time she reached the bottom, the air had turned stale, thick with smoke. She covered her nose as she stepped into the chamber.

The Tall Dark Man waited within. The torches along the walls burned low and blue. His coat hung open, and the runes across his back glowed faint red beneath the fabric. He didn't turn when she entered.

"You followed her."

"Yes, my lord."

"Speak."

"She's begun to pull away. She seeks the relic. She called to the spirits in the bay, and they answered." Thessara kept her voice steady, though her throat tightened under his presence. "The coin rose to her hand."

He turned at last. The brim of his hat shadowed his eyes, but the scar along his cheek caught the firelight.

"And?"

"She dropped it. She defied the call."

The silence that followed seemed to tilt the room.

He exhaled once. The torches flickered out, then flared back brighter.

"Defiance," he said softly. "How quickly they forget who gave them life."

Thessara lowered her head. "Shall I bring her back?"

"No." He stepped closer. "A stray must be allowed to believe herself free. She will lead us where the relic sleeps."

One gloved hand brushed the edge of her jaw. "You have done well, my sweet."

The mark at her hip burned, the serpent brightening beneath her skin. "I live to serve."

"Then serve me again. The Queen stirs in the islands. The wolves howl in the north. Everything moves toward her." He looked past Thessara, toward the tunnel's black mouth. "We will move faster."

"How, my lord?"

He smiled beneath the shadow of his hat. "We will give the angel a reason to fall the rest of the way."

The floor trembled. Somewhere above, thunder rolled through the earth, the echo of a distant howl answered by something older.

Thessara whispered, "The pack."

"The pack," he repeated, the word a promise. "Bring me one alive. I will make it mine to replace the one who left. I will trap them and bend them to serve me as they were meant to."

He turned back to the fire. As he raised his hand, the flames curved inward, forming the shape of black feathered wings rising behind him.

"Go," he said.

Thessara bowed and disappeared into the smoke.

When she was gone, he traced the air where the wings had burned, the ghost of heat lingering on his gloved fingers.

"Soon," he murmured. "Soon they will all remember my prophecy is the true one. Theirs was only an illusion to prepare them for my mercy."

The flames collapsed, leaving the chamber in darkness.

CHAPTER 14

BROKEN PROMISES

*Marcus, The Forest, Present
Night*

The forest watched them.

Marcus felt it in the way branches leaned closer, how every leaf seemed to tilt toward the heat of their breath. The fog hung lower now, heavy and wet, clinging to skin like a second atmosphere.

He had led them deeper than before, beyond where natural light reached, into a place where time moved differently.

McPherson stayed close, rifle tight to his shoulder. "You sure we're still followin' her trail?"

Marcus didn't answer. The ache in his chest told him everything. Zaraquel was still here, somewhere beneath the skin of the world, and she was hurting. It wasn't sight or sound guiding him, but something older. Blood. Bond.

Nimue's spell light shimmered ahead, soft and trembling as if it feared what waited. Garnet Rose's fire burned lower than before, crawling over her fingers in thin ribbons, gasping for fuel. Black Wind moved first, Sabre behind, both wolves silent, yellow eyes cutting through the dark.

The mist opened into a clearing that was too perfect.

Moonlight fell straight down through the canopy, white and cold. In the center hung a shape suspended between roots, glowing faintly.

A girl.

Wings spread wide. Hair tangled in branches. Face half-hidden.

"Zara..." Marcus's voice broke as he stepped forward.

She stirred. Her head turned. Pale gold eyes opened beneath the shadows.

"Father," she whispered. "Help me."

Nimue's light faltered.

Marcus dropped to his knees beside the roots, reaching out. The glow from her skin pulsed once, twice, and he felt her heartbeat match his own.

For a moment, everything aligned.

Then the pulse twisted.

The warmth turned sharp, biting into his palm. The illusion began to unravel. Her face blurred, skin splitting into streams of red light.

The sound that followed wasn't a scream. It was tearing. Something precious ripping apart.

Marcus clutched his chest and gasped. A burn seared across his ribs, deep and cold at once.

Their bond.

Breaking.

Nimue staggered back, hands clutching her heart. "Marcus—what's happening?"

"She's gone," he choked. "They've cut her from me. I can't feel her. If I can't feel her, Chloe will feel it too."

The figure in the roots dissolved into ash that scattered in the wind. The clearing dimmed. The forest fell silent.

Then laughter drifted from beyond the trees, low, female, familiar.

Witch Anne stepped from the mist, white hair faintly luminous in the dark. Her eyes were calm and bright.

"You came all this way for a ghost," she said. "How sweet."

Marcus surged to his feet, blade drawn, but Nimue caught his arm.

"Don't," she whispered. "It's her forest now."

Anne tilted her head as if admiring a painting. "She's with him, where she belongs. You should be proud. Not every father raises an angel fit for a king."

Marcus's voice was raw. "You did this."

"I only gave her what she asked for. Freedom. Power. Purpose. Things you never could."

He stepped forward, fury burning bright, but the air thickened around him. Roots shifted, drawing closer, their tips sharp as blades.

Anne looked toward the treetops, listening to something only she could hear.

"He's watching," she murmured. "He wanted you to see. To know how it feels when the light you love chooses the dark instead."

Marcus's breath came ragged. The wolves growled low, teeth flashing. Chloe knelt trembling, her hands glowing faint blue as she tried to heal a wound she couldn't see. Nimue whispered under her breath, straining to hold the barrier steady, but the spell cracked.

Anne's smile widened. "You should leave now. The forest has no mercy left for you."

The mist surged forward, swallowing her shape. When it cleared, she was gone.

Marcus fell to his knees again, pressing his hand to the soil still warm from Zaraquel's fading light.

The pulse was gone.

The blood between them was silent.

A single crow called in the distance, its cry echoing like a mourning bell.

"Zara," he whispered.

No answer.

He had once promised to surrender himself to the Tall Dark Man. Evil had broken that promise first.

Now it was his turn.

He would no longer surrender. He would fight until his daughter was home, where she belonged.

Marcus knelt in the dirt, fist pressed to his heart, and swore a vampire's oath to serve the blood prophecy and Amber, the one true Queen, or die trying.

Anne, The Underground, Present Night

Anne entered without hesitation. Her bare feet made no sound against the black floor. Her white hair clung damply to her shoulders.

She carried Zaraquel's broken light cupped in her palms. It burned faint red, not warm but alive, an ember of what had once been pure.

The Tall Dark Man stood near the altar where molten glass still radiated heat. He didn't speak at first. When he turned, his shadow cut the light in half.

"You severed the bond," he said.

Anne bowed her head. "Yes, my lord. The father cannot reach her now. His pain feeds the forest. Her heart beats only for you."

He studied her for a long moment.

"You've served me better than the others," he said at last. "Even Thessara doubts in whispers. But you..."

His voice softened, sweetness curling around the words.

"You remember what loyalty costs."

Anne straightened. "You promised me a reward when the child's light fell. I've come to claim it."

He moved toward her slowly, gloved hand brushing the air beside her face without touching.

"You were once powerful beyond measure," he said. "They called you storm-bearer, witch of the northern sea. You made kings kneel and priests burn. Then you chose to bear my demons and forgot yourself."

"I never forgot," she said. "You took that from me."

His smile did not reach his eyes. "I take nothing that isn't already mine."

He gestured to the ember in her hands.

"You hold the proof. A piece of the prophecy's heart."

His voice dropped lower.

"You want your gift? Take it back."

Anne looked down at the ember.

It felt alive. When she lifted it closer, the light crawled up her wrists, threading through her veins. She gasped.

It hurt. Not surface pain, but something deeper, a burn beneath her skin. The light reached her throat, her temples, her eyes.

She saw flashes of her past.

The sea boiling under black skies. Ships torn apart. Men screaming her name in prayer and curse alike. The storms she had once commanded roared back into her blood.

She fell to her knees, hands shaking. "What did you do to me?"

He crouched beside her, his coat brushing the floor. "I kept my promise. I gave you back what you lost. But gifts from me come with memory, and memory is power you must learn to control again."

He leaned closer, the brim of his hat shadowing his face.

"You wanted more than motherhood. You wanted dominion. Be careful what you remember, witch."

Anne lifted her eyes. The veins beneath her skin glowed faint blue now, lightning threading through them.

"What would you have me do?" she asked, her voice trembling.

He stood and looked toward the ceiling, where faint tremors of Zaraquel's red light flickered through the rock.

"The angel will need a mother to guide her through what she's becoming. Teach her what it means to love me."

Anne pressed her hands to the ground and forced herself to rise. "And if she resists?"

"Then remind her what her heart already knows," he said. "Pain is devotion. Devotion is freedom."

The torches flared white-hot. Anne's silhouette sharpened, her shadow stretching across the wall until it touched his boots.

She bowed her head again. The last traces of the old witch were gone, replaced by the storm that once drowned a king.

"Yes, my lord," she whispered. "I will make her love you."

***

He watched her leave, her figure dissolving into the light.

When she was gone, the Tall Dark Man lifted one hand. The air trembled.

He could still feel the father's rage burning in the distance, the Queen's call across the sea, the wolves' answering cry. It was all converging now—the angel's fall, the blood oath, the storm reborn.

He smiled, soft and certain, and whispered into the dark:

"Let them think they've won their vows. I've already written mine in fire. It's time they learn the rest of my prophecy. I will fulfill it and devour the Queen before them all. Only then will they understand and submit to my true power."

CHAPTER 15

AWAKENINGS

Amber, Hōnaunau, Present
Night

The ocean had gone quiet, but nothing about it felt calm.

Amber stood at the edge of the lava shelf, wind tangling her hair, salt burning in her throat. Behind her, torches hissed in the damp air. The kaimoni gathered again, their forms drawn from steam and coral light, warriors of the old sea standing shoulder to shoulder along the tide.

Between them rose Kanaloa, taller than the rest, his skin black as cooled stone streaked with veins of blue fire. His eyes were the color of deep water where sunlight never reached.

"You come again," he said. "The island bleeds because you woke what should have slept."

Amber stepped forward until her feet touched the wet line where sea met land.

"I come to bind it before it breaks. I ask not for your mercy, but for your hand."

The kaimoni murmured, the sound like surf breaking over rock.

Kawika moved behind her, chanting under his breath, calling the names of the four winds and the nine currents. Malia scattered salt and black sand into the air so the ancestors would hear. Chloe stood opposite Amber in the circle, hands raised, voice weaving Hawaiian and Latin into one prayer that turned the air hot.

Kanaloa's gaze drifted to Chloe. "You bring outsiders to our altar."

Amber answered steadily. "They carry the blood that made me Queen. They stand as my ʻohana now."

The god considered her, then lowered his head.

"So be it. But every covenant demands a price. Give me a memory—the moment that made you Queen."

Amber hesitated. The request carried weight.

Memory was more than thought. It was the thread binding soul to body. To give it was to carve herself open.

"If that is the cost," she said quietly, "I give it freely."

Kawika's chant rose, deep and rhythmic, like ocean striking hollow stone. The circle brightened. Sand fused to glass beneath their feet.

Amber closed her eyes.

She saw Michael's face in moonlight, pale and fading. Felt his hand slip from hers in that final battle centuries ago. Heard the roar of fire. The scream that split her first life in half. The taste of blood and salt filled her mouth.

When she spoke, her voice carried both love and agony.

"I remember the day the light died, and I was born again."

The gods answered.

The ocean surged in one breathless rise, lifting her from her feet. Waves spiraled around the circle without breaking. Within the water, figures formed—men, women, children of every generation who had guarded the islands.

Their eyes burned blue.

The kaimoni stood in full number now, hundreds strong, chanting the ancient names of power. The sound shook the cliffs. Even the stars seemed to flicker.

Kanaloa stepped deeper into the sea until water reached his waist. He raised one hand, and a column of ocean rose with him, spiraling upward like a living tower.

From within it echoed the old chant:

E ala, e ala, e ke ahi o ke kai,

E ala, e ka mōʻī wahine o ka honua!

(Rise, rise, fire of the sea, rise, Queen of the earth.)

Amber reached for him. The moment her fingers touched the water, pain burst through her chest. Her heartbeat stuttered. Memory fled—not only of Michael's death, but of his smile, his voice, the first word he ever said to her. It was gone, leaving a clean ache behind.

The light from the column shot through her body, searing every vein until it met the mark on her throat. The serpent and the sun merged there, burning gold and red. The light spread outward, touching Chloe, Kawika, and Malia in turn. They fell to their knees, their faces lit by it.

Kanaloa's voice rolled through the surf. "The covenant is sealed. The land and the sea remember Illyris, born again in the blood of men. When she calls, the land and the sea will answer her. The island will serve the queen as long as she remains true. If she fails to bring honor to our land and our people, the kaimoni will have their fill of revenge."

The kaimoni lifted their weapons—spears of coral, blades of obsidian—and struck them once against the water. The sound carried across the sea like thunder. The circle burst into white fire. For a heartbeat, the island glowed from its heart outward. Birds rose from the cliffs; the forest answered with wind.

When the light faded, only Amber stood within the smoke. The water at her feet had turned clear and still. The mark on her throat no longer burned, but a faint blue light pulsed beneath it like a second heartbeat.

Chloe reached her first. "Amber—your eyes."

She blinked. The reflection in Chloe's gaze showed gold burning where red had been. "He took it," Amber said softly. "The memory. I can feel the hole he left."

Kawika's voice came low. "But he gave somethin' back, yeah? Feel dat mana? Da island is alive again."

Amber looked toward the horizon. The sky was paling, the first edge of dawn breaking over the water. "He gave me the land and the sea," she said. "And I gave him the past. Now we see what the world does with the trade."

The torches guttered out. The smell of salt lingered. Beneath the calm, the island was now a part of her, and she was part of the island. Together, they were one.

Zaraquel, The Witch's Forest,
Beneath

She woke to the sound of water. Not rain. Not the sea she remembered from Hawai'i. Something different. It dripped from the ceiling and slid over her face, warm as blood.

The forest around her glowed with a faint blue light. The trees had no bark. Each passing moment sent another ripple through the air, making her feel scared and alone, yet the world reshaped itself in response.

She could not tell how long she had been bound. Her arms ached from the weight of silver roots wound around them, alive and tightening each time she tried to move. The air was thick with the smell of salt and decay, making her nauseous. Somewhere close, Witch Anne was singing in a voice gone hoarse with hunger.

Zaraquel lifted her head. Above the canopy, through miles of water and stone, she felt something shift. It wasn't from this world or from down here. It was a call.

A surge of power struck through her bones, stirring a deep, seething rage unlike anything she had ever felt. But it was rage and power, and as she felt it, she understood what it was.

"Amber," she whispered. The word came out raw, broken by thirst.

She knew it wasn't her mother's light she felt, but the same source that fed her family's blood. Illyris's fire joined to the island's mana, an echo of her own divine core. She remembered Amber speaking about her past life as Illyris and how it had all begun with her. The fire was powerful, too powerful. It nearly made her pass out.

Anne stopped singing.

"You felt that, didn't you?"

Zaraquel didn't answer. She stared at the witch across the chamber. Anne looked smaller now, her eyes rimmed in black, her hands trembling as she clutched the crystal that still held the last fragment of Zaraquel's light. The glow inside it flickered weaker each time the earth above them shook.

"The Queen has made her bargain," Anne said. "She burns what is left of the old gods. Foolish woman. She does not know she feeds him."

Zaraquel's voice cracked. "Who?"

Anne smiled without teeth. "The one who never sleeps. The Tall Dark Man."

The sound of his name twisted the air. The silver roots writhed tighter, biting into Zaraquel's skin until blood ran down her wrists. The forest turned cold, as if something had shifted the moment she heard his name.

A voice followed—a whisper that wasn't Anne's, or any mortal's. It was a voice she knew.

Child of light, open your eyes.

The command cut through her skull. She screamed, and the forest seemed to scream with her. Every tree bent toward her. Every drop of blood she shed turned to fire when it hit the ground. The silver roots blackened and fell away.

Open them.

She obeyed.

The world ignited. Blue flame spiraled through darkness. She saw Anne's face melt into shadow and reform into something older, the witch's true self stripped bare. She saw the Tower beneath the sea, the Hunter standing within it, his eyes white and blind, his chest moving with her breath. She saw her father's hand reaching for her through a hundred miles of ash.

"Marcus," she said, and the sound of his name shattered what remained of the binding.

The crystal in Anne's grasp shattered, and Zaraquel's light rushed back into her body. It no longer felt pure. It burned red at the edges, touched by the serpent's flame Amber had awakened above.

Anne fell to her knees, clutching her throat. "You can't take it back," she rasped. "It belongs to him now."

Zaraquel rose. The blood on her hands steamed where it struck the ground. "Then he will have to take it from me himself. No matter how dark my light becomes, even if I lose myself, I am still the true Avenging Angel of the highest order. I serve the prophecy, but first I serve the Order."

The chamber split open behind her. Water poured in from nowhere, filling the forest rapidly. Zaraquel did not fight it. She let it lift her, carry her upward through collapsing roots and stone until she broke into the current that linked the underworld to the island.

She became one with the water as it surged forward, moving too fast for anything else to follow. The light above was blinding. For one breathless moment, she felt Amber's heartbeat echo her own, the mana running between them like a thread of fire and salt.

Then the current snapped, and she was gone, drawn toward whatever waited between realms.

Marcus, The Forest Between Realms

The forest looked no different than moments before. Zaraquel's light still lingered, though dimmer now. The pain in Marcus's chest had grown nearly unbearable.

He stood at the center, listening, searching.

It wasn't sound that reached him first, but a feeling—a rhythm buried deep within the ground. It throbbed once, twice, then again.

A memory surfaced: Chloe teaching him spells, showing him how to listen to the magic around him. He chuckled softly, remembering her promise that it would one day come in handy.

"Stop," he said quietly.

The wolves froze. Sabre's nostrils flared as he lifted his head toward the unseen sky. McPherson lowered the lantern he carried, its light bending under the thick mist. Nimue stood slightly apart, her face pale, the white streak in her hair catching the glow like frost.

"What is it?" she asked.

Marcus turned slowly in a circle. The scent of magic and blood filled the air. "She's awake."

No one spoke.

The ground trembled beneath them, not with danger, but with something older. Far away, a low roar echoed, a sound not meant for mortal ears. He felt Zaraquel's light pressing through the layers of this place, breaking apart the illusion that had held them prisoner for who knew how long.

"She's coming back," he whispered.

Nimue stepped closer. "Then we must be ready for what she brings with her."

He met her eyes. "She's my daughter. I'll take whatever comes."

A sudden flash of red split the fog ahead. For a moment, Marcus thought he saw her—a shape of fire within the mist, wings unfurling where no sky existed. The vision struck him so hard his knees buckled. Blood filled his mouth, the price of their bond reopening.

McPherson caught him before he fell. "Easy, brother."

Marcus shook his head, breathing through the pain. "No. Let it come."

The night felt different now. His blood was trying to tell him something. He tried to ignore it, but he couldn't. Closing his eyes, he reached through the blood bond toward Zaraquel.

She was here.

Then she was gone.

When he opened his eyes, the trees tore themselves from the earth, roots twisting into spirals of bone and vine. A wave of water followed, rolling through the undergrowth. The wolves leapt aside. The lantern went out.

In the darkness, Zaraquel's voice filled the space—not as sound, but as thought.

I am coming, Father.

The words struck him like lightning down his spine. The Totem of Death at his belt pulsed once, burning cold. The trees snapped in half.

He rose to his feet, eyes black with power, fangs bared. "Then the way is open."

Nimue drew her staff. "The veil won't hold long. When she crosses, he will feel it too."

Marcus nodded. "Then we move now."

Sabre and Black Wind shifted back to their half-forms, claws gleaming. McPherson lifted his staff and began chanting the old druidic prayer that steadied worlds when they broke. The words bent the mist around them into a tunnel of pale green light.

Marcus stepped forward first. The totem's light spread outward, tracing veins of silver through the roots beneath them. "Zaraquel," he murmured. "Follow it home."

For a breath, the mist parted. Through it he saw her again, rising in the current of water, her wings aflame, her face a mixture of rage and sorrow. Their eyes met through the veil.

He smiled, even as blood ran from his nose. "There you are."

The vision shattered. The forest closed behind it. Only the feeling in his heart guided him forward. His promise to Chloe to bring their daughter home was one he would not break, even if it meant giving up everything else that mattered.

Malakai, The Blue Mountains,
Present Night

The wind off the peaks carried the scent of burnt pine and rain, the smell of a world caught between storms. Malakai stood where the ridge fell into shadow, looking down at the valley that had once been green. Firelight glowed far below—villages, camps, hunters' fires—but what he felt in his chest was not man-made.

It came from deep beneath the earth, a vibration that rolled through stone and marrow like a drumbeat.

The island across the sea was calling.

He felt the Queen's mana rise with the tides, her new covenant rippling through every living thing that still remembered the first fire.

The pack waited behind him, silent shapes against the slope. Kael, scarred and watchful, paced near the edge, his breath misting in the cold.

"You hear her too," Kael said.

Malakai nodded once. "I hear her. I just don't trust what follows."

Kael tilted his head. "Then you forgot who you are."

Malakai almost smiled. "No. I remember too well."

He turned away from the pack and let his eyes drift to the dark east, where the mountains met the clouds. A memory pressed up from the earth—snow falling on iron, the smell of blood in a frozen field, Nikoli standing over him, his hands covered in fur and flame. The old king's voice came as clearly as the wind.

You don't master the wolf, boy. You make peace with it. The moment you fear it, it owns you.

Malakai had not shifted since that night. The last time he did, he lost three brothers before he came back to himself. He had seen his reflection in their blood and vowed never to become that creature again. Even now, centuries later, his hands still shook at the thought.

Kael watched him with the eyes of a challenger. "If you won't lead, I will."

The words hit harder than the wind. He remembered Amber's face the last time he saw her, the way she whispered his name before the chains closed, and he realized the truth he'd been avoiding—the world didn't need the man who feared himself. It needed the wolf who could stand beside the Queen.

He dropped to his knees.

The first crack of bone echoed across the ridge. Pain tore through his ribs, white and blinding. Claws burst from his hands. His skin split along the scars of the old chains. The pack drew back, not in fear, but in reverence.

His body stretched and twisted, muscles folding beneath fur the color of ash and stormlight. When he lifted his head, his eyes burned gold.

Kael bowed low. "Alpha," he said.

Malakai's growl rolled through the mountains. It was not rage this time. It was promise.

The sound carried through every valley, across rivers and forests, until it reached the ocean's edge. Somewhere far beyond, Amber felt it in her bones.

The pack answered him, ten voices rising into the cold night. The mountains shook. Snow slid from the peaks.

When the echoes faded, he turned his muzzle toward the south, where the air smelled of salt and heat.

We run for her.

He bounded forward, the others falling into stride beside him. The earth kept their rhythm, and for the first time in years, Malakai felt whole—man and beast, king and servant, fear and faith running as one.

Kupa'aike'e, Hōnaunau, Island
of Hawaii, 1795

The night the island chose its king, the people wept with joy. At last, they had a ruler to bring fertility, loyalty, and love to both the land and its people. Fear no longer ruled their sleep.

Kupa'aike'e stood barefoot on the black rock terrace of Pu'uhonua o Hōnaunau, the Place of Refuge, his hands painted in ash and oil. Below him, canoes filled with warriors crowded the shore, their torches reflecting in blood-colored water. Kamehameha's fleet waited for dawn to strike the final blow against the southern chiefs, yet even the war drums had gone silent.

Something older was coming.

He had felt it hours before—the mana trembling beneath the stone, the ocean turning against itself. The priests had fled inland, whispering that the gods were restless. Only Kupaʻaikeʻe remained. He was kahuna of the deep, keeper of the old chants no one dared speak anymore.

His ancestors had warned him: the waters were not always kind. Even the gods must bow when something greater rose from below. They had also warned him of a day when the land would revolt, turning dry and barren.

He knelt at the terrace's edge and pressed both palms to the wet stone. His chant began slowly, then strengthened, each word reopening an ancient wound.

"E ala e, e ala e, e ke ahi o ke kai, e ala e."
(Rise, fire of the sea, rise.)
The ocean answered.

The waves withdrew until the reef stood bare, glistening in torchlight. The sound that followed was not surf, but breathing—deep and heavy—as though the island itself had lungs.

Something was changing.

The torches flickered blue. The men in the canoes cried out.

A column of water rose from the deep, twisting like a living serpent, its body made of storm and flame.

Kupaʻaikeʻe did not run.

He lifted his face to the towering shape and shouted over the roar, "Who claims the fire of the sea?"

The answer came in a voice that was neither thunder nor man.

"I am the darkness that waits beneath your gods. I am Ka Kāne ʻEleʻele Loa."

The Tall Dark Man stepped from the water as though born from it. His skin shimmered with scales of shadow. His eyes were pale as a moon drowned in rain. The air grew heavy. Thunder shook the sky.

The people hid in terror. Only one remained standing.

He looked at Kupaʻaikeʻe with something like amusement. "You called for power to save your islands. I have come to grant it."

Kupaʻaikeʻe trembled but did not retreat. "You are no akua I know. The gods of this land protect their own."

"Do they?" the dark one asked softly. "Where are they now? Sleeping in the mountains while men burn their temples? I bring a covenant, kahuna. One that will make your chiefs immortal."

He reached into the water and drew out a blade—black and curved, its edge gleaming with red fire.

"Blood for balance. The sea for dominion. Swear to it, and your people will rule the waves until the world ends."

Kupaʻaikeʻe hesitated. He felt the mana bleeding from the earth beneath him, the island's heart faltering. As kahuna, his soul was bound to the land. What the land felt, he felt.

Behind him, the cries of Kamehameha's warriors rose on the wind.

"And if I refuse?"

The Tall Dark Man smiled.

"Then your island sinks tonight."

Lightning split the sky. The serpent of water coiled higher, its roar shaking the cliffs.

Kupaʻaikeʻe fell to his knees, pressing his forehead to the stone. "Then I bind this covenant in the name of life," he whispered. "Not of darkness."

He took the blade.

Fire shot up his arm, searing his skin in the shape of a spiral serpent. The Tall Dark Man pressed his hand over the mark, sealing it.

"It is done. The Shadow Covenant is born."

The ocean surged forward, swallowing sand, canoes, screams.

Kupaʻaikeʻe felt himself lifted and drowned at once. Through red water he saw the god's eyes watching him, calm and endless.

When he awoke, the sea was still. Dawn painted the horizon.

The mark burned on his arm. Beneath the surface, the serpent's shadow writhed.

He understood then what he had unleashed.

The gods of the island were bound to a foreign darkness. Every generation after him would bear the debt.

Far above, the volcano answered with a deep, sorrowful tremor. The island shook once, as though remembering what it had lost.

And the kahuna wondered whether he had saved his people—or doomed them.

Philip II of Macedon, The First
Covenant, 338 B.C.

The war had ended, but the earth still reeked of iron.

Macedon's hills glowed dull red in the aftermath, torches burning low where men buried their dead. Philip walked among them without crown or guard, the serpent standard fallen from his hand.

The wind carried ash and olive wood, mingled with the blood of men who had called him king.

He had given them victory.

He had also given them ruin.

He stopped beside a broken wall that had once marked the border of Thebes—his teacher's city.

Epaminondas lay long dead, yet Philip still heard his voice as clearly as the day he first took up a spear.

Power without wisdom burns its bearer first.

He had believed those words once.

Then kingship taught him that wisdom without power meant nothing at all.

He picked up a stone from the ground and turned it in his hand. Carved into it was an older symbol—two serpents twined around a crown.

The mark had been there before the battle. Older than Greece. Older than any name for God.

"Is this what you left me?" he murmured. "A world too small for the man who wins it?"

From the dark horizon shimmered something like fire, though no flame touched the earth. It drew closer, shaping itself into a man—taller than any soldier, draped in smoke and silver. His eyes glowed pale and steady, like moonlight holding its breath before dawn.

"Who are you?" Philip asked, though part of him already knew.

The figure smiled. "Once, they called me teacher too. You have been asking the same question your master did—how does a man make the world obey?"

Philip dropped the stone. "Epaminondas is dead."

"I wear his memory," the stranger replied. "And many others. I am Ka Kāne 'Ele'ele Loa, the dark god of all oaths. I come to answer the question that haunts kings."

Philip's throat tightened. "And what question is that?"

"How to remain remembered."

The god stepped closer.

"Your name will fade. Your son will outshine you. But I can give you a kingdom no death can unseat. A serpent's bloodline. Power to rule long after Greece has turned to dust."

Philip looked at his scarred, trembling hands. "At what price?"

The Tall Dark Man drew a dagger from shadow. Its blade was dark glass. Its hilt gleamed gold.

"All covenants are the same. Blood for balance. Dominion for devotion. Swear it, and you will bear my mark. Refuse, and your line vanishes into silence."

He should have turned away.

Instead, he reached for the blade.

"Then let my sons remember."

The dagger cut his palm. Blood struck the dust and began to bubble. The serpent carved in stone flared red.

The Tall Dark Man pressed his hand over Philip's wound. The blood smoked, shaping itself into scales that crawled up his arm.

"It is done," the god said. "Your blood will coil through empires—through witches and angels alike. When the Queen of Reconciliation rises, your serpent will rise with her. The blade will know your name."

Philip's breath came heavy. "And my soul?"

The god smiled.

"That was never yours to keep."

When the light faded, Philip stood alone. His hand still bled, the mark pulsing beneath his skin.

Thunder rolled across the sky—the same sky that would one day carry Illyris to death and rebirth.

He looked toward Olympus, its peak lost in cloud, and felt the serpent move beneath his flesh.

"So this is what it means to rule forever," he whispered.

The covenant had been sealed. The blood of kings had begun its march through time.

And the man who sealed his fate didn't yet realize that the god he met would one day become his nemesis.

CHAPTER 16

WHERE THE DARKNESS SETTLES

The Tall Dark Man, The
Underground, Present Night

The chamber seemed darker than before as he paraded through the inner halls. The walls were sticky with trails of blood. He removed a glove and let his finger touch the warm liquid. His Underground was beginning to feel different somehow.

The Tall Dark Man stood in the center of the hall where the Hunter's cradle had once rested. It was shattered now, the glass melted inward, the blood run dry. He could feel it, the pull of something that was once his. A queen's fire. A witch's chant. The mana of an island he had long ago claimed. The memory of it burned through his chest like a wound that refused to close.

The queen was acting on impulse, and it connected her to him in an unusual way, forcing memories from long ago to surface. Her power had increased, and he didn't like that. There could only be one person to rule the dark prophecy, and that was him.

"The Queen trades memory for dominion," he said. His voice rumbled low, each word shaking dust from the ceiling. "And believes herself unbound."

Tituba knelt beside the altar, her eyes shadowed by exhaustion. "She bound the island's gods. The island now carries her mark."

"She carries mine," he replied. "She calls to the old powers, but all the old powers answer to me. I rule them all."

He reached for the Hunter, the body of a man grown too soon, his skin gray, his veins glowing red like magma in stone. When the god's hand met the boy's chest, a pulse of heat tore through the room. Stone cracked. The altar split. From the fissures, creatures crawled, men of marrow and smoke, their spines bent backward, mouths open in silent hunger.

"The marrow-born will be my eyes," the Tall Dark Man said. "They will feed on her light until she crawls to me for mercy."

Tituba watched as the creatures gathered. "She will fight."

He turned toward her. "Then she will fall, just like the angel. They will bow down to me."

He traced a circle in the air, and in its center a vision formed. Amber on the shore of Hawai'i, her eyes gold, her mark glowing faintly blue.

"She awakens what I built to sleep. Her Queen's fire calls the angel home." His mouth curved into something between a smile and pain. "So be it."

He pressed his palm to the altar. Shadows flooded upward, spinning into a spiral of red smoke that raced toward the surface world.

"Let the Queen see the cost of her awakening."

The Hunter stirred, his breath rising shallow and quick. His eyes opened, white and sightless.

"Rise," the Tall Dark Man whispered. "Find her. Bring her to me. Bring the queen and the angel bride both. The light will kneel before the dark once more."

The walls split with a sound like thunder. The marrow-born screamed as they ascended, crawling through the cracks toward the world above. When silence returned, only the Tall Dark Man and Tituba remained. His form shimmered, growing less human, edges blurring into smoke.

"The covenants are awake," he said, almost to himself. "Now let the world remember who made them."

Marcus, The Rift Between Worlds, Present Night

The world felt under siege. Marcus's vampiric instincts were on high alert. Every sense pointed in the direction he needed to go.

Marcus drove his claws into the ground to stay upright as the forest began to change. It was no longer quiet and peaceful. Instead, it was filled with anger and tension, something he had felt for a while. The wolves braced against the pull, fur lifting in waves. McPherson raised his staff high, light flaring in the old runes that still obeyed him.

"Hold your ground!" Marcus shouted, though his voice was swallowed by the quake.

From the fog ahead came a noise like bone scraping glass. Then they saw them. The first of the marrow-born. Creatures with bodies half-formed, their ribs twisted into spines, faces smooth except for mouths that gaped open in hunger. They crawled across the ground, smoke trailing from the joints where limbs met.

Nimue moved first. She thrust her staff into the soil, the veins in her hands lighting gold as she whispered the druidic seal. The earth buckled upward in a jagged wall, slowing the nearest wave.

"They're not real flesh," she said. "They're bound souls, like pieces torn from the dark."

Marcus bared his teeth. "Then they can die again."

He drew the Totem of Death from his belt. The moment it touched his palm, everything around them darkened and grew still. Over time, he had begun to see the effects of the Totem of Death when he held it in his hands. The world would darken as if life in all beings were slowly dying. When he had more time, he planned to ask McPherson about this strange behavior.

The wolves lunged together. Sabre tore through the first creature's neck. Its body burst into gray ash, the scent of burnt marrow thick enough to choke them. More followed, too many to count.

McPherson planted the staff beside Marcus. "If they breach the tunnel, the worlds will bleed."

"They already are." Marcus's eyes burned black.

He swung the totem like a blade. It didn't do anything at first, but with the second swing, it shone a bright red light that cut through everything around them. Every creature it touched vanished, its scream caught before exploding. The ground quaked harder.

A light broke through the ceiling of mist, blue and red, swirling like a storm. Zaraquel fell through it, wings folded, fire dripping from the tips of her feathers. She hit the ground hard enough to crack the stone. For a moment she didn't move. Then she looked up, her eyes burning with both fury and confusion.

"Daddy," she said.

He stepped through the carnage toward her. "You're home."

The creatures turned on her at once, drawn by the light pulsing beneath her skin. She didn't hesitate. She opened her hands, and what came out was not pure light anymore. It was light touched by something deeper. Every blast tore through the marrow-born like glass under pressure, leaving smears of molten dust behind.

Nimue watched her in awe and fear. "She's not what she was."

Marcus didn't look away. "No. She's way more."

The rift above them began to close, edges collapsing in a swirl of violet fire. McPherson's voice cracked from strain. "If we don't move now, we're trapped!"

Marcus reached for Zaraquel. "You lead. I'll cover."

They ran, wolves at their sides, Nimue behind them, the last of the marrow-born pouring in from every direction. Zaraquel spread her wings once, and the rush of heat from them drove the front line back into shadow. Marcus swung the totem again, carving open a path of silver light through the dark.

When they reached the threshold, the rift shuddered. The tunnel of mist narrowed to a single line of brightness. Marcus looked back once. The forest was gone. In its place, a red glow pulsed from the depths, the Tall Dark Man's mark burning through the ground like veins of fire.

Zaraquel's hand closed around his wrist. "Don't look back."

He nodded. Together they leapt.

The rift sealed behind them with a sound that made them shudder. The silence that followed was worse than the noise. For a long moment, nothing moved.

Then Marcus felt her grip tighten. He looked down and realized they weren't standing anywhere at all. The mist below them stretched endless and black. Zaraquel's wings unfurled on instinct. She caught him before he fell, her fire casting long shadows against the void.

"We're not free yet," she said.

Marcus smiled, blood still running from the corner of his mouth. "Then we fight until we are."

The void made him uneasy, and there was something ancient stirring below.

The battle was only beginning.

Raven Hexham, Transylvania,
Present Night

The night wind crawled through the broken windows of the fortress, bringing with it a cold breeze that chilled her to the bone. Raven sat in the center of the hall that had once been a chapel, her hands resting on the stones where the altar used to be. Every prayer carved into the walls had been defaced long ago, but she could still feel the echo of what they once meant.

The mark on her wrist burned again, a serpent of shadow twisting beneath her skin. She bit down on a cry. The fire spreading through her veins wasn't his call. It was something else, older and deeper.

She saw flashes she couldn't explain. Blue light from an island far away. A Queen crowned in coral and flame. The pulse of blood meeting blood and a fire that wouldn't stop burning.

Then came the voice.

You feel it too.

It wasn't the Tall Dark Man. It was a woman's voice, calm and sharp as glass.

"Who are you?" Raven whispered.

You already know. You carry my line.

The vision sharpened. For an instant, she saw Chloe Tudor standing in a circle of light, her hands raised over a grimoire that bled symbols across the page. Between them hung a thread of red light that vibrated like a heartbeat.

Break the mark, Chloe said. *Or it will take what's left of you.*

Raven gripped her wrist. "It's bound by his blood."

Then burn it with your own.

The light vanished. The silence that followed waited for her to answer, but she didn't. She stood, trembling. The mark writhed as if it knew what she meant to do.

Around her, shadows gathered, the Tall Dark Man's watchers, thin as smoke, heads tilted in mock reverence.

"He says you belong to him," one hissed.

Raven smiled through the pain. "Tell him he's wrong."

She tore the dagger from her belt and drove it into her wrist. Blood hit the stone and burned black. The mark flared once, brilliant and wild, before exploding in a burst of red light. The watchers screamed as the fire spread, eating their shapes until nothing remained but ash.

When it was done, Raven fell to her knees. The wound sealed instantly, leaving a faint scar shaped like a spiral serpent biting its tail. Her breath came ragged, but her mind was clear for the first time in years.

"Chloe," she whispered. "You were right."

A faint shimmer answered her, a reflection in the air, the ghost of a connection still alive. Chloe's voice carried through it, tired but steady.

You're free now. Come to me. The Queen needs every hand that still remembers the light. You still have light in you. I can feel it. It's faint, but it's alive. Come to me, and I will make it burn brighter than ever.

Raven rose. Her eyes glowed faint violet, the color of a spell half dark, half redeemed.

"Tell her I'm coming. But I don't fight for redemption."

Then fight for blood, Chloe said.

The link snapped.

The fortress around her shook as the last of the old shadows fled. For the first time since her birth, Raven Hexham felt the world's weight shift without his will pressing on her. She smiled at the start of her freedom. Her choice to rebel.

"Let him come," she said. "This time I'll burn first."

The Hunter, The Underground,
Present Night

He woke to silence. Not the silence of rest, but the kind that makes a person uneasy before a disaster strikes.

His chest rose and fell as if remembering how to breathe, a strong sensation of pain and rage threading through him. The air around him was thick with dust and the scent of burning blood flooding his nostrils. Shadows clung to the walls like living things.

He looked down at his hands. They were not children's hands anymore. The skin was gray, veined with red lines that pulsed faintly with each heartbeat, running from his forearms to his fingertips. When he flexed his fingers, sparks of light crawled across his knuckles and vanished again.

He did not know his name. He knew the word *father*, and it filled him with heat he couldn't understand. Somewhere beyond the walls, someone was calling, a voice he almost recognized. It was soft and bright, the sound of a life he had never lived.

"Amber," he whispered, though he didn't know where the word came from. It tasted like longing and fire, yet the feeling gave him unease and a rage that needed to be freed.

Chains rattled above him. The chamber's ceiling shook as the last of the marrow-born climbed through the cracks to the world above. He tried to follow, but the weight of something unseen pressed down on his shoulders, keeping him still, unable to move.

"Not yet," a voice murmured inside his head. "Your time is measured in blood, and it has not come yet."

He closed his eyes. The darkness that answered was not empty. It was alive. Faces formed within it, flashes of battle and light, an angel's wings burning red. He saw her fall through the rift, and the sight made something inside him ache.

When he opened his eyes again, the world had sharpened. He could see the threads of power running through the stone. He could hear the heartbeat of the earth miles above. His voice came low, almost reverent.

"I will find her."

The chamber's torches flared one by one, feeding on air that should not have burned. His shadow moved along the wall until it touched the altar where the Tall Dark Man had stood.

He rose, tall and steady, the last trace of youth gone from his face. His eyes turned white, and the red veins in his body glowed brighter, burning through his skin like living fire.

"Father," he whispered, though the word no longer meant mercy.

The sound of footsteps echoed from somewhere unseen. The Hunter took one breath, and the entire room exhaled with him.

Then the lights went out.

CHAPTER 17

WHAT THE WORLD COSTS

Chloe, Hawaii, Dawn

Chloe woke with her heart already racing, her body slick with sweat as though she had been running. The room was still dark, the faint sound of the ocean drifting through the open windows, calm enough to be cruel.

For a moment she lay there, staring at the ceiling, trying to convince herself that the weight pressing against her chest was only the echo of a dream. It wasn't. Her magic hummed under her skin, restless and sharp, the way it only did when something had already happened and the world was too slow to catch up.

She sat up and pressed her palm to the floor. The stone beneath her hand felt warm, not from the sun but from power that had not yet finished moving through the island.

Somewhere close by, Amber slept in her coffin. Chloe could feel her presence the way one feels gravity, steady and immense, but altered. Something had been taken from her. Something had been added. Chloe did not need to look to know that both were true.

The vision came without warning.

She was standing in water up to her knees, black and glassy, reflecting a sky that did not belong to any world she recognized. Marcus stood a short distance away, whole and breathing, his expression calm in a way that made her chest ache. He reached for her, and for a breath she believed this was the future she had been promised.

Then she saw the space behind him.

It wasn't empty. It was missing.

Zaraquel knelt in that absence, her wings folded tight against her back, her head bowed not in defeat but in acceptance. Chains circled her wrists and throat, glowing faintly as though the chains were alive. She was not crying.

That was the worst part.

Chloe gasped, and the vision shattered.

She doubled over, breath tearing from her lungs as if she had been struck. The room spun. When she finally forced herself upright, tears streaked her face, though she could not remember when they had begun. She wrapped her arms around herself and rocked once, twice, grounding the way McPherson had taught her.

The sight had been clear. Too clear to dismiss.

Someone had paid a price.

And it was not Marcus.

Amber Stone, Hōnaunau, Hours
Before the Dawn

Amber woke to silence and knew immediately that it was wrong. The island had always spoken to her, even before she understood what she was, the memory of life among the people and their history threaded through the land. The mana lay coiled and attentive, waiting for her to move.

She rose slowly and stepped outside, barefoot on the cooling stone. Her throat tingled where the mark rested beneath her skin. When she touched it, it answered her like it was truly part of her.

She did not think of Michael when she woke anymore. The space where his memory had lived was quiet and clean, an absence that did not bleed. That frightened her more than grief ever had.

Philip stood at the edge of the terrace, his back to her, hands folded behind him like a courtier waiting to be addressed. He had not slept. She could tell by the tension in his shoulders, by the way he stood as though braced against a blow.

"You feel it too," she said.

He inclined his head. "The covenants have tightened."

Amber joined him, her gaze fixed on the sea. "Something has been taken."

Philip exhaled slowly and shook his head. "Not taken. Offered."

She turned then, studying him. The serpent's presence clung to him more closely now, restless and alert. "You've known this was coming."

"Yes," he said. "Just not who would bleed for it."

Amber's jaw tightened. "I did not ask for this."

"No," Philip replied. "But the world did."

The words settled between them, heavy with implication.

Amber looked back toward the water, her expression hardening into resolve. Whatever had been set in motion would not be undone by regret. If the Tall Dark Man believed this action would weaken her, he had miscalculated. She would learn its cost. And then she would decide what it bought.

What unsettled her was not fear, but knowledge half withheld. The Blood Prophecy had always promised balance, yet something else now moved beneath it, older and harder to name. A shadow layered beneath the words she had sworn to serve.

She stood alone on the terrace longer than she meant to. Malakai's absence pressed harder than the unanswered prophecy. A queen could rule without a king, but she had never wanted to.

Marcus, The Threshold, Present Night

Marcus stood at the edge of a place he could not name. It was not the forest and not the world beyond it, but a narrow veil where reality felt thin enough to tear if struck too hard.

The constant ache beneath his ribs had eased, leaving behind a strange hollowness that made him uneasy. McPherson moved nearby, quiet and watchful. The wolves lingered at a respectful distance, still and alert.

No one spoke.

Marcus flexed his hands, testing the familiar strength in them. Everything felt intact. Too intact. He had learned long ago that survival without cost was rarely a gift. There was always a cost.

He closed his eyes and reached inward, searching for the bond that had once burned in his chest. Zaraquel was still there. Distant, muted, but present.

He let out a breath he had not realized he was holding.

She's alive, he told himself. That had to be enough.

When he opened his eyes, the threshold shimmered faintly, as if something had passed through it and left no trace behind. Marcus stared at it for a long moment, a chill creeping up his spine.

Somewhere far away, the door had closed.

Zaraquel, Beyond the Threshold,
Present Night

The space she stood in had no walls, no ground, no sky. It was built of memory and promise, a place that responded not to fear but to certainty.

Zaraquel stood at its center, her wings folded, her hands steady at her sides. The fire within her no longer raged. It was silent, contained, waiting.

He did not arrive in smoke or shadow. He stepped into sight as though the space itself had been holding him, his presence settling the air around her into stillness. His eyes were calm, patient, almost kind.

"You know why you're here," the Tall Dark Man said.

"Yes," Zaraquel replied.

He studied her without haste. "Your father walks free."

Her throat tightened. "He does."

"And you understand the exchange."

She lifted her chin, her gaze steady. "I do."

For the first time, something like approval touched his expression. "You were always meant to choose."

Zaraquel's wings trembled once, then stilled. "Then let it be me."

The words did not echo. They did not need to.

The space sealed around them, ancient power locking into place with the quiet certainty of a law older than any world she had known. Far away, the world continued unaware of what it had accepted.

Zaraquel closed her eyes as the chains formed, not in fear, but in resolve.

Somewhere beyond the veil, the Queen rose, unaware that the angel had already fallen for her crown.

CHAPTER 18

AN ANGEL'S SILENCE

Amber Stone, Ala Moana
Center, Honolulu, Present Night

Amber had never trusted quiet in a place built for noise.

At night, Ala Moana was usually a living machine: feet on tile, music spilling from open doors, laughter rising and falling in waves, the smell of perfume and fried food. Tonight, the sound was still there, but it felt wrong, as if someone had pulled the soul out of it and left the body walking.

She stood just inside the main concourse and let her eyes track the crowd without looking like she was tracking anything at all. Chloe stayed close, hood up, her black hair tucked in, a woman trying not to be seen in a place designed to see everyone. Philip lingered a few steps behind them, hands in his pockets, the posture of a man pretending to be human while the serpent under his skin was ready to strike.

Amber touched her throat without thinking. The mark beneath her skin answered her touch with something like acknowledgment. The bargain with Kanaloa had not faded with distance. It had settled into her the way hunger settles into a vampire, quiet until it decides to speak.

She did not remember Michael's face anymore. She remembered that she had once loved someone enough to break for him, and that was all. The emptiness was clean.

That was what frightened her.

Grief would have been easier. Grief meant something still lived there.

Chloe leaned toward her, keeping her voice low so it disappeared into the mall's hum. "You feel it again."

Amber did not nod. She did not want anyone to see anything that looked like agreement. "It is not the land moving," she said. "It is something beneath it."

Philip's gaze fixed on a polished stone column near a jewelry store. A hairline crack had formed midway up the surface, so thin it could have been a vein in the marble. He moved closer, slow and casual, like a man admiring his reflection in the glass.

The crack spread another inch.

"This is not settling," Philip said. His voice stayed calm, but Amber heard the tension beneath it. "This is pressure looking for release."

A child laughed somewhere to their left. The laugh cut off too quickly, replaced by a sharp cry. Amber turned and saw the child's mother bend, confused, reaching for a dropped toy, then freeze as the floor beneath her shoes vibrated.

It was subtle, barely more than the tremor of a large truck passing outside. Most of the crowd did not notice. The ones who did glanced down and kept walking, because that is what people do when they want the world to stay normal.

The vibration returned, stronger.

A long fluorescent light fixture over the concourse flickered once, then steadied. Two more flickered farther down the hall. Chloe's hand tightened around Amber's wrist.

"This is him," Chloe whispered.

Amber's jaw locked. "No. This is what he sent."

The first real sound came from above them. It was so deep it seemed to rise from the foundation of the building itself. Heads lifted. Conversations paused. Somewhere, a store alarm chirped and then died.

Amber looked up and saw a seam in the ceiling panels widen, the thin black line stretching like a mouth opening. Dust sifted down, fine and pale, landing in hair and on shoulders like a soft warning.

A chunk of ceiling panel dropped, hit the floor, and shattered into fragments.

People screamed.

A wave of bodies surged backward.

Amber stepped forward into the panic without thinking, moving against the flow, barely keeping her claws intact. Another section fell, then another. The lights stuttered. The concourse dimmed, brightened, dimmed again, each flicker turning faces into masks.

"Chloe," Amber said, and the name carried the same authority as a command and a prayer. "Get them out."

Chloe's eyes were already glowing faintly, not bright enough to draw attention from anyone who was not watching for it. She raised a hand and whispered something under her breath, a binding spell meant for structure and motion, the kind that asked the world to hold itself together for one more minute.

Amber felt the cost immediately. The air thickened around them, heavy with strain, as if a storm were about to break.

Philip moved toward a group of teenagers frozen near the escalator, their phones raised like shields, filming instead of running. His voice cut through the chaos, sharp and human. "Move. Now."

He shoved one of them hard enough to break the trance, and once one ran, the others followed.

The escalator jerked.

It did not stop gently. It seized, metal teeth grinding, then lurched backward half a step as if the motor had been yanked by invisible hands. A woman near the edge stumbled, caught herself, screamed.

Amber crossed the space faster than a human eye could track and braced the woman with one arm, pulling her away just as the escalator railing snapped with a sound like bone breaking. The broken piece whipped through the air and struck a glass storefront. The window spiderwebbed, then collapsed outward in a roaring cascade of shards.

People ran. Some fell. Some were trampled. The noise became too loud, too layered, too full of fear to understand.

Amber stood in the center of it and tried to listen past it, to find the pattern underneath, the true source. It was coming from beneath the shopping center. She felt something crawl through the building's foundation, not an earthquake, not geology, but something deliberate moving through stone like thought.

Chloe shouted, "Amber, behind you."

Amber turned and saw the marble column Philip had watched split from top to bottom, the crack widening until it became a seam of darkness. From that crack, something pushed outward, not a creature climbing through, but a shape forming from the gap itself.

It looked wrong against the bright commercial lights. It had no face, only a mouth that opened too wide. Its ribs were visible, like the suggestion of a skeleton drawn in smoke. It moved on all fours, then rose into a half crouch, joints popping as if reality itself resented giving it form.

It was a marrow-born.

Amber's anger came first, hot and clean. It was a relief to see an enemy with edges.

She stepped toward it, and the crowd between them scattered as if sensing something inhuman had entered their world. The creature lunged.

Amber caught it by the throat with one hand. Its skin felt like ash pressed into shape. It snapped at her wrist, teeth scraping her skin, but it did not break her.

She slammed it backward into the cracked column and felt the building shudder in response, as if the structure recognized violence and offered more. The creature did not die. It folded, then tried to rise again, smoke leaking from its joints.

"Not here," Amber murmured, and pressed her palm to its chest.

The mark at her throat pulsed. A faint blue light, the same hue Kanaloa had left beneath her skin, ran down her neck and into her arm. It did not explode. It did not flare theatrically. It entered the creature like cold water entering hot rock, and the marrow-born began to fracture from within, its form cracking into thin lines that glowed briefly before turning to dust.

It collapsed soundlessly at her feet, leaving only a smear of ash on the tile.

Another seam opened farther down the hall. Then another.

Chloe swore under her breath, not a curse, but a prayer turned sharp. "There are more. This is a breach."

Philip's eyes narrowed. "He is testing you."

Amber looked at the crowd, at the bodies pressed toward exits too narrow for panic, at the security guard on the floor holding his bleeding head in both hands, at a woman pinned beneath a fallen display rack screaming for help in a voice that was turning hoarse.

"This is not a test," Amber said. "This is punishment."

Chloe grabbed her shoulder. "We cannot hold the whole building."

Amber knew it. She could feel the strain already, the way the mall was beginning to fail in layers. One collapse pulled on another. Stress traveled through beams and joints, multiplying faster than any spell could mend.

If they stayed here trying to save everyone, they would save no one.

Amber swallowed the bitter truth and forced her mind to narrow. Queens did not get the luxury of wanting everything. Queens chose. Queens paid.

"Take the west concourse," Amber told Chloe. "Hold it long enough for them to get out."

Chloe met her gaze, and Amber saw the fear there, not for herself, but for the cost Chloe would pay for holding anything at all. Chloe nodded once anyway. "And you?"

"I will break the breaches," Amber said.

Philip stepped closer. "You cannot chase all of them."

Amber did not look at him. "Then we make one place safe."

Philip understood. He shifted his weight, eyes scanning the crowd. "Where?"

Amber looked toward the central atrium, where the ceiling rose higher, where the largest concentration of people had gathered, trapped by confusion and blocked exits. She could feel the building's stress lines converging there. If that atrium fell, it would take people with it like a mouth swallowing.

"There," she said.

She moved first, cutting through the crush of bodies with inhuman speed, not shoving, not trampling, threading through gaps that did not seem to exist until she made them exist.

Philip followed, fast for a man, unnatural in his own way.

Chloe peeled away toward the west corridor, raising both hands, whispering a spell that tasted like blood even before she paid for it.

Amber reached the atrium and saw the ceiling above it sagging. A long beam groaned. A cluster of people stood frozen beneath it, staring up as if looking could stop gravity.

Amber stepped into their space and let her voice cut through the panic, loud enough to be heard, steady enough to be obeyed.

"Move," she said. "Now. This way."

Some listened because her tone carried command. Some listened because Philip grabbed them and shoved them into motion. Some listened because Amber's eyes were gold, and they felt something ancient in that gaze that made their bodies obey before their minds understood.

The beam cracked.

Amber threw herself upward, hands slamming into the underside of the failing structure. For an instant she felt the full weight of the building, not the physical weight alone, but the weight of what had been built here, human arrogance layered in steel and glass, believing it could defy anything if it sold enough.

Her arms trembled. The mark at her throat flared with cold light. The beam held, but she felt it trying to tear free anyway, the way a jaw tries to bite even when held shut.

Philip looked back at her, eyes sharp. "Amber."

"Go," she hissed. "Get them out."

He did not argue. He moved.

Amber held the beam and listened to the building. She listened past the screams, past the alarms that had started again in a broken, stuttering rhythm. She listened for the marrow-born, for the places where darkness pressed up from below like a hand against skin.

She could feel three more breaches forming. One near the food court. One near the parking levels. One deeper, beneath the foundation, larger than the rest, a wound being widened by something patient.

The Tall Dark Man did not need to be here for this to be him. His work was enough. His rules were enough.

Amber's lips curled back from her teeth. She held the beam a second longer, long enough for the last cluster of civilians to clear the space beneath her. Then she released the structure and let it fall behind her, choosing collapse where collapse would cost less life.

The crash shook the building. Dust filled the air. People screamed again, but they were moving now. They were alive.

Amber turned toward the deeper breach and started running.

Chloe Tudor, Ala Moana Center,
Honolulu, Present Night

Chloe had held walls in place before. She had held doors shut against things that wanted to enter. She had held a dying girl's heartbeat steady with her hands shaking and her mouth full of prayers. Holding a public building together while thousands of people ran through it was a different kind of terror.

It was impersonal, and that made it worse.

There were too many lives to count, too many chances to fail, too many ways for one wrong breath to become a body on the floor.

She reached the west concourse and felt the breach before she saw it. The temperature dipped. The lights in a row of stores flickered blue, then died. People surged toward her, faces wet with fear, hands out, as if she could physically carry them out of the place.

"Keep moving," Chloe said, forcing her voice to stay calm. "Do not stop."

She planted her feet on the tile and raised both hands. The spell she used was old, older than the words she spoke for it now. It came from the part of her bloodline that believed law could be written into the world if you paid enough.

Her palms burned as she pulled on her own life to feed it, and she tasted copper at the back of her throat almost immediately.

The floor beneath her shuddered. A seam opened at the base of a support column, and the marrow-born began to crawl out one after another, not fully formed yet, like nightmares learning how to stand.

Chloe did not give them time to find their shape.

She drove her hands downward and spoke the binding again, forcing the seam closed. The first creature screamed without a voice as it was crushed back into the gap. Another forced itself through anyway, elbows and ribs tearing against reality until it gained enough purchase to lunge.

Chloe's heart kicked hard. For one moment she wanted to turn and run like everyone else, to be human, to be only a mother who had already lost too much.

Then she remembered Zaraquel's face the last time she saw her, and the fear became anger.

Chloe stepped forward and swung her hand through the air as if she were slamming a door shut. Light cracked from her palm, not bright and pure, but sharp and cutting. It struck the creature's chest and split it open like paper.

The marrow-born fell apart on the floor, collapsing into ash that drifted beneath the feet of fleeing shoppers.

A man fell near her, tripped by the crowd. Someone stepped on his hand. He screamed.

Chloe dropped her hands long enough to grab his arm and drag him toward the wall, pulling him out of the crush.

"Get up," she told him. Her voice shook. "Get up and run."

He stared at her, eyes wild. "What is happening?"

Chloe wanted to tell him the truth. She wanted to tell him that gods were awake, that darkness had rules, and that the world had never been safe.

Instead, she said, "Move."

He moved.

The spell line in her body began to fray. She felt it in the tremor of her fingers, in the way her vision started to blur at the edges. She could hold the concourse for another minute, maybe two. After that she would begin to pay in things she could not get back.

The floor shuddered again and the seam opened wider, not where she had sealed it, but ten feet away, as if the darkness leaned and adjusted.

Another marrow-born pushed through. This one rose higher, taller, more stable, its mouth opening as if tasting the panic.

Chloe's pendant at her throat pulsed once, faint and wrong. She thought of the cracked stone she had carried for so long. She thought of Eve, of lava light and warnings spoken in a voice too old. She felt the Tall Dark Man's presence in the shape of the breach, in the cruelty of doing this in a place full of civilians, in the certainty that he wanted them to choose.

She lifted her hands again and whispered, "Not this way."

The light that came from her was not a flare. It was a thread, fine and violent, a line of force that wrapped around the marrow-born's neck and snapped it back into the seam it had crawled from.

Chloe drove the seam shut with both palms and felt something inside her chest tear slightly, a small rip she did not have time to acknowledge.

She leaned against the wall for half a heartbeat, eyes closing.

In that half beat, the world shifted.

It was not a vision like the ones that came to her in dreams or in smoke. It hit her like a knife.

She saw Zaraquel standing in a place without walls, wings folded, face calm, lips parting to speak words Chloe did not hear but understood anyway. She saw Marcus walking free and unaware. She felt the cost of that freedom, the exchange sealed somewhere beyond law.

Chloe's eyes flew open. Her breath caught. Her hands began to shake.

"No," she whispered, and she did not know if she meant no to the vision or no to what she already knew was true.

A scream rose behind her. A woman clutched her arm, blood running down her sleeve from a shard of glass.

Chloe reached out without thinking, pressed her palm to the wound, and let healing flow. The woman sobbed and stumbled away, alive.

Chloe stood upright again. She forced her face blank. She forced her body to keep working.

She could break later. She could mourn later. She could hate later.

Right now, she had to keep people breathing.

Philip II of Macedon, Ala
Moana Center, Honolulu,
Present Night

Philip had stood on battlefields where the ground was slick with blood and the sky itself rained ash. He had seen boys die with their mouths open, still surprised. He had seen cities burn because one ruler wanted to be remembered.

None of that prepared him for the sound of civilians panicking inside a modern palace of glass.

Fear smelled the same in every century, but here it carried perfume and soap and fried sugar. It was obscene to him.

His breathing staggered at the sight, but as a warrior he pulled it together.

He was the Serpent King.

He dragged a teenage girl away from a broken storefront just as another sheet of glass collapsed inward. A man tried to turn back for a shopping bag, and Philip grabbed him by the collar and shoved him toward the exit hard enough to make him stumble.

"Your life is not in that bag," Philip snapped.

The man stared at him, shocked, then ran.

Philip moved through the concourse looking for Amber. He could feel her presence the way he had once felt storms building when he was still mortal. The serpent mark beneath his skin pulled toward her like iron to a magnet. It resented it. It wanted to coil around her power and claim it as his own.

Philip kept his jaw clenched and forced the serpent into stillness through sheer will, the way he had once forced armies to obey.

He found her near the collapsed atrium beam, dust in her hair, eyes bright with fury. She looked like a queen out of old myth, and for a moment he understood why men once worshiped and feared Illyris.

Then he saw the strain on her shoulders, the tightness around her mouth, the way she kept glancing toward the deeper parts of the building as if listening to a threat only she could hear.

As a vampire, she impressed him. As a queen, he admired her.

"You cannot hold all of it," Philip said, stepping close enough that his voice would reach her alone.

Amber did not look at him. "I am not trying to."

Philip followed her gaze and felt it then, the larger breach beneath the foundation, the one that did not belong to this mall alone. It was connected to something older, darker, and deeper, something that did not care about this building, only about what it represented.

A city.

A people.

A soft target.

"He wants you to choose," Philip said.

Amber's eyes cut to him. "He wants me to fail."

Philip swallowed the bitter truth that tasted like his own past. "He wants you to become the kind of ruler who does not hesitate to sacrifice."

Amber's expression did not soften. "Then he will be disappointed."

She moved again, heading toward the deeper tremor. Philip followed, because whatever he was, whatever curse he carried, his blood had always led him to her.

He had once bartered kingdoms for power. Now he was running through a collapsing shopping center because a queen was trying to keep strangers alive.

The irony tasted bittersweet.

As they reached a service corridor, the lights died completely. Emergency illumination flickered on, painting the hall in sickly red. The deeper breach pulsed. Philip heard something scrape beneath the floor, like claws searching for the weakest point.

Amber paused and looked at the concrete beneath her feet as if she could see through it.

Philip knew that look. It was the look of a commander calculating loss.

"Amber," he said more quietly now. "If you go down there and the breach is rooted deeper than this building, you may not come back up."

Amber's voice came cold. "Then I will not come back up."

Philip's serpent mark flared, angry, hungry, afraid. He clenched his fists until his nails cut his palms, using pain to anchor his will.

"Then you will not go alone," he said.

Amber looked at him for a heartbeat that felt too long. Then she nodded once.

Together, they stepped toward the place where the darkness was pressing up from below like a hand against a throat.

The Tall Dark Man, The Underground, Present Night

He felt the fracture before the first scream reached the surface. Stone remembered him. It always had. Long before men learned to stack it into temples and markets, before they believed glass could protect them from consequence, the earth had learned his name and kept it close. His name and his twin sister's.

The breach beneath Honolulu opened exactly where it should have. Not at the heart of the city. Not deep enough to kill indiscriminately. But close enough to teach.

Pain, when applied without purpose, was a waste. Pain applied with restraint became instruction.

He stood alone in the chamber where the walls still carried the heat of the Hunter's awakening. The marrow-born had already climbed. He did not watch them go. He did not need to. Their hunger was simple, and obedience required no supervision.

"They will call this an attack," he said quietly.

Tituba knelt several paces away, her head bowed, her hands folded in her lap to keep them from shaking. "They always do."

"Yes," he replied. "They prefer language that absolves them."

He reached out and rested his palm against the stone floor. Through it, he felt the Queen moving. Fast. Decisive. Choosing where to stand and where to let the world break.

She was learning faster than he had expected.

That pleased him.

"She holds the weight," Tituba said. "She does not turn away."

"No," he agreed. "She does not."

He closed his eyes and let his awareness widen, touching the corridors where the witch bled herself thin to hold strangers together, touching the Serpent King as he forced his ancient curse into silence, touching the civilians who would live long enough to tell the story wrong.

Above all of them, deeper than fear, he felt the angel.

Broken, but she yielded.

Zaraquel did not resist the chain when it settled. That was the truth no one else understood. Resistance created suffering. Acceptance created law. She had chosen law.

A city shook. Glass broke. Bones fractured but did not end.

The balance held.

"This is mercy," Tituba whispered, though her voice carried doubt.

"This is restraint," he corrected. "Mercy comes later."

He opened his eyes.

"They believe I want her to fail," he continued. "They believe this is punishment."

He almost smiled. "Failure teaches nothing. Only survival does."

The Queen would emerge from this bloodied but standing. The witch would feel the cost of vision sharpen into resolve. The Serpent King would edge closer to the sacrifice he pretended not to want. And the angel would remain silent, her choice buried so deeply that when it surfaced it would shatter what they believed about balance and their prophecy.

It was his prophecy that was meant to rule.

He withdrew his hand from the stone.

"Let them gather," he said. "Let them believe they are moving toward unity."

Tituba lifted her head. "And when they reach her?"

"Then they will understand," he replied calmly, "that the world was never saved by light alone."

Far above, concrete cracked again. Sirens wailed. The Queen descended toward darkness with a king at her side.

The Tall Dark Man remained where he was.

Order did not chase chaos.

Chaos always came home to order.

CHAPTER 19

UNFORGIVEN

Marcus, The Order, Present
Night

Marcus had taken the watch alone.

As he stood guard, he couldn't help but think of everything he had gone through just to make it back to the Order. His body felt ragged. Hunger loomed, and he knew there had been no other choice but to bring them back here.

Recalling his memories of Eliza, Michael, Kabos, and others, he smiled at them, because each had helped shape him into the vampire he was today.

And then there was Chloe.

Their initial meeting had been rocky, considering he and Michael had only wanted the Queen. But as time went on, his heart had fallen in love with his witch.

Knowing what Zaraquel was going through just to bring Rae back brought tears to his eyes. Blood tears ran down his cheeks as he bared his fangs.

They slept in turns tonight. Wolves curled near the outer threshold, their bodies still while their breathing remained slow, ears twitching at sounds that never came. McPherson had sealed the inner wards hours earlier, the kind of careful magic that did not announce itself but settled into the walls, giving off only a fraction of light to reassure everyone.

Even the Totem of Life had gone quiet, its hum reduced to something Marcus felt more than heard.

That silence should have comforted him.

Instead, it pressed against his ribs like weight.

The Totem of Life should never be silent, unlike the Totem of Death he carried in his pocket.

He stood near the edge of the upper hall where the walls thinned and the world outside pressed close. The forest beyond the Order's veil was dark and motionless, trees standing still as if no breeze stirred their leaves.

Marcus rested one hand against the stone and let his other fall near the Totem of Death at his side. He took it out to hold.

It did not answer him.

It had done that more often lately, not resisting, not flaring, simply acknowledging his presence and choosing stillness.

He did not try to call Zaraquel.

He had learned what that cost.

Something shifted behind him, not a sound, not a footstep.

The change came as absence, the way a room knows when it is no longer alone.

Marcus did not turn right away. He breathed once, steady and unnecessary, and felt his body align into readiness without fear.

When he did turn, she was already there.

The woman stood where the light from the high windows thinned, neither fully shadowed nor touched by it. She wore no crown, no armor, no sign of rank or threat. Her hair fell loose down her back, dark as wet earth, her face calm in a way that had nothing to do with mercy.

She did not look old.

She looked young.

She looked permanent.

Marcus did not kneel. He did not reach for a blade. Something inside him recognized her.

"Diana," he said, not as a question.

She inclined her head slightly, as if acknowledging something already decided.

"You know my older name," she replied. Her voice was low, measured, shaped by centuries in which men learned to listen or die. "That matters."

"Macedonia taught its kings to recognize silence," Marcus said. "Not gods."

A faint curve touched her mouth, not quite a smile. "Macedonia taught its kings that gods arrive after the choice, not before."

She stepped closer, stopping a few paces away, close enough that Marcus could see the faint scars along her forearms, old marks left by bows drawn too many times, by wars that did not remember the names of the dead.

"The Queen holds the light," Diana said. "The angel holds the balance. But neither of them carries what comes after."

Marcus felt it then, a tightening behind his sternum that had nothing to do with breath or blood. "And you're here to tell me that I do."

"I am here," she corrected, "because the world has already begun to place the weight you carry."

She turned her gaze toward the forest beyond the Order, toward the dark where Zaraquel's silence now echoed louder than her screams ever had.

"When Macedon fell, it did not break because the king died. It broke because no one stood where the king had been, willing to be cursed by continuity."

Marcus's jaw tightened. "I'm not a king."

"No," Diana said. "You are worse."

The word settled between them without cruelty. She did not explain it. She did not soften it.

"Kings are remembered," she continued. "Martyrs are forgiven. Gods are feared. But the ones who keep the world from tearing open when those things fail are erased by necessity. They do not get statues. They do not get songs. They do not get absolution."

Marcus looked down at his hands. They were steady. That disturbed him more than rage ever could have.

"You're telling me there's no path where this ends clean," he said.

Diana's eyes held his, unflinching. "There has never been such a path. Only paths where fewer die."

Silence stretched. The Order did not stir. The Totem of Death remained still, as if it were listening.

Marcus lifted his gaze again. "Whatever I choose," he said slowly, "they'll call it wrong."

"Yes."

"And it won't be forgiven."

"No."

He nodded once, a small motion that carried no hesitation. "Then it will hold."

For the first time, Diana stepped back. The space she vacated felt colder, thinner.

"That is all I was sent to witness," she said. "Not your power. Your refusal to look away."

She did not fade. She did not vanish. She simply was not there anymore, the hall returning to itself as if it had never been interrupted.

Marcus stood alone again, the forest unchanged, the silence intact.

But the weight had settled.

And he did not try to set it down.

Chloe, Honolulu, Present Night

The first sirens reached Ala Moana before the last screams finished echoing through the corridors.

Chloe stood with her back to a concrete wall that had not cracked yet, her palm still pressed to the tile where she had forced it shut. She could taste the spell in her mouth like she had bitten down on a penny and never let go.

People kept running past her in waves. Some were bleeding. Some carried children who had gone silent from shock. A few were still filming, hands shaking, eyes wide, as if proof could keep them safe later.

Chloe watched their faces and did not let herself feel the urge to grab them and shake sense into them. She did not have the luxury of anger.

She had minutes, and she was already paying for every second.

The west concourse gave another tremor, then a smaller one, like an aftershock. Chloe held the line again, not with a grand gesture but with her shoulders squared and her breath forced steady. The spell was simple in shape and brutal in cost. She anchored it through her own body and dared the building to stay whole.

Her vision blurred at the edges. She blinked hard until the world returned.

Another crack tried to open near a kiosk, a dark, thin cut at the base of the wall pushing outward like pressure beneath skin. Chloe did not let it become a mouth. She snapped her hand downward and felt something in her chest give in a small, sharp way.

Pain did not bloom.

It sank.

That was worse.

When the last of the crowd cleared far enough that the crush thinned, Chloe let the spell loosen. She did not drop it fully. She couldn't. She shifted it from a hard seal to a strained hold, something that would delay collapse instead of defeating it.

Her arms trembled. Her palms felt scraped raw from magic that did not care about tenderness.

She leaned her head back against the wall and closed her eyes for one breath.

Just one.

In that breath, she felt the world change.

It was not the mall. It was not the city.

It was the thread that had always tied her heart to Marcus, the quiet cord of knowing that had survived death and war and the kind of love that makes people call each other foolish.

That thread did not snap.

It did not burn.

It simply went still, the way a pulse goes still when a body stops fighting.

Chloe opened her eyes so fast the lights above her streaked.

Her first thought was Zaraquel.

Her second thought was worse.

She tried to reach for Marcus the way she always had, not with words, not with a spell, but with the small inner motion of trust.

The bond answered.

But it answered wrong.

Marcus was there. She could feel the shape of him, the weight of his presence, the imprint of his hunger and his will.

And yet it did not feel like him.

It felt like a door she had opened a thousand times, and suddenly the room on the other side had been emptied and repainted and locked from within.

The emptiness hurt, even though she was still connected to him.

Chloe took a step away from the wall and almost fell. Her knees did not buckle from weakness. They buckled from recognition.

Amber appeared out of the haze of dust and emergency lighting, her hair streaked with pale powder, her eyes a clean gold that did not belong to any human story.

She looked at Chloe once and stopped moving, the way predators stop when they sense a shift in another predator.

Amber's birthmark began to glow, a faint blue that did not flash or flare before returning to its normal color. It was different, and Chloe recognized it immediately from her days with her family's coven in Yakima.

It was a sign of change.

Something was coming.

"You felt it," Amber said.

Chloe tried to speak and failed. Her mouth opened and the sound that came out was thin, not a sob, not a word, just breath that would not become language.

She swallowed hard. "He is alive," she said, because she needed to say something true before she broke. "Marcus is alive."

Amber held Chloe's gaze and did not soften. That was love from Amber, not cruelty. The Queen did not lie to comfort.

"Yes," Amber said. "But something has moved."

Chloe looked past Amber toward the corridor where Philip had disappeared with the last of the civilians. She saw security guards trying to direct people outside. She saw a woman sitting on the floor holding her own wrist as if she could keep it attached by force. She saw blood on a child's shoe.

Chloe wanted to kneel beside them. She wanted to be the healer she had trained herself to be.

Instead, she stood there and listened inward again to the bond that should have been warm and messy and human even inside vampiric power.

Chloe's pendant rested against her throat, faintly warm. It had not done that in weeks, not since the first cracks of this cycle began.

She lifted it with shaking fingers.

The stone should have steadied her.

It didn't.

It felt like it was waiting for her to ignite it.

A second tremor ran through the building. Somewhere, metal screamed.

Amber turned, shoulders tense, ready to move again, but Chloe caught her wrist.

"Wait," Chloe said.

Amber's eyes narrowed. "Chloe."

"I need one second," Chloe said. She hated the pleading in her voice, but she forced it out. "Just one. Something is wrong with Marcus."

Amber went still. The air around them did not change, but Chloe felt the way Amber's attention sharpened until it became a blade.

"Explain."

Chloe closed her eyes again. She did not reach for Marcus like a lover. She reached for him like a witch, with precision and cruelty toward her own fear.

She followed the thread.

It led her across distance and wards and seas, past the pulse of the island, past the heavy pressure that belonged to the Tall Dark Man. It ended at a place that felt like stone and old vows.

The Order.

Marcus stood there, alone, holding the Totem of Death.

Chloe saw him in her mind with such clarity that for a moment she smelled the cold of his skin and the faint iron scent of his blood tears. He was not moving. He was watching something Chloe could not see, listening to someone who was not there.

His face did not look afraid.

It looked determined.

Something in her stomach turned over as if she had swallowed seawater.

There was a presence with him.

Not McPherson. Not the wolves. Not Nimue. Not any living thing Chloe had ever faced.

A woman's shape. Calm. Fixed. A myth wearing skin.

Chloe did not see the woman's face clearly. She saw only the sense of her, the weight of her attention, the way the air around Marcus seemed to hold itself so the moment could be written.

Chloe knew without knowing how.

Diana.

Chloe's eyes flew open.

Amber was staring at her, and Chloe realized she had been silent too long.

"Someone came to him," Chloe said. "Not like a ghost. Not like Rae. This is older. This is prophecy old."

Amber's expression tightened. "Diana."

Chloe flinched at hearing the name spoken aloud. "You felt it too."

Amber nodded once. "The island taught me the taste of old gods. This feels like that. Not the same. But close."

Chloe's hands began to shake again, and she hated herself for it. She had faced demons. She had bled herself into wards. She had watched her daughter disappear into dark roots and kept breathing.

This fear was different.

It was domestic.

It was the fear of waking up beside someone you love and realizing they have already left, even though their body is still there.

"He is choosing something," Chloe whispered. "I cannot see what. I only feel the shape of the choice."

Amber's voice was quiet. "Marcus always chooses the greater good."

Chloe laughed once, sharp and broken. "That is what scares me."

Amber did not argue. She glanced toward the corridor again, toward the deeper breach beneath the mall, and Chloe saw the weight behind her eyes.

Queens chose.

They paid.

Chloe understood that. She had paid in blood, in sleep, in the softness that used to make her human.

But this felt like a payment that would not leave a scar.

It would leave absence.

Chloe tilted her head slightly, listening past the building's groans. She could still sense the marrow-born in the structure, not many now, not pushing through in swarms, but lingering like embers where the seams had been forced open.

The Tall Dark Man was not satisfied.

He was teaching.

It made Chloe want to vomit.

Amber's hand settled on Chloe's shoulder, firm. "We move," Amber said. "We do not let him control the rhythm of our fear."

Chloe nodded. She could obey that. Action was easier than thought.

"Philip is with the last civilians," Chloe said. "We need to leave before the next breach opens."

They moved together through a service corridor that still held, stepping over shattered glass and fallen panels. A firefighter ran past them, face streaked with sweat, shouting into a radio.

Chloe kept her eyes down and her shoulders tight, forcing her body to look like a terrified civilian instead of a witch carrying a war inside her chest.

At the exit, the humid night air hit her like a wave.

The parking lot was chaos. Ambulances arrived. People sat on curbs holding strangers' hands. The world tried to return to normal through procedure and sirens.

Chloe should have felt relief.

Instead, she felt the bond again, tugging at her like a question.

She reached for Marcus one more time, more carefully. She did not push. She did not demand. She simply touched the edge of him.

The answer came as a faint pressure, an image that was not a vision but a certainty.

Marcus standing in the Order's upper hall, alone.

Marcus holding the Totem of Death as if it were no longer a weapon but a contract.

Marcus listening to Diana's last words as if they were not prophecy but sentence.

Chloe's throat tightened. She pressed her fingers against her pendant until it hurt.

"He is going to make himself something else," she whispered.

Amber looked at her, eyes steady. "More."

Chloe swallowed. "Less," she said. "More powerful. Less human."

Amber did not deny it. She did not soften it. "He will do it because he believes he has to."

Chloe stared at the line of palm trees beyond the parking lot, their fronds barely moving in the heavy air. She forced herself not to search the sky for signs. She had learned the hard way that signs did not stop fate.

"If Marcus changes," Chloe said, her voice low, "then Zaraquel's silence is not the only silence we are living with."

Amber's jaw tightened. "Then we do not let his sacrifice become a weapon in the Tall Dark Man's hand."

Chloe nodded, but she did not feel steadier.

Her fear was not about the Tall Dark Man in this moment.

It was about Marcus.

The man she loved.

The father of her child.

The vampire who still tried to hold on to humanity even while the world demanded he become a monster in service of the greater good.

Chloe closed her eyes and tried to pray. Not to gods. Not to saints. Not to anything outside herself.

She prayed to the only thing she trusted.

Blood.

If blood remembered love, then Marcus would not vanish completely.

If blood remembered mercy, then the choice he was about to make would not hollow him out.

If blood remembered her, then she would find him after, even if the world called him unforgiven.

Chloe opened her eyes.

Amber was already moving, already directing Kawika's people toward safer ground, already thinking ten steps ahead.

Chloe followed, because she had always followed Queens into the worst nights.

But inside her chest, where the bond to Marcus should have been warm and alive, something remained still.

Waiting.

Chloe understood with a clarity that felt like grief.

Marcus had not asked her permission.

He had not said goodbye.

And that was how she knew it was real.

The Tall Dark Man, The
Underground, Present Night

Thessara waited where she had been told to wait.

Not kneeling. Not standing at attention.

Simply present.

He required stillness, not theater. When he spoke, it would be because the moment demanded speech, not because silence needed filling.

The Tall Dark Man stood with his back to her, hands folded loosely behind him. He was not watching the chamber.

He was listening to the shape of what had shifted.

The world did not announce such changes. It never had. Only those who survived long enough learned when the rules were broken and reset. To them, it was law.

"Marcus has accepted it," he said at last.

Thessara did not ask how he knew. She had learned that knowledge, when offered without invitation, was already settled.

"Accepted what, my lord?"

"The position," he replied. "Not the power."

He paused.

"The burden."

That distinction mattered. It amused him that it mattered. He turned then, slowly, so that she could see his face. There was no anger, no triumph. Only consideration, as if he were studying a pattern that had repeated one time too many and finally demanded annotation.

"They always misunderstand this part," he continued. "They believe sacrifice must end in absolution. That if one suffers enough, the world will forgive the act." He shook his head once. "Forgiveness is a human indulgence. It has no structural value."

Thessara lowered her eyes. She felt the weight of the words settle into her bones, heavy and instructive. "And he will not be forgiven."

"No," the Tall Dark Man agreed. "Which is why it will hold and break them all."

He walked past her then, not touching her, not acknowledging her flinch. His pace was unhurried. There was no need for urgency. The choice had already been made. Consequences were now mechanical.

"Prepare the crossings," he said. "Not the large ones. The small fractures. Places where people still believe safety is permanent."

Thessara lifted her head. "Which cities?"

"Not cities," he corrected. "Institutions. Schools. Hospitals. Courts. Anywhere faith has been outsourced to systems instead of belief."

She nodded and committed it to memory. "And the angel?"

The Tall Dark Man paused. She also mattered, at least to him, in reaching his endgame.

"She remains silent," he said. "Which is what I need from her right now. She needs to make not a single sound, not even a cry."

He turned slightly, enough that Thessara could see his profile now, the calm certainty carved into it by centuries of being right too often. "Zaraquel believes she has chosen restraint. In truth, she has chosen continuity. She will learn the difference."

"And Marcus," Thessara asked carefully. "If he has bound himself?"

"He has not bound himself to me," the Tall Dark Man said. "That would be submission. He has bound himself to the rule I represent."

Thessara's breath caught before she could stop it.

"Yes," he said, acknowledging it. "That should frighten you."

He moved again, stopping at the edge of the chamber where the Hunter slept beyond walls Thessara was never permitted to approach.

"Marcus believes endurance without dominion is moral. He believes suffering without ownership redeems the act."

A faint, almost imperceptible curve touched the Tall Dark Man's mouth. "That belief will either make him indispensable, or it will hollow him until even his gods or his prophecy can't recognize what remains."

"And if it works?" Thessara asked.

The Tall Dark Man looked at her fully now. His gaze did not threaten. It weighed.

"Then I will adapt," he said. "I always do."

She swallowed. "You sound almost pleased."

"I am," he replied. "The world becomes stale when no one is willing to stand where history rots. Marcus has stepped into that place willingly."

He turned away from her, dismissing her without gesture. "Begin the preparations. The Queen will descend. The witch will bleed herself thinner. The Serpent will circle closer to sacrifice. And the angel will learn what silence costs."

Thessara bowed and left without another word.

The Tall Dark Man remained where he was. For the first time in a very long while, the future did not feel obedient. It felt negotiable.

He welcomed that.

Heroes were born from resistance. Villains were born from fear. What came next would require something rarer. Someone who could endure being unforgiven.

CHAPTER 20

BORROWED FLESH

The Hunter, The Underground,
Present Night

He woke with a sense of calm that washed over him, as if something had shifted within his body and soul. The chamber remained the same around him, stone, dark glass, the old geometry of control, but he did not feel contained the way he had before. His body no longer felt strange and useless. It felt alive for the first time.

He sat up slowly, palms on the floor, and listened without moving. There were no voices in the hall. No footsteps. No chanting. No maternal whisper.

The silence was baffling, yet alluring at the same time.

That was the first thing he understood without being taught. Silence could be a weapon.

His weapon.

He looked down at his hands and saw the red lines under his skin again, veins that did not belong to a living man but to a monster. When he flexed his fingers, the lines brightened as if they responded to his mind instead of blood. His nails were normal now, not claws, not childlike, not monstrous. The skin across his knuckles was smooth.

When he touched his face, the curve of his cheekbone, the bridge of his nose, he felt features settling into place, as if his body had been waiting to become something recognizable, more humanlike. He did not know what the recognition meant, only that it came with a hunger that did not ask for food.

It asked for a name.

He tried to remember his own. Nothing came. Not a childhood. Not a first breath. Not a mother holding him. Only the word Father, heavy in his skull, and beneath it the faint impression of another word that made his throat tighten as if it wanted to become a plea.

Amber.

He did not understand why the sound of it made him feel both heat and anger, like a wound that healed wrong and still ached when touched.

The stones around him did not speak to his mind like they used to. They simply remained silent now, which meant they were waiting for him to obey the boundaries that had been set but that he did not yet understand.

He stood anyway.

When he rose to his full height, the chamber felt smaller. He walked to the edge of the melted cradle that had once held him and studied the fractured glass. His reflection was there, but it did not settle into a single shape at first. It wavered, as if the surface could not decide what it was allowed to show.

Then, slowly, his face sharpened into one version and stayed.

Blond hair, shoulder length, strands falling forward the way a young man might have styled it without thinking too hard. Blue eyes, too bright against the dark. A jaw that looked carved by confidence rather than suffering. A body built for war and beauty both, broad shoulders, long torso, muscles that did not come from training but were naturally sculpted.

He stared as if the reflection might disappear, but it did not. It simply existed.

Something inside him tightened, as if he knew this face all too well. It was not a new face. This was a face the world had already held once and lost.

He did not know how he knew that, but the knowledge brought pressure behind his eyes that felt like grief trying to become fury, a pain that filled his head with a magnitude of suffering he had never experienced and yet somehow recognized.

He lifted his arm. On the upper left, the tattoo appeared as if ink had always lived there, a pyramid with an eye that seemed to look back when he moved.

He touched it and felt a memory that was not his.

A wagon wheel turning in mud. A woman singing low in a tongue that did not belong to this place. A man laughing quietly while blood dried on his fingers.

The images vanished before he could grasp them, but the impression remained. Someone had carried this mark before him. Someone had believed in something beyond survival.

He turned away from the reflection as the chamber's torches flared in sequence, not bright, not dramatic, simply awake.

The light did not comfort him.

It clarified the fact that he was not alone.

A figure stood near the entrance, not where it would have been convenient for the guards, but where it would have been noticed only by someone who looked without fear.

The visitor wore a long coat the color of old ash, not ceremonial, not fashionable, simply chosen to disappear into the edges of rooms. Their hair was dark and braided tight down their back, the way people braid hair when they intend to keep it from being grabbed in a fight. The face was plain at first glance and impossible to forget at second, not because it was beautiful, but because it held no familiarity.

Their eyes met the Hunter's and did not lower.

"You are awake," the figure said.

The Hunter did not answer immediately. He felt the urge to speak the word Father again, to call for the hand that had shaped him, because that was what his body expected. Instead, the word caught in his throat and turned to something else.

"Who are you?" It came out rough, unused.

The figure stepped closer, slow enough to be read as respect.

"I keep what others try to bury," they said. "I am sent when forgetting becomes dangerous."

He frowned. "Sent by him?"

The figure's mouth moved slightly, not quite a smile, not quite contempt.

"He believes everything is sent by him." They paused, then spoke with care, as if choosing what to reveal were a form of violence. "I serve the covenant. Not the man."

The Hunter felt the words sink into him and catch on something sharp.

Covenant.

That word was older than the name *Father*. It made his spine straighten. It made the red lines under his skin warm.

"What covenant?"

The figure's gaze stayed steady on his face, on the borrowed beauty that was no longer borrowed. "The covenant that keeps things in check," they said. "The covenant that remembers what was taken and what was considered consequence."

He did not like the words *taken* or *consequence*. They made him feel as if he were standing over a grave with his heart ripped out, though he did not clearly understand the feeling. He took one step forward.

The figure did not stop him.

That was another lesson he learned quickly.

"You said forgetting becomes dangerous," he said. "What am I supposed to remember?"

The figure reached into their coat and drew out a small object, not a weapon, not a relic glowing with power, just a simple thing wrapped in dark cloth.

They unwrapped it slowly and revealed a red silk shirt, folded neatly, the kind a man might wear when he wanted to feel alive.

The color struck the Hunter like a blow. Not because it was bright, but because it was familiar.

He reached out for the shirt, but the figure pulled it away.

The name in his mind became clear as day.

Amber.

His breath caught. He did not know why it hurt. His fingers twitched at his side as if they wanted to reach for the shirt again and tear it apart just to stop the feeling.

"That was his," the figure said. "Before he died."

He stared at the shirt.

The word died did not land as a concept. It landed as an insult.

"He," the Hunter repeated.

The figure did not look away. "Michael," they said softly, and the name moved through the chamber like a key turning in a lock, waiting to spill some secret. "Machiel. King. Keeper. The one your father hated most because he would not be owned."

The Hunter's stomach turned, not with nausea, but with the rising need to break something. His hands clenched. The red lines in his arms brightened.

"I am not him," he said, though he was no longer sure why he said it.

"No," the figure agreed. "You are the answer to him."

That hit the Hunter hard. His vision sharpened until every edge in the room became precise. The tattoo on his arm seemed to tighten against his skin as if it wanted to crawl off.

He tried to breathe and realized his body did not need to. He breathed anyway, because something about rage felt more real when it rode on breath.

"Why do I look like him?" he asked.

His voice was quieter now, and that was worse than shouting.

The figure folded the shirt back into the cloth and held it like an offering.

"Because the Tall Dark Man cannot stand to be opposed without possessing the shape of what opposed him," they said. "He does not only want victory. He wants replacement. He wants the world to look at you and feel the absence of what they loved. He wants their grief to become obedience."

The Hunter felt the truth of it in his bones, and something deep in him flinched, not from guilt, but from the realization that he had been built as a message.

Not a person.

A message.

The figure stepped closer until they were within reach, close enough that the Hunter could take the cloth, close enough that he could snap their neck if he chose.

"You are not a child," they said. "You are not a man. You are what comes after his first failure. You are the key he wants to control."

He stared at the cloth. "What do you want from me?"

"I want you to remember," the figure said, and their voice hardened slightly, the first sign of emotion. "Not what he tells you to remember. What the world tries to forget so it can sleep. Every bargain. Every sacrifice. Every time the light bled itself thin and hoped it was enough. I want you to remember that there are always two sides. Two prophecies."

The Hunter's jaw tightened. "And when I remember, then what?"

The figure's eyes stayed locked on his. "Then you will understand why evil does not die," they said. "It survives long enough to make the living pay again."

The Hunter took the wrapped cloth from their hands and held it carefully, not gently, but with the strange caution of someone holding something that could change him.

He did not understand why a shirt mattered.

He only knew it did.

He felt a presence somewhere beyond the chamber walls, distant but attentive, like a man listening at a door. He did not turn toward it. He did not call for it.

He kept his gaze on the figure who had entered without permission and spoken as if permission were irrelevant.

"Who are you?" he asked again, because the answer mattered now.

The figure hesitated for the first time, as if names carried risk.

Then they said, "They call me Zahraem."

The Hunter looked down at the cloth one more time, and when he looked back up, his eyes had changed, not in color, but in intention.

"Show me," he said.

Zahraem nodded once, as if this were the only outcome that had ever existed.

"Then come," they replied. "Your father thinks he made you to serve his future. I am here to give you the past so that your future is yours to write. Both sides of the prophecy will clash, but it cannot do so under restraint."

The Hunter stepped forward, following.

The chamber did not stop him.

Behind them, the torches dimmed again, leaving the melted cradle in shadow. He did not look back.

Whatever he had been before had already been paid for.

Zaraquel, Beyond the Veil,
Present Night

She did not wake during her fall. When she did, she realized there was no ground beneath her feet, no ceiling above her head.

Zaraquel stood alone at the center, wings folded tight against her back, their weight familiar and yet wrong, as if they remembered something she had chosen not to be.

The fire inside her was quiet.

Not gone.

Just silent.

And that frightened her more than pain ever had.

She had learned that silence was not empty. It was restraint given a body. That teaching was one of the first lessons she and Rae learned from McPherson.

She closed her eyes and reached, not outward, not toward the Tall Dark Man, not toward her father or her mother or the world that still moved without her consent.

She reached inward.

And then back.

To the places that remembered her before she remembered herself.

Blood answered first.

Then something colder.

"Kabos," she said.

The name did not echo. It did not need to.

Suddenly he was there, standing a few steps away, solid in the way ghosts become when summoned by truth rather than grief or fear. He looked as he always had at the end. Not young. Not old. A man who had lived centuries to understand and serve the prophecy.

His eyes softened when he saw her, not with pity, but recognition.

"You shouldn't be here alone," he said quietly.

"I am," Zaraquel replied. "That's part of it."

Kabos inclined his head, conceding the point without argument. He glanced past her shoulder, toward a presence that had not yet shaped itself.

"Rowe," Zaraquel said.

The air changed again, subtler this time. He did not arrive with ceremony. He simply existed where existence was permitted. Tall, indistinct at first, then resolving into the familiar outline of a man whose face had been worn by centuries and never claimed by any of them.

His eyes were calm. Not kind. Not cruel. Always truthful.

She knew Rowe's true form.

The legend himself.

Merlin.

"You called for witnesses," Rowe said.

"I called for truth," Zaraquel answered. "Witnesses are what remain after."

Rowe accepted that without comment.

Zaraquel turned slowly, taking in the space around them. Images moved at the edges, not visions, not memories, but impressions.

Blood on stone. Wings unfolding for the first time. The rush of power that came with justified certainty. The knowledge of who deserved to die and why the world would be cleaner for it.

She had lived those moments.

She had believed in them.

She looked at her hands.

They were steady.

And that, more than anything, told her what had changed.

"Kabos," she said, and this time there was no command in his name. Only need. "You served the prophecy. You believed in justice that cut deep enough to end the cycle."

Kabos did not deny it. "I believed in consequence," he said. "Justice was what we called it when we could still live with ourselves afterward."

Rowe's gaze did not move. "And when you could not," he added, not unkindly.

Zaraquel's mouth tightened. She turned back to the open space, to the sense of weight pressing in from all sides.

"I was born for that," she said. "To end what returned. To destroy what refused to stay buried. That was my role." Her voice did not shake. "That was the Avenging Angel."

Neither of them corrected her.

She laughed once, sharp and short, the sound of something breaking cleanly instead of tearing.

"Do you know what I thought silence would be?" she asked. "I thought it would be mercy. I thought restraint would preserve something worth saving."

Kabos looked at her then, truly looked. "And does it?"

She swallowed. The answer was already there, heavy and undeniable.

She felt the Hunter's movement like a distant bruise. She felt her father hardening into something the world would never thank. She felt the Tall Dark Man's patience stretching, pleased and dangerous.

The world had not been preserved.

It had been delayed.

Rowe spoke, gently now. "What does an Avenging Angel do when the choice is offered?"

"She ends it," Zaraquel said immediately.

Then she stopped.

"She ends it," Zaraquel repeated, slower this time. "She breaks the cycle so it cannot return. She does not bargain with continuity. She does not preserve the structure that allows evil to wait."

Her wings trembled once. She did not let them unfold.

"I did not end it," Zaraquel said. The words landed between them like stone. "I chose restraint. I chose silence. I chose to let the world continue instead of forcing it to change."

Kabos closed his eyes, not in sorrow, but in understanding. Rowe remained still.

Zaraquel lifted her chin. Her eyes burned, not with rage, but with a clarity that hurt more than fury ever had.

"An Avenging Angel would have destroyed this," she said. "She would have taken the cost and ended it."

She drew a breath she did not need.

"I didn't."

The silence that followed was absolute and brutal at the same time.

Rowe inclined his head, a motion so small it could have been missed by anyone not watching for truth. "Then you understand," he said.

Kabos's voice was rough when he spoke again. "Understanding doesn't absolve you."

"I know," Zaraquel replied. Tears traced heatless paths down her face, evaporating before they could fall. "That's the price."

She looked at her wings at last. They were not white. Not red. Not black. They were something quieter now, something unresolved. A promise unanswered instead of fulfilled.

"I was an Avenging Angel," Zaraquel said aloud, and the words mattered because they were spoken. "And by choosing silence, I stepped out of that role."

Kabos did not argue. Rowe did not object.

That was how she knew it was true.

Zaraquel closed her eyes and stood in it, in the loss, in the consequence, in the knowledge that good intentions did not erase outcomes.

Somewhere beyond this place, the Hunter walked wearing borrowed flesh. Somewhere else, her father carried a burden that would never be forgiven. Somewhere, the Tall Dark Man waited.

When she opened her eyes again, the space had begun to thin.

"I will live with this," she said quietly. "But I will not forget it."

Rowe's voice followed her as the vision began to release.

"Good," he said. "Forgetting is how we all survive."

Kabos did not speak again. He did not need to.

Zaraquel let the silence take her, not as refuge, but as a vow.

CHAPTER 21

WITHOUT MERCY

Chloe Tudor, Hawaii, Pre-Dawn

Chloe didn't cry when she noticed the sky was different.

It was almost dawn, but it still looked like the dead of night.

She noticed it the way a witch notices small changes that signal something is wrong. The sky stayed darker than normal for that hour, and the light over the water was dim, to say the least. It looked as if dawn wanted to come but couldn't.

Then she recalled several nuances from times when this had happened before.

Chloe stood barefoot on the lanai, one hand braced against the railing, the other pressed flat against her sternum where the bond should have been warm and responsive.

Instinct drove her to call her coven, but her heart already knew the answer, or at least she thought she did.

Marcus was still there in a distant way, but the closeness wasn't.

Her feelings for Marcus hadn't changed.

But something had.

The connection no longer reached her the way it always had before. It felt distant. Formal. As if something essential had been placed behind glass.

She could sense his existence the way one senses a family member, but not a soulmate. Not a lover. Not a husband. Not a father.

Three words came to her immediately.

Immovable. Present. Unreachable.

Chloe inhaled slowly and tasted salt and damp earth.

Hawaii breathed around her, alive and watchful, but the island did not intrude. It never did when grief was honest.

She closed her eyes and reached again, carefully this time. Not like a wife. Not like a lover. But like a powerful witch with nothing left to lose.

The bond answered with pressure instead of warmth. With endurance instead of love.

There was no hunger in it now. No ache. No pull.

It was simply an answer to a witch's call.

A tear fell from her eye.

"No," Chloe whispered, the word breaking as soon as it left her mouth.

She pressed her palm harder against her chest, as if pressure alone could force feeling and love back into place.

"You don't get to do this without telling me."

The wind moved through the palms. Somewhere down the beach, a bird cried once and then went quiet.

Chloe laughed under her breath, sharp and humorless. "Coward," she said, though she did not know whether she meant Marcus or herself.

She felt it then.

Not Marcus.

Something else.

A presence that did not arrive like magic and did not announce itself like one of the Hawaiian gods.

Footsteps on stone.

She could hear them coming closer.

Something powerful.

Yet motherly.

"You standing like that gonna make your heart worse, not better."

Chloe turned.

Kawika's grandmother, known as Tutu, stood at the edge of the lanai, wrapped in a faded shawl, bare feet solid on the stone as if the house had grown around her instead of the other way around.

Tutu's hair was silver and pulled back tight, her face carved by sun and years and survival. Her eyes, sharp and dark, missed nothing.

Chloe swallowed. "I didn't hear you come in."

Tutu snorted softly. "That's because I didn't announce myself. The dead announce. The dangerous announce. I don't."

She stepped closer.

"You lost something."

Chloe shook her head immediately. "No. He's alive."

Tutu nodded once. "I didn't say dead."

That landed harder than Chloe expected.

She felt her knees weaken and caught herself on the railing again, suddenly furious that her body insisted on betraying her at the worst moments.

"He made a choice," Chloe said. "I don't know what it is yet, but I can feel it. He moved somewhere I can't follow."

Tutu's gaze drifted toward the ocean, where the horizon still refused to brighten. "Men who do that don't disappear," she said. "They step onto a different path. Our laws are different from mortal laws."

Chloe looked at her sharply. "You know?"

"I know the shape of it," Tutu replied. "I've seen it before. Not your man. But the choice."

She reached out then and took Chloe's wrist, her grip firm, grounding, undeniably human. Chloe felt the magic in it immediately, not spell work, not invocation, but something older. Ancestral authority. The kind that did not need permission to show its true power. Chloe had felt that once before, and only from her stepfather, who guided her secretly and urged her to never forget her true roots. He was the only one who knew her destiny and even tried to convince the coven that her power was limitless and unstoppable, especially if they would spend more time guiding her than punishing her. Chloe thought fondly of him. She loved her stepfather, who had always protected her from the shadows.

"Listen to me," Tutu said. "When a man chooses to carry something meant for gods, the people who love him feel the absence first. That's the cost of proximity."

Chloe's throat burned. "He didn't ask me."

Tutu met her eyes without flinching. "Of course he didn't. This kind of choice doesn't survive negotiation or discussion. It is something that happens when it needs to be done."

The words were not unkind. They were worse. They were true.

Chloe pulled her hand free and turned back toward the sea, blinking hard. "I can still feel him," she said. "But it's wrong. It's like he flattened himself. Like something essential was sanded down to almost nothing, like a sandcastle a child builds on the beach and the waves come and tear it down."

Tutu was quiet for a moment. When she spoke again, her voice was lower. "Hunger gone?"

Chloe stiffened. "Yes."

"Desire?"

"Yes."

"Love?"

Chloe hesitated. That hesitation answered the question for both of them.

Tutu exhaled slowly. "That's a boundary being crossed," she said. "Not broken. Crossed."

Chloe turned back, anger flashing through the grief. "Then fix it."

Tutu's expression hardened, just slightly. "No."

The word hit like a slap.

"You don't fix vows made to keep the world standing," Tutu continued. "You survive them. Or you don't."

Chloe's magic stirred, sharp and defensive. "I am not a bystander in my own life. I'm supposed to be the most powerful witch in the world. There is no one greater, or at least none that I know of."

Tutu stepped closer, her presence suddenly heavy enough that Chloe felt her loss. "And you are not the center of the balance," she said calmly. "That's the test. Whether you can love someone who chose the greater good without being forgiven for it."

Chloe stared at her, her breath unsteady. Somewhere deep inside, something old and proud and terrified recognized the truth and hated it. She recognized the feeling. It was the same as a vision she once had from Sarah Good, her ancestor.

"So what am I supposed to do?" Chloe asked, her voice barely holding back her tears. "Just accept it?"

Tutu's gaze softened then, not with comfort, but with respect. "No," she said. "You're supposed to remember who you are while he becomes something else. That's harder to live with, but it is required if you both want to save your child. My sweet child, you loved a man who is more than what he seems. He is willing to risk it all for you and your child. The question you must ask yourself is whether you will stop him or help him."

The first line of sunlight finally broke over the horizon, thin and pale, cutting across the water. Chloe watched it and felt nothing ease. That was how she knew the war had already begun.

Marcus, The Order, Before
Dawn

Marcus felt the change had completed right before dawn. Not as pain or loss, but as completion of a purpose. Ever since Kabos and Michael took him in, he had always wanted a purpose. He thought he had found it once. The tug toward something more had never stopped. He just didn't know what it was until now.

The Order was quiet in the way places become quiet after something irreversible has been decided within their walls. The Order had been built to protect and to recognize when protection was no longer enough. The wards held. The wolves slept. Even the Totem of Life remained subdued, its presence distant, respectful, as if it understood that this was no longer its domain to influence.

Marcus stood alone in the upper hall, hands folded loosely in front of him, posture relaxed in a way that would have unsettled anyone who knew him well. He did not feel hunger. That absence was precise. Clean. Where hunger for blood had ruled his survival before, it no longer called to him the way it used to. The thought of feeding carried no desire. Instead, it registered as function alone.

Marcus reached inward, not searching, not demanding. He touched the bond the way a hand touches a sealed door, aware of its presence without expecting it to open. Chloe was there. He could feel her life, her power, the shape of her love. It remained intact, vivid, fiercely alive, yet it no longer reached out to touch him.

His heart began to ache. That was the cost he had agreed to without negotiation, driven only by the desire to answer the call of his true purpose.

"I know," he said quietly, though there was no one to hear him. His dark hair hung down around his eyes, hiding the tears that began to fall. When his finger touched the warm wetness on his cheek, he looked at his fingertip. It was wet but not stained with blood as it used to be. The tears were clear. Something deeper than loss had shifted.

He crossed the hall and rested his hand briefly against the stone wall, grounding himself out of habit rather than necessity. The stone felt cool. Marcus understood why he had been brought here, to this place between worlds and vows. He finally understood why Diana had not asked for consent. There were choices that ceased to be choices once they were seen clearly.

He closed his eyes and thought of Chloe as she had been the first time he saw her truly angry, magic sparking under her skin, daring the world to challenge her authority. He thought of her hands, always steady when everything else fell apart. He thought of the sound of her laugh when she forgot, just for a moment, how much she carried.

He did not reach for her. That boundary had already been crossed. To test it now would be cruelty for both of them.

Marcus turned his attention instead to the Totem of Death, resting where he had placed it hours earlier. It no longer pulsed in response to him. It did not resist. It did not warn. It simply acknowledged his presence, as if recognizing that its function had changed.

"You're quieter," Marcus observed.

The Totem did not answer. He almost smiled.

This was what Diana had meant. Not power. Not elevation. Responsibility without relief. Endurance without recognition.

To exist as a constant rather than a participant. To hold a line no one else could see and never be thanked for holding it.

He did not know what to call himself now. Only what he was not.

He straightened, shoulders settling into a posture that was no longer defensive, no longer predatory. Whatever he was now, it was not driven by instinct or desire. It was driven by necessity.

Somewhere far beyond the Order, he felt the Tall Dark Man's awareness brush against the shape of his choice, testing it, measuring it. Marcus did not react. He did not shield. He did not provoke. He could feel him, but he wasn't afraid.

Marcus had not bound himself to the Tall Dark Man. He had bound himself to the prophecy that made both sides survive. That was the difference. That was why it would never be forgiven.

He exhaled slowly, a habit rather than a need, and accepted the stillness that followed. The world did not feel lighter to him. It felt heavier. And different.

Marcus turned away from the hall and began walking toward the lower chambers, toward the places where they created the most tightly controlled magic to protect the world. There would be no announcement about his change, no explanation offered to those who would soon feel the loss and fear the outcome.

That was his final sacrifice.

To be known not as savior or king or hero, but as the man who stood where the world threatened to break and did not move.

The Tall Dark Man, The Underground, Before Dawn

He felt it before the light reached Hawaii. The change that would not be known until it was too late. A power shift in the prophecies, but which one?

The Underground did not collapse. Its protection spells did not break. No alarms were raised. That was how he knew the change was significant. Catastrophic shifts never announced themselves. They came differently to their kind. They settled into place quietly and forced everything else to adjust around them. That was supernatural law.

Marcus had crossed the boundary. Whatever promise the Tall Dark Man believed existed no longer applied.

The Tall Dark Man stood alone in the inner chamber, hands folded behind his back, gaze unfocused, turned inward toward the invisible geometry of power that mapped the world and charted his climb to rule it. He did not need mirrors or scrying bowls. He did not need servants whispering reports. This was blood work. Covenant work. Old law responding to new law.

He smiled faintly. "Not bound," he murmured. "Aligned."

Servants bent to his will. Martyrs broke under his will. Kings demanded worship. Marcus had done none of these. He had chosen position without dominion, burden without authority, endurance without reward. That was rarer. And more dangerous.

The Tall Dark Man had built entire centuries around preventing that choice from being made again.

And yet here it was.

He reached outward lightly, trying to feel the change in Marcus, but there was no resistance. No fear. No challenge. Just presence. Immovable. A line drawn not in opposition, but in refusal.

Interesting, he thought, a quiet chuckle leaving him. A witch in the corner began to tremble.

"Diana warned them," he said softly, though no one would hear him. "And still they chose it."

He turned his attention next to the angel.

Zaraquel's silence had shifted as well. Not weakened. She no longer stood at the edge of execution. She stood at the edge of consequence, fully aware of what she had relinquished.

That awareness would either hollow her or harden her into something far less predictable than an avenging angel.

That made her even more interesting than Marcus.

And she still had to become his bride.

He approved of unpredictability. It kept the game alive. Yet the player who still must fall is the queen. That remained constant. His prophecy would not be undone by the choice Marcus had made.

The Hunter stirred beneath layers of stone and spell, his borrowed flesh settling more completely into form. The Tall Dark Man did not look toward him. He did not need to. Zahraem's interference had been anticipated. Memory was always the counterweight to control.

He allowed it.

He needed the Hunter to *understand* what he was wearing. Only then would the resemblance become unbearable.

His gaze lifted, distant now, tracking the Queen's fire across the islands, the witch's grief at the edge of collapse, the kahuna lines tightening in response to ancestral law.

Everything was moving exactly as it should.

Except Marcus.

The Tall Dark Man's smile faded, not into anger, but into thought.

"This will cost you," he said to the empty chamber, voice almost contemplative. "They will never forgive you. Not your wife. Not your child. Not the world you are preserving."

He paused, then added quietly, "But you already know that."

He straightened. War was not announced by shouting. It was announced by patience.

"Let them grieve," he continued. "Let them mistake endurance for safety."

The Underground remained still. The rules had shifted, but the game was far from over. Evil did not die. It rose, adapted, and learned to wait for the right moment.

And somewhere above, dawn finally began to break over a world that has yet to see the consequences of its choices.

CHAPTER 22

PAIN

Kawika Kekahuna, Oʻahu,
Morning

Kawika had learned as a child that the land did not cry when something important was about to happen. The land reacted differently. It called to its protectors, the kahunas.

That morning, he felt the land calling.

He stood barefoot in the quiet service corridor behind the exhibit hall, the concrete cool beneath his feet, the museum still closed to the public. Beyond the walls, tourists would later stand in neat lines and read placards written by people who believed history could be contained in glass.

Kawika knew better.

History did not live behind barriers. It waited.

The figure of Kūka'ilimoku stood where it always had, carved from darkened breadfruit wood, mouth open in that unmistakable expression that unsettled those who did not understand what they were seeing. The god of war did not look violent. He looked attentive.

Kawika had always understood the difference. Violence was impulse. Kū was law.

"You came before sunrise," Tutu said behind him.

Kawika did not turn. "The land was awake already."

Tutu stepped to his side, her presence familiar in the way only ancestral authority could be. She followed his gaze to the figure.

Everything he knew that mattered had come from her.

"He remembers," she said.

"So do we," Kawika replied.

They stood in silence. Not reverent. Not fearful. Listening.

"The sky wouldn't break last night," Kawika said finally. "The same stillness we felt at Ala Moana. The same pressure in the ground."

Tutu nodded once. "Ea was held."

He glanced at her. "Held?"

"Not lost," she clarified. "Not broken. Suspended. When the breath of the land pauses, it means something is being weighed."

Kawika swallowed. "Pono."

"Yes," Tutu said. "Always pono. People misunderstand that word. They think it means goodness. It doesn't. It means balance that costs."

She shifted her weight, eyes never leaving Kū.

"When Kamehameha raised these figures, he wasn't begging for victory. He was acknowledging law. Ua mau ke ea o ka ʻāina i ka pono was never a promise. It was a warning."

Kawika felt the truth settle into his chest. "The life of the land endures only if balance is paid for."

Tutu glanced at him then, approving. "Good. You were listening. People translate it as righteousness," she continued. "We know it means balance."

She gestured subtly toward the figure. "Kūkaʻilimoku was not built to speak. He was built to receive. A vessel. A threshold. The kahuna knew that if Kū entered fully, the land would unify, yes. But it would also remember blood long after the battles ended."

Kawika thought of fractured stone. Of silence that followed screams. "And now?"

"Now the land recognizes the same conditions," Tutu said. "A queen who carries many bloodlines. A serpent stirring. A witch breaking under grief. A man choosing endurance instead of dominion."

Kawika's jaw tightened.

"Marcus."

Tutu did not confirm it. She did not need to.

"When ea is held like this," she continued, "it means the land is waiting to see who will act in pono and who will act in hunger."

"And us?" Kawika asked quietly.

Tutu placed her palm over his heart, firm and grounding. "We remember. We guard. We do not force doors open that were meant to test restraint."

Kawika nodded slowly. "And if the Queen seeks power she doesn't yet understand?"

Tutu's gaze hardened slightly. "Then Kū will not give it freely. He never has."

She stepped back, already turning away. "The land does not choose sides," she said over her shoulder. "It chooses balance."

Left alone again, Kawika faced the figure of Kūkaʻilimoku and felt no comfort, no fear. Only responsibility. The breath of the land remained held, waiting.

And somewhere beyond the island, the world continued moving toward a reckoning it would not recognize until it arrived.

Philip II of Macedon, Elsewhere,
Morning

Philip had learned long ago how to stand in places that did not belong to time. Kings who survived long enough developed that skill out of necessity. History was rarely linear when bloodlines and oaths were involved.

He felt the change without seeking it. Not a surge. Not a tremor. Something different.

Philip did not move. He closed his eyes and let the sensation finish arranging itself so he could understand what came next. The Serpent's mark beneath his skin stirred once, irritated, then went still.

That alone told him this was not victory.

"This is not dominion," Philip said quietly.

He had built his life around dominion. Armies. Borders. Obedience. Even his pact had been rooted in control, the belief that order required force and that force required a king willing to be feared.

What he felt now carried none of that shape. It outweighed anything he had ever commanded.

There was only one person he believed capable of that kind of power, and it wasn't the Queen.

It was Marcus.

The name formed without resistance. Philip did not try to reach him. He knew better than to intrude on a position that was not meant to be shared. Some roles collapsed the moment they were acknowledged by more than one soul.

Philip exhaled slowly. "He chose endurance," he murmured. "Without authority."

That choice unsettled the Serpent within him. The curse had never understood restraint. It responded to ambition, to hierarchy, to hunger sharpened into purpose.

Marcus had stripped all of that away and still stood.

Philip opened his eyes. Once, long ago, he had been offered something similar. Not by a goddess. Not by prophecy. By consequence. A moment stepping aside would have preserved balance at the cost of memory.

He had turned away.

Kings were not trained to disappear.

Marcus had stepped forward instead.

"They will never forgive you," Philip said, not as condemnation, but as certainty. "Not the woman you love. Not the world you stabilize."

The world around him remained silent. That silence confirmed the truth he now understood.

Philip felt the Tall Dark Man's attention drift, distant and precise, testing the edges of this new alignment. There was no clash. No resistance. Just a line that could not be crossed because it was not drawn in opposition.

Alignment.

That frightened him more than war ever had.

Philip turned inward, examining the Serpent's mark with a clarity he had avoided for centuries. Once, he had believed survival required dominance. Now he understood that survival sometimes required someone willing to be erased.

He stepped back from the threshold he could sense but not see.

"I was not strong enough," Philip said quietly. "But you are."

For the first time since his pact was made, Philip did not attempt to influence what came next. He let the moment stand.

And in doing so, he finally learned what kind of king he had never been.

Raven Hexham, Romania,
Present Night

Raven couldn't sleep. She had learned the difference between vigilance and fear long ago, and this was neither, but it kept her awake.

The room around her was stone and shadowed, familiar enough that she did not bother to look. The fire in the hearth had burned down to embers, but she had not tended it. Heat was optional. Silence was not.

Arioch stood where he always did, near the far wall, unmoving, massive, patient. His stone skin caught the low light in uneven planes, his eyes dull and obedient. He had been forged to protect her.

He did that without question.

That was the problem.

"You feel it too," Raven said quietly.

Arioch did not answer. He never did unless commanded. His loyalty was not conversational. It was structural.

She hated herself for how much she relied on it.

Raven pressed her fingers into the arm of the chair, grounding herself in sensation. Something had changed in the world.

Not in her mark. Not directly. The Tall Dark Man's influence remained heavy and constant, like pressure at the base of her skull.

But beneath that, something else had settled into place.

Something that did not feel like him.

Someone else.

After a moment, she realized who it was.

Marcus.

The name came unbidden, sharp and unwelcome. She had not spoken it in months. She had tried not to think it.

Marcus represented too many things she did not want to face. Choice. Consequence. A man who had once looked at her and seen not a weapon, not a resource, but a person who could still turn back.

She swallowed hard. Her mark burned faintly, a warning, then dulled again.

"That shouldn't happen," Raven muttered.

The Tall Dark Man's law did not allow confusion. Orders were clear. Roles were defined.

Yet here she was, sitting in the quiet, feeling something she could not report, could not explain.

Marcus had changed.

She could sense it the way one senses gravity shift underfoot. Not death.

Something worse.

Endurance.

She laughed once, bitter. "Of course it would be you."

Raven stood and paced the length of the chamber, boots echoing softly against stone. Arioch turned his head to track her movement, waiting. Always waiting.

"You would make it harder," she said. "You would choose something no one could praise."

She stopped abruptly, breath catching as another presence brushed the edge of her awareness.

Malakai.

Not physically. Just the thought of him, chained somewhere deep below, his will still resisting despite everything she had done to put him there.

Guilt flared, hot and immediate.

Raven turned on Arioch, anger snapping sharp. "Stop looking at me like that."

Arioch's gaze did not change. That was worse.

"I didn't betray him for pleasure," she said, the words tumbling out before she could stop them. "I did it because I thought it mattered. Because I thought choosing the winning side would end this faster."

Her mark pulsed again, stronger this time, and she felt the Tall Dark Man's attention sharpen somewhere far away. He wasn't focused on her yet. Just aware that something in his network had faltered.

Raven went still.

This was the moment. The one she had avoided for months. The moment when she decided whether she would continue lying by action or begin lying by omission.

She could call him. She could report the shift. She could tell him Marcus had chosen something that might undermine the structure he was building. She could regain favor.

Instead, she did nothing.

The realization settled into her chest like a stone dropped into water.

She was withholding information.

That was a betrayal all its own.

Arioch took one careful step forward. A question, not a threat.

Raven closed her eyes. "No," she said softly. "Not yet."

She did not know why she said it. Only that she could not give Marcus's choice away as if it were nothing.

Her mark burned hotter now, anger bleeding through command. The Tall Dark Man did not like delay. He tolerated disobedience even less.

Raven forced herself to breathe, jaw clenched.

"Endurance without dominion," she whispered. "What does that even look like?"

She saw it then, in the shape of her own future if she continued this path.

One word surfaced.

Dispensable.

She was dispensable in the end.

She thought of Malakai's eyes the last time she saw him, full of disappointment. That hurt more than punishment ever could.

Raven opened her eyes and looked at Arioch again.

"If I tell him," she said, voice steady now, "everything moves faster. More people die, including the ones he claims he's protecting."

Arioch did not respond. He would follow whatever order came next.

Raven straightened.

"We wait," she said. "That's the order."

The mark flared, then receded, as if recording the defiance without fully understanding it.

Somewhere far away, the Tall Dark Man would feel it eventually.

Raven turned back toward the hearth and knelt, feeding the embers just enough to keep them alive.

Not enough to burn bright.

Endurance, she thought bitterly.

She did not yet know whether she was capable of it.

But for the first time since she had chosen her side, Raven Hexham did not act in hunger.

And the silence that followed was heavier than any command she had ever obeyed.

CHAPTER 23

GATHERING BEFORE THE STORM

*Malakai, Over the Pacific, Before
Dawn*

The ocean below him was dark and unbroken, a wide stretch of water that had swallowed centuries of war and carried them anyway. Malakai ran above it, his body cutting through the night air in long, tireless strides, wolf and man no longer separate things but a single rhythm learned through pain. The moon hung low, pale and distant, and he did not look at it. He had learned long ago that the sky never answers back.

He had not meant to return this way. Still, whenever he ran, Nikoli and Miriam surfaced without invitation, the memory of their voices pacing him as steadily as his breath.

That truth sat heavy in his chest, heavier than the salt air, heavier than the memory of chains biting into his skin in the Underground. He had left Seattle once believing distance would protect her and that if he stood apart from Amber's crown and fire he could preserve something of himself that still belonged to him. That belief had not survived captivity. It had not survived the Tall Dark Man's patience or the way the world had changed while he was bound. Amber had stood without him. That was the wound. Not betrayal. Not absence. The fact that she had endured everything so far without him.

Malakai slowed as the islands rose from the dark, their shapes familiar enough for him to recognize. He felt the land before he saw it, the way a wolf feels territory through bone and breath rather than sight. Hawai'i did not welcome him. It did not reject him either. It simply recognized him, the way ancient things do when they decide whether something still belongs.

He knew this feeling all too well.

He crossed the shoreline without ceremony and let his pace ease, boots touching ground at last. The earth was warm beneath his feet, faint heat bleeding upward, restrained but present. Pele was awake. She always was. That knowledge settled his nerves more than any prayer ever had.

Amber was already here. He knew that without searching. He felt her the way one feels their lover nearby. Her fire had changed since the last time he stood beside her. It was deeper now, less forgiving, and threaded with something colder than rage. It was not rage that threaded her fire now. It was something colder. Something that did not reach for comfort.

Malakai moved inland, following the pull of gathering voices, of footsteps not yet taken but already decided. He felt witches moving like quiet weather, their magic tight and inward. He felt the wolves farther off, Sabre and Black Wind's presence familiar and steady, their loyalty not loud but absolute. He felt McPherson's wards settling behind him like doors closing with intention, the Order choosing to move rather than wait.

Most of all, he felt the land holding its breath the way he was.

He wanted to feel clean and ready, but his soul had already been torn by the Tall Dark Man's captivity. He had survived chains, silence, and the Tall Dark Man's patience. What he did not know how to survive was the possibility that Amber might look at him and no longer need him there.

Kawika stood at the center, barefoot, spine straight, eyes forward. His family ringed him in a loose circle, not arranged, not formal, each person standing where they had always stood in his life. Aunties with arms folded, uncles with hands clasped behind their backs, cousins quiet and alert. Tutu stood nearest, shawl pulled tight, gaze sharp enough to cut through doubt.

None of them looked surprised to see Malakai. No one shifted. No one asked why he had come. The family simply made space, as if his arrival had been counted long before it happened.

Amber stood just beyond the circle, Chloe at her side. Chloe's face was drawn, her power held so tightly it hummed under her skin like a wire pulled too taut. Amber did not look at Malakai when he arrived. She did not need to. Her awareness shifted anyway, fire answering fire, recognizing balance restored even if nothing between them had been spoken yet.

Malakai stopped at the edge of the gathering. He did not step forward. This was not his ground to claim.

Kawika lifted his chin slightly as Malakai arrived, acknowledgment without interruption. The ritual did not pause. It was not fragile enough to be broken by presence.

Tutu spoke then, her voice low, carrying without effort. She did not invoke gods by name. She stated lineage, land, and consequence, each word placed with the care of someone who understood the islands and their people across generations.

Kawika listened. That, Malakai realized, was the moment. Not when Kawika would speak. But now, while he chose to hear everything he could no longer pretend not to know.

When Kawika finally spoke, his voice did not shake. He did not claim power. He did not ask for protection. He named what he was giving up. The life that could have stayed small. The future that might have remained untouched. The safety of neutrality. Each loss was named plainly, without flourish.

The land did not answer. The sky did not move. Kūka'ilimoku's carved face remained fixed and watchful, receiving without reaction.

That silence was the agreement.

Malakai felt it settle into place, the way a battlefield settles after the last line is drawn. This was not the rise of a king. It was the acceptance of law.

Amber's fire grew beside him. He turned his head then and met her gaze at last. There was no accusation there. No relief. Only recognition. They had both changed. Whatever passed between them next would have to be built from truth, not memories.

Kawika finished speaking. No one applauded. No one bowed. The family did not move to embrace him. They remained where they were, witnesses rather than comforters.

That, Malakai understood, was love sharpened into duty.

As the circle slowly loosened, as people began to breathe again, Malakai stepped forward at last. He did not enter the center. He stopped beside Amber instead, shoulder to shoulder, the way wolves stand when guarding something that matters more than territory.

"This is where it turns," he said quietly.

Amber nodded once. "It already has."

Above them, the sky began to pale, dawn finally permitted to arrive. It did not feel like relief.

The storm was coming. And no one here intended to move out of its path.

Kawika Kekahuna, Oʻahu,
Before Dawn

Kawika had always known the difference between standing near something sacred and standing nowhere near it. This was the second kind.

The ground beneath his feet was cool stone, worn smooth by generations who had come here before sunrise for reasons they never explained to outsiders. He did not look down. He did not need to. His body knew exactly where it was.

The air smelled faintly of salt and old wood, something that reminded him of what ancient Hawai'i might have been like. Somewhere behind him, the island breathed, shallow and careful, as if waiting to see whether he would flinch. He felt the island more than before, but he did not flinch.

His family stood around him in a loose ring, not arranged by rank or ceremony, but by memory. Aunties who had scolded him as a child. Uncles who had taught him when to speak and when silence mattered more. Cousins who had watched him choose books over bravado, history over spectacle.

None of them reached for him. None of them offered comfort. That was how he knew this was real.

Tutu stood closest. She had not touched him since they arrived. She would not. Her presence was enough. It always had been.

Kūka'ilimoku loomed just beyond the circle, carved from dark wood that still held the echo of fire. The god of war did not threaten. He never had. He waited.

Kawika felt the weight of that waiting settle across his shoulders, not as fear, but as responsibility finally acknowledged.

He thought of the life he could have kept. The museum halls. The quiet authority of scholarship. The ability to leave at the end of the day and let the past remain behind glass. That life slipped away from him without drama. No one took it. He set it down himself.

When he spoke, his voice was steady because it had already accepted what his body understood. He named what he was giving up. Not in poetry. Not in prayer. He named it the way one names land boundaries or the dead. Simple and clear, without permission.

The land did not answer him. That was the agreement.

The silence pressed in, dense but not hostile, the kind of quiet that comes when something ancient has been satisfied without needing to be impressed. Kawika felt it lock into place, a line drawn not through conquest, but through continuity.

He was not becoming something new. He was stepping back into something that had been waiting for a long time.

Only then did he become aware of the others.

What Kawika felt in that moment was everything because of the ritual, because of the choice he had made.

The Queen stood beyond the circle, fire held tight behind her ribs. He did not look at her directly, but he felt her recognition settle like heat against his spine. She understood what this cost. That mattered.

Beside her, the witch carried grief like a blade she refused to drop. Kawika respected that. Grief sharpened judgment when it was not allowed to rule.

Farther back, just at the edge of things, the wolf stood still. Malakai did not intrude. He did not lower his head. He simply remained present in the way guardians are present when something larger than territory is at stake.

Kawika felt the alignment click into place.

When the moment ended, it did not end loudly. His family did not move to him. They did not embrace him or say his name. They let him stand alone because that was now required of him.

Love did not disappear. It hardened into duty.

The breath of the island eased, just slightly, and he felt more alive with the island and the people.

Kawika exhaled for the first time since arriving and understood with a clarity that did not ask for approval that this was not a coronation.

It was a return.

And returns, he knew, always demanded more than arrivals ever did.

*Amber Stone, O'ahu, Before
Dawn*

Amber felt the approach of dawn the way she felt pressure changes in the ocean. Not light yet. Not danger. But it was coming, the moment when night stopped belonging entirely to her.

She stood just beyond the circle, careful not to intrude. This was not her ground. Not her law.

The island did not answer her the way it answered Kawika, and she understood why. Queens commanded allegiance. The land demanded obedience of a different kind. That was why she observed everything Kawika had done out of respect for the land.

What Kawika had done settled into her slowly, not as awe, not as fear, but as recognition. He had not reached for power. He had allowed himself to be claimed by it.

Amber knew that choice. She had made it once, long ago, with blood on her hands and fire in her chest, and she had never been thanked for it. She did not expect Kawika to be either.

Chloe stood beside her, silent, grief held so tightly it radiated heat. Amber could feel the strain in her the way she felt fractures in her bones before they repaired themselves.

Amber did not touch her. Comfort was not what either of them needed right now.

And then there was Malakai.

Amber did not turn when he arrived. She did not need to. The fire inside shifted anyway, recognizing the shape of him before her eyes ever did.

Wolf. Warrior. Survivor. Lover.

The one who had stood apart because he believed distance was mercy.

She felt the truth of his return land between them without words. Not forgiveness. Not reunion.

Just presence.

That would have to be enough for now.

As the ritual ended, the island eased. Only slightly. Enough to be noticed by those who listened to such things.

Amber listened. She always had. It was how she had survived becoming something she never meant to be.

The sky began to pale at the edges, not brightening, just loosening. Amber felt the first warning touch her skin, a subtle tightening, wards warming in response. Illyris stirred beneath her ribs, not restless, not hungry.

Something was coming.

She turned away from the gathering, and her gaze caught on the object resting where it had been placed hours earlier, wrapped and waiting, unremarkable to anyone who did not know what it was.

The mirror.

McPherson had given it to her when she became Queen, not as a weapon, not as reassurance. A reminder. He had told her only that she would know when the time was right. Amber had not touched it since.

Now, standing at the edge of night, with the land choosing law and the people choosing sides, she felt its presence like a weight she had been carrying without realizing it.

Not yet, she thought. But soon. Amber drew a slow breath she did not need and turned back toward the others as dawn finally edged closer, permitted but unwelcome.

This was not the storm.

This was the gathering.

And whatever came next would demand more than blood, more than crown, more than fire.

For the first time since she had accepted the name Queen, Amber understood with quiet certainty that she was standing at the edge of a realm she did not yet rule, and the world was about to ask her to.

CHAPTER 24

THE TURNING OF WITCHES

Chloe Tudor, O'ahu, Night
Holding

Chloe knew something had changed because magic did not argue with her. It should have.

Even the smallest working usually did, a brief tightening before yielding, a reminder that power always demanded acknowledgment before obedience. This one did neither. It rose when she called it, thin and pale, and then hovered as if uncertain where it belonged.

Her power was still under her control, but something was off.

Chloe let the words trail away. She lowered her hands slowly, carefully, as though sudden movement might startle the spell into collapse. It dissolved without complaint, bleeding back into the earth in a way that felt unfinished.

No backlash came, no sting in her palms, no echo in her bones.

That was wrong.

She stood still and listened, not with her ears but with the part of herself that had learned long ago how to feel absence. Around her, the other witches did the same.

No one spoke at first. Sand shifted under bare feet. A breath caught and released too quickly. Someone folded their arms, not in defense, but restraint.

"This should've held," a woman near the edge said quietly.

Chloe nodded once. "It should have."

The night pressed in, heavy but watchful. The island did not push back against them. It did not withdraw either. It simply waited, the way it always did when humans mistook delay for permission.

Chloe frowned slightly.

Another witch spoke, older, her voice worn smooth by years of compromise. "Has anyone heard from Anne?"

The name landed without ceremony. No one flinched. That alone told Chloe how long the question had been circling without being asked.

"Not directly," someone answered.

Chloe felt the shape of that phrase and disliked it immediately. Anne commanded. She punished. Silence had never been her tool. She also carried a quiet disdain for that witch for what she had done to Zaraquel.

Chloe reached inward, searching for the familiar pressure that always accompanied Anne's oversight, the subtle sense of being watched even when alone.

There was nothing.

No resistance. No reinforcement. Just a hollow where authority had once lived.

"She hasn't spoken at all," Chloe said finally.

The admission moved through the group like a draft through a closed room. Not panic. Not relief. Something quieter. Calculation.

A younger witch swallowed. "Then maybe we wait."

Chloe tasted the word and felt her stomach turn. Waiting was how things curdled. Waiting was how women like Elizabeth Hexham convinced themselves they were choosing safety when they were really choosing surrender.

"No," Chloe said.

Every head turned toward her.

"No," she repeated, softer now. "Waiting is still a choice."

No one argued. No one stepped away either.

Chloe felt the truth settle into her chest, heavy and undeniable. Anne's silence had not freed them. It had stripped away the illusion that obedience was protection.

Whatever came next would not be decided together. There would be no clean line between right and wrong, only movement and consequence.

She thought of Marcus, distant in a way that had nothing to do with space. Thought of Zaraquel, silent beyond reach, her absence louder than any scream. Thought of Amber standing with the land, learning a law that did not bend for crowns or grief.

Balance required consent.

And that consent was gone.

Chloe drew a slow breath and let the last of the unused magic sink harmlessly into the ground. When she looked up again, her voice was steady, even if her heart was not.

"Those who intend to wait," she said, "should step back now."

No one moved.

Chloe nodded once.

That was answer enough.

Whatever this became, it would not be called unity. It would be called choice.

And choice, she knew, always demanded payment in one form or another.

Her stomach tightened at the thought of what that payment could be.

Raven Hexham, Romania,
Night

Raven knew something had changed in their world because the mark did not bite her like usual.

It should have.

Any delay, any refusal, any moment of hesitation usually earned her pain sharp enough to remind her where obedience lived. The mark on her wrist had always been efficient that way. Command. Consequence. Compliance. All in one.

Tonight, when she paused mid-step in the stone corridor and felt the familiar tightening of thought that preceded instruction, nothing followed.

There was no burn, no pressure, no correction.

Raven stopped walking.

Arioch stood a few paces behind her, massive and patient, his stone frame catching the low firelight in dull planes. He waited because that was what he did when she stopped. He did not ask questions. He did not need reassurance. He simply existed as proof that orders still worked on some things.

Raven flexed her fingers slowly, testing herself.

The mark remained warm but dormant, like a scar that remembered pain without delivering it. She pressed her thumb against it harder than necessary.

Still nothing.

"That's not right," she murmured.

The Underground had not changed. The walls still hummed with layered spells, each one reinforcing the Tall Dark Man's authority through repetition rather than force.

Everything looked the same.

That was what unsettled her.

Power did not disappear loudly.

Raven reached inward, careful, the way one does when checking a wound they are afraid to name. She did not call him. She did not dare. She simply brushed the edge of where his presence usually pressed against her thoughts, constant and undeniable.

There was distance.

The Tall Dark Man had not withdrawn. He was still there, vast and patient and dangerous. But his attention was not threaded through her the way it always had been. She felt no immediate expectation, no corrective pressure shaping her intent before she could finish forming it.

For the first time since she had accepted his mark, her thoughts reached the end of themselves without being interrupted.

Raven exhaled shakily.

She thought of Chloe then, unbidden. The witch who still believed in balance as something chosen rather than enforced. Raven had mocked that once. She had told herself that belief was a luxury for those who had never been cornered.

Now she wondered if Chloe had simply been stronger than she was.

Arioch shifted, stone grinding softly.

Raven turned toward him more sharply than she meant to. "Don't," she said, even though he hadn't moved toward her.

Her voice echoed faintly off the walls. She hated how exposed it sounded.

Arioch went still again, obedience without judgment.

The contrast made her chest ache.

Something tugged at the edge of her awareness then. A disturbance traveled through the witch lines like a low vibration underfoot. Raven recognized the sensation from centuries-old texts and half-buried memories passed through blood.

Coven movement.

Not gathering.

Fragmentation.

"They're moving," Raven whispered. "Not together. Separately."

She understood immediately what that meant.

Anne had always been the hinge. Cruel. Precise. Unwavering. If Anne enforced, witches oriented themselves around her presence, even in defiance. Even in hatred.

Silence from someone like that was not mercy.

It was destabilization.

Anne had gone quiet.

Raven swallowed hard. "What did you do?" she asked the empty corridor, not sure whether she meant Anne or the power that had allowed it.

For the first time, a dangerous thought completed itself without interruption. *I could wait.* Not obey. Not defy. Just wait.

The realization frightened her more than any punishment ever had. Waiting meant choosing not to move when movement was expected. Waiting meant holding information. Raven knew exactly how that ended for people like her: dispensable, removed when convenient.

She thought of Malakai then, chained and furious and still refusing to break. Thought of Marcus standing alone where no one else would. Thought of Zaraquel, light stripped and reshaped by hands that claimed to know better.

Raven closed her eyes.

"I'm not ready," she said quietly to no one and everyone. "I'm not brave enough to turn."

The mark pulsed once, faint and unreadable, then settled again. No punishment followed.

Raven opened her eyes. "Then I'll hesitate," she decided. "And let that be enough for tonight."

Arioch remained where he was as Raven turned away from the corridor and chose a path that led neither deeper into command nor outward into defiance. Somewhere far away, witches were making choices that would not be forgiven. Somewhere closer, silence was being mistaken for safety.

Raven walked on, carrying the weight of a decision she had not yet made, and understood with cold clarity that the turning had already begun.

Tabitha Ward, Seattle, Night

Tabitha did not believe in forgiveness. She believed in leverage.

Mary slept badly. That was the first thing Tabitha noticed once the silence settled into her bones. Tabitha lay awake on the narrow bed across the room, eyes open, breathing shallow, listening to the uneven rhythm of Mary's sleep and the softer sound beneath it. The baby lay there awake, not crying and not moving. Tabitha thought that was the most dangerous state of all.

Her power had been taken cleanly. Tabitha still remembered the moment with perfect clarity: the wrong warmth, the brief vertigo. Mary's hands had been steady and apologetic, as if that made the theft righteous, as if intention mattered more than outcome. It had not hurt enough to kill her. That was the cruelty of it.

Tabitha flexed her fingers slowly. There was no answering pull from the currents she once commanded. No hum in her bones. Only a thin echo, like standing in a room where music had just stopped. She had learned quickly what that meant. Power was still near. Close enough to taste. Just not hers.

The Tall Dark Man had sent her here to watch, to report, to endure. He had not promised restoration. He had promised relevance. Tabitha had accepted because relevance was survival. But relevance without power was just another word for expendable.

She turned her head slightly and studied Mary in the dim light. Mary's face looked softer in sleep. Younger. Less haunted. That was the problem. Mary believed she had been forgiven, that the world had rewritten her sins because she had a child now. Tabitha almost laughed.

The mark on Tabitha's inner wrist warmed faintly, not in warning and not in command. Just awareness. The Tall Dark Man was not watching closely tonight. His attention was stretched thin. Witches were moving. Lines were breaking. He trusted Mary because Mary was useful. He trusted Tabitha because she was quiet.

He had never understood what quiet people did when they were left alone too long.

Tabitha slid from the bed without a sound. She did not reach for a blade. She did not need one. What she needed was proximity.

She moved to the crib and looked down at the child. Elijah's face was slack with sleep, mouth parted, one small fist curled against his chest. He was warm. Real. Anchored.

Tabitha felt the echo in her bones respond to that anchor with a low, aching pull.

So that's where you put it, she thought. Clever.

Mary stirred, murmured something unintelligible, then settled again. Tabitha did not flinch. Fear wasted energy.

She placed one hand lightly on the edge of the crib, the other against her own sternum, and reached. Not with a spell and not with words, but with intent sharpened into focus. She did not ask for her power back. She claimed it.

The air tightened. The echo inside her flared, thin at first, then stronger as it recognized itself. Tabitha felt the familiar burn return, threading through muscle and marrow, reasserting ownership.

Somewhere in the room, Mary gasped in her sleep, breathing hard enough to wake herself.

"No," Mary whispered, eyes flying open. "No, wait—"

Tabitha turned slowly.

Mary sat up, clutching her chest, eyes wide with dawning comprehension. She could feel it now. The loss. The reversal. The child whimpered softly, unsettled by the shift, but did not cry.

Tabitha whispered where no one else could hear, "That was mercy, bitch."

"You took what wasn't yours," Tabitha said calmly. "I'm taking it back."

Mary shook her head, tears already spilling, hands outstretched as if pleading could undo physics. "He'll kill you," she said. "You don't understand what I'm holding together."

Tabitha smiled then. It was small and precise.

"I understand exactly," she replied. "You were holding it together with my blood."

She stepped back as Mary collapsed inward, scrambling, already diminished, already reaching for a protection that was no longer there.

Tabitha felt whole again. Whole. The difference mattered.

She did not stay to finish it. Death was unnecessary. Mary's usefulness had just expired. That was enough.

As Tabitha slipped into the night, power settling back into her bones with familiar intimacy, she made no vow and felt no guilt. Betrayal was not a moral act. It was a correction.

Somewhere far away, witches were choosing sides. Somewhere closer, silence was being mistaken for safety.

Tabitha did not intend to be either.

She intended to survive.

CHAPTER 25

INHERITANCE

The Tall Dark Man, The Underground, Present Night

He did not feel the betrayals as wounds. Wounds implied surprise, pain, or loss. This was none of those things. This was variance. Difference.

The Underground remained intact. The geometry held. The old spells did not fracture or scream. That was how he knew the problem was not structural. Not yet. It was behavioral.

He stood at the center of the chamber where the stone still remembered fire, hands folded loosely behind his back, long coat draped around him, his attention turned inward toward the lattice of bloodlines and obligations that had governed the world for centuries.

Threads shifted. Some loosened. One snapped entirely and did not reattach.

Anne.

Not her death. Not her absence.

Her inefficiency.

Silence had spread outward from her position, not as obedience but as drift. Commands were delayed. Enforcement softened. Fear misplaced. He had tolerated much from her over the years because she understood necessity and because she never confused cruelty with indulgence. But silence was not restraint when it came from a tool designed to speak. Silence was abandonment of function.

He traced the consequence without touching it. Witches were no longer behaving as a body. They were behaving as individuals. That was always the beginning of collapse. Systems failed when fear stopped being shared.

Tabitha's correction registered next. Not as defiance, but as reclamation.

He allowed himself the briefest consideration of that choice before discarding it. Tabitha had been quiet for too long. Quiet people eventually remembered what they were owed. That was not a flaw. It was predictable.

Anne, however, had miscalculated.

She believed herself essential.

He did not turn when the infernal channels withdrew from her. There was no need to watch. The Mother of Devils did not cease to be. The permission that routed creation through her simply ended.

Devils would still rise. They would just no longer arrive ordered, shaped, or taught to wait.

Chaos was not a punishment. It was an adjustment.

Anne would understand that shortly.

Or she would not.

Either way, her usefulness was concluded.

He shifted his attention next to Tituba.

That thread remained taut. Human. Annoyingly resilient. He had accounted for her survival from the moment the Hunter drew breath. Covenants made with blood always left residue. Tituba was that residue. She could not be erased without cost. Not yet.

So he moved her instead.

Distance was kinder than death and far more effective. Containment replaced proximity. Voice was replaced with silence. Influence was removed without severing life.

He felt her awareness of the removal now, the sharp recognition of someone who understood exactly what was being done to them.

He approved of that.

Ignorance dulled suffering. Understanding refined it.

The Hunter reacted.

That was unexpected.

No movement. No rebellion. Pain. Raw and immediate, unfiltered by command or prophecy. It crossed the bond not as information but as sensation, sudden enough to stagger him for half a breath.

Maternal pain. Untaught. Unshaped. A consequence transmitted without permission.

Interesting.

He cataloged it quickly, already adjusting his expectations.

The Hunter did not act. He did not reach. He did not defy. He simply absorbed it and went still, his presence tightening rather than expanding.

That was not submission.

That was not obedience either.

The Tall Dark Man allowed the moment to pass.

Anne was finished. Tituba was contained. Witches were no longer reliable. The world had grown noisier, less efficient, and therefore more honest.

He turned his attention to where it now belonged.

To the angel.

Zaraquel remained silent, bound by her own understanding of consequences. She had chosen restraint, believing it preserved something worth saving. She would learn, as all angels eventually did, that restraint only delayed ownership.

The board had shifted. Enforcement removed. Mothers sidelined. Tools reassigned.

The next structure would not be built from fear or obedience.

It would be built from union.

He smiled faintly, already certain of the outcome.

The bride was no longer a question of if.

Anne, The Witch's Cottage,
Present Night

Anne felt absence first.

Not pain. Not resistance.

Absence had always come before punishment.

She stood alone in the inner chamber where her sigils had never failed her, hands resting lightly on the stone altar that had answered her voice for centuries. The wards were still there. The symbols still burned faintly in their grooves.

Everything looked correct.

That was the problem.

She spoke a single word. Not a command. Just a test.

The shadows did not bend. Nothing answered.

Anne frowned, a small, precise movement that had once been enough to make lesser witches falter.

She tried again, sharper this time, letting intent edge the sound.

The chamber remained unchanged.

For the first time in longer than she could remember, Anne felt her own weight.

She drew a slow breath and reached inward toward the familiar conduit that had always responded when she required it.

There was no resistance.

There was also no connection.

It was as if the structure had been quietly rerouted around her, leaving her standing inside an intact shell that no longer belonged to her.

"No," she said softly.

She had worked too hard for this to be an accident. She had been precise. Loyal and efficient. She had broken witches who needed breaking and preserved those who still served a purpose. She had understood restraint. She had understood silence.

The realization arrived without drama and without mercy.

Silence had not been restraint.

Silence had been delay.

Delay had become drift.

Drift had become variance.

It flowed together completely.

She had mistaken patience for indispensability.

Anne straightened, spine stiff with pride that had never learned how to kneel.

Somewhere beyond her chamber, she felt the infernal lattice still functioning, still producing, still feeding the world what it demanded. Devils were being born. Contracts were being honored. Chaos was spreading exactly as it always had.

Just not through her.

The Mother of Devils had not been destroyed.

She had been bypassed.

Anne's fingers curled slowly against the stone.

There was no fury in her now. Fury was useless without leverage.

There was only a cold, narrowing clarity.

She had been a structure, not a source. Enforcement, not law. A tool.

And tools, when worn, were set aside.

She stood alone as the truth finished settling around her, understanding at last that there would be no summons, no correction, no explanation offered.

Not because she was hated.

But because she was finished.

He was finished with her.

Anne did not scream. She did not beg.

Those were the sounds of people who still believed they were being heard.

The chamber remained silent.

Tituba, The Underground,
Present Night

Tituba woke knowing she had been moved.

Not dragged. Not carried.

Moved the way objects were moved when they were still useful but no longer important.

The chamber was smaller than the one she had occupied before, narrower, the stone closer to her skin. The light was wrong. It did not flicker or breathe. It was pale and steady, denying time its usual softness.

She sat up slowly, a hand pressed to her chest.

The first thing she reached for was not fear.

It was him.

The bond answered, and it nearly dropped her to her knees.

Pain surged through her without shape or warning, sharp enough to steal her breath, deep enough to feel ancient.

It was not her pain alone.

She knew that instantly.

This was something being *shared*, something crossing the bond sideways, stripped of command and intention.

She tasted iron and salt and something colder beneath it.

"My son," she whispered.

There was no echo. No voice answered her. The Underground remained silent and dim.

She pressed her palm to the stone floor and tried to ground herself, tried to reach again more carefully, the way she had learned to do when he was still small and the bond was fragile.

The connection held. That was the cruelty of it. It had not been severed. It had been tightened, compressed until sensation traveled faster than meaning.

Tituba understood then what had been done. Not death. Just pure containment and distance. They had taken her *position*, not her life. Her nearness. Her ability to soften what passed between the Tall Dark Man and the Hunter. She had been allowed to remain alive only because blood remembered too much to be discarded cleanly, and parental bonds remained.

She laughed once, low and broken. "You never could stand witnesses," she murmured to the stone.

The pain surged again, stronger this time, and she knew he felt it now. Not as a message, but as a raw sensation, unshaped and unfiltered by prophecy. She clutched at her ribs as if she could pull the feeling back into herself, as if she could keep it from reaching him.

"I'm here," she said, louder now. "You hear me. You feel me."

The bond tightened in response. It was only recognition.

Tituba closed her eyes, letting the pain settle into something she could endure. She had survived worse. She had survived centuries of being used, named, rewritten. This was not new. What was new was the knowledge that the Tall Dark Man had miscalculated something small and human. Pain taught faster than command. Somewhere beyond the walls, her son was learning what it meant to feel without permission, to absorb suffering without instruction, and to remain still not because he was ordered to, but because he chose to hold it.

Tituba pressed her forehead to the stone and breathed through the ache.

"That's it," she whispered, not knowing whether he could hear the words or only the intent behind them. "Hold it. Don't give it back yet."

The Underground remained silent. But for the first time since his birth, the silence did not belong entirely to the Tall Dark Man.

The Hunter, The Underground,
Present Night

He did not scream. That was the first failure.

The pain arrived without warning, without shape, without instruction. It tore through him sideways, not like an order and not like a vision, but like something real breaking inside flesh that had only recently learned how to feel. His body jerked against the restraints before his mind caught up, chains ringing once, sharp and loud in the chamber. Stone bit into his back.

His breath tore out of him in a sound that did not yet know how to be a word.

Then he went still.

But the pain did not stop. It deepened. It carried weight. Memory. A familiarity that did not belong to him but knew him anyway. His hands curled slowly, fingers digging into his palms hard enough that skin split and dark blood welled, hot and bright. He watched it run without reacting. That surprised him. He had been taught to react.

Mother.

The word surfaced without permission, without command. It was not given to him. He did not reach for it. It simply rose, fully formed, and lodged itself behind his teeth like a blade he did not yet know how to wield.

"Stop," he said hoarsely.

The word echoed wrong in the chamber. Nothing answered.

The pain surged again, sharper now, focused. He felt it in his ribs, in his spine, in the places where bone met something older than bone. He understood then that it was not meant to shape him. It was meant to pass through him. To teach him endurance through saturation.

That was the mistake.

He did not push it back. He did not offer it up. Instead, he held on to it. The chains creaked as his body adjusted, shoulders settling instead of straining. His breathing slowed deliberately, uneven at first, then measured. Each inhale dragged the pain deeper instead of letting it spill outward. His jaw clenched. A low sound escaped him, half breath, half restraint.

"I feel her," he said.

The words were not loud. They did not need to be. They were not meant for the Tall Dark Man. They were meant for the bond that made them blood and consequence.

The pain answered immediately, flaring hotter, more insistent. He let his head fall back against the stone, eyes burning, vision fracturing at the edges. For a moment, something almost like anger flickered through him. Not toward the source. Toward the system that had decided pain was a tool instead of a consequence.

"Good," he whispered, his voice breaking on the word. That was the second failure. Pain was not supposed to be welcomed.

Something shifted then, subtle but real. The pain changed shape, no longer sharp, no longer clean. It became dense, heavy, something that could be carried instead of endured. He felt it settle into him the way weight settles into muscle over time, altering balance without asking permission.

He exhaled slowly.

The Tall Dark Man's presence brushed against him, testing. The Hunter did not look for it. He did not react to it. He remained where he was, blood running freely now from his palms, breathing steadily, eyes open and focused on nothing.

When he spoke again, his voice was different. Not stronger. Quieter.

"She's still alive," he said.

There was no question about it.

Silence followed. And for the first time since his awakening, the Hunter understood that pain could be a language no one had taught him to speak, and that meant it belonged to him.

He closed his eyes and held it. Not forever, but just long enough.

CHAPTER 26

THE MOMENT OF CHOICE

The Tall Dark Man, Where
Zaraquel Is Held, Present Night

The parchment lay open across the stone table where he had studied it a thousand times before, its edges brittle, its ink darkened by centuries of handling. Blood had been used in its making. That much he had always respected. Blood remembered the truth even when a prophecy lied by omission.

He read the lines again, slower this time, not for meaning but for what was missing. There were the births. There were bloodlines. There were the unions and the betrayals he himself had authored and corrected and repeated across centuries. There was an angel. There was the bride. There was a fire that would not be extinguished.

What there was not—what had never been written—was *this*.

No passage accounted for witches who delayed instead of obeyed. No margin note warned of tools that mistook silence for restraint. No line acknowledged maternal bonds persisting where control should have erased them.

He closed his hand over the parchment, fingers tightening just enough to crease the page.

"Inefficient," he said aloud.

The Dark Prophecy had never been wrong about outcome. But it had always underestimated resistance that came without rebellion. Endurance without dominion, or pain without direction, were not variables prophecy handled well.

Anne's name did not appear anywhere on the page. That omission no longer irritated him. Her relevance had already been corrected. Tituba appeared only once, referenced as a vessel, not a variable. That, too, was a miscalculation, but one he could still manage. The Hunter was mentioned only obliquely. A continuation. A shadow of a shadow.

He turned the parchment slightly, scanning the final section again. The section was devoted to the angel.

Zaraquel.

Her role was clear. Her function was precise. Her surrender was inevitable.

What the prophecy did not account for was *delay*.

He exhaled slowly and folded the parchment with care. Anger was useless when correction was required. He did not tear the page. He did not burn it. He set it aside.

Then he stood.

The Underground did not resist him. It never had. Wards did not fail as he moved. They adjusted.

When he arrived where Zaraquel was bound, he did not announce himself. He did not need to. The restraints that held her did not break. He looked at her then, not as a conqueror and not as a god, but as an architect correcting a flaw that had been allowed to persist too long.

"The prophecy never mentioned hesitation," he said calmly. "That was my mistake. Not yours."

He stepped closer.

"Even angels run out of time."

Zaraquel, Where She Is Bound,
Present Night

Time did not stop when he said it. That was the lie she had still been holding onto. Somewhere inside her, something had believed that if she delayed long enough, the world would hesitate with her, that it would wait. Instead, everything kept moving, and she was the only thing standing still.

Even angels run out of time.

The words did not resonate. They did not need to. They lodged themselves inside her chest and began to burn outward, not like fire but like something corrosive eating through her flesh.

Her light reacted before she could. It flared hard and wrong, slamming into the limits that held her, spilling sideways instead of rising. Pain followed immediately, sharp and humiliating. Not the pain of punishment, but the pain of loss of control.

She dragged in a breath that felt too shallow to be useful.

He was gone. She knew that without looking. His presence had receded the way certainty did when it finished what it came to do. What remained was not silence.

Bride.

The word rose unbidden, and she hated how easily it fit, how neatly it slid into the spaces she had been guarding. She pressed her hands against the restraints, not to break them but to feel something solid, something that still answered her effort, something that showed her she hadn't lost all control yet.

The stone beneath her palms was warm now, heat bleeding into it from her light whether she wanted it to or not. A hairline fracture crept along the surface, and she jerked her hands back as if burned.

Stop, she told herself. *Hold it.*

But her light did not listen to her the way it once had. It pulsed erratically, bright then dim, as if it no longer trusted her to know what to do with it. That frightened her more than his words had. Power slipping was one thing. Power deciding on its own was another.

She thought of her mother. The image came sharp and immediate, her mother's face drawn tight with restraint, grief turned into structure because that was how witches survived. Zaraquel felt the pull of that bond weaken slightly, like a thread fraying under too much tension. It wasn't severed, at least not yet, but no longer reliable or constant.

If I refuse, she thought, and the thought completed itself without her permission, *this is what happens to her.*

Marcus followed, just as unbidden. Her father's fury, his refusal to bend even when it broke him. She felt the echo of that fury stir in her blood and recoiled from it. Rage would not save anyone. Rage was exactly what he expected.

Amber's fire burned next in her awareness, deeper now, more predatory. The Queen was already moving toward something she had sworn she would never claim. Zaraquel understood that with sudden clarity. The cost of her refusal would not be abstract. It would be paid in pieces of the people who loved her.

Her light surged again, uncontrolled, and this time the restraint did not merely strain. It cracked. A sharp sound split the air as stone fractured behind her, a jagged scar spreading outward like a wound.

Zaraquel cried out despite herself and immediately bit the sound off, ashamed of it.

This was the first time she understood what he meant.

Not a bride as a reward, but a bride as containment.

The Avenging Angel role had always required balance, restraint, distance. She felt that slipping now, not because she had chosen otherwise, but because exhaustion had eroded the space where choice used to live. Love was the pressure point. It always had been.

"I don't want this," she whispered to no one.

The words felt small and insignificant.

Her light dimmed suddenly, not extinguished but pulled inward so hard it made her dizzy. She sagged against the restraints, breath shaking, vision blurring at the edges.

Delay had been her last defense. Now even that had been taken from her.

Zaraquel closed her eyes and held herself still, not because she was ready, but because there was nowhere left to retreat. Time had not stopped. It had simply moved past her.

The Hunter, The Underground,
Present Night

The pain came first. It felt sudden and wrong, dropping through him like a collapsed ceiling. His body reacted before thought, muscles locking hard enough that the chains bit deep, iron screaming once as stone anchors shifted under the strain. The sound echoed sharp and ugly through the chamber.

He did not cry out. He bent forward instead, shoulders rounding, breath sawing out of him in short, controlled pulls.

The pain was not his. He knew that immediately. It carried direction, memory, and something rawer than fear.

It was her.

The bond flared hot and uneven, no longer filtered, no longer guided. Zaraquel's distress hit him sideways, not as image or prophecy, but as rupture. Something breaking under pressure that had been held too long. His jaw clenched hard enough that his teeth ground.

"Enough," he said, low and hoarse.

Nothing answered.

The Tall Dark Man's presence was there, vast and watchful, but distant. He didn't intervene or try to control. The Hunter felt that distance as clearly as the chains around his wrists.

The pain surged again, and this time he understood the lesson it was meant to teach him.

Endure. Absorb. Remain aligned.

He did none of those things.

He didn't let it pass through him. Instinct pulled it inward instead. His breathing slowed deliberately, each inhale dragging the sensation deeper, compacting it instead of dispersing it. His muscles adjusted around the restraints, not fighting them but learning their limits. One of the chains shifted but held firmly. That surprised him. He felt something *give*, not break.

Another wave hit, and this time it carried clarity.

She will be taken.

The knowledge settled without drama. Without argument. Zaraquel's fate was no longer conditional. The structure of it was already in motion. He tasted blood and realized he had bitten through his lip.

"No," he said, quieter now.

The word was not rebellion. It was refusal without movement. Acceptance of consequence without consent.

The Tall Dark Man's attention sharpened briefly, brushing against him like a hand testing a blade's edge.

The Hunter did not look up. He did not strain. He held the pain where it was, dense and burning, and let it change him instead of shaping him.

"She's still alive," he said.

The Hunter leaned back against the stone, breathing steadily now, blood running warm down his chin, hands clenched tight enough to shake.

He understood something then that no one had taught him. Pain could be carried.

And anything that could be carried could be used.

Amber Stone, Oʻahu, Night

Amber felt it before the island reacted. Her mark burned once beneath her skin, not flaring, not awakening, but tightening, as if something had just been claimed without asking permission.

She stayed where she stood. The night around them remained intact. The ocean did not surge. The land did not cry out. That was how she knew it was real. The gods did not announce inevitability. They waited for mortals to notice they were already too late.

Chloe was beside her, quiet, focused inward, her magic drawn tight like a wire under strain. Amber did not speak. She did not reach for the mirror resting where it had been placed, wrapped and patient. She did not need confirmation.

He had moved.

Not through threat. Not through force. Through proximity.

The Tall Dark Man had stopped arranging the board and stepped onto it.

Amber felt the consequences ripple outward immediately, pressure traveling through old covenants and newer promises alike. Diplomacy had ended without anyone declaring it finished.

Her fire shifted in response, not rising but sharpening. It felt heavier now, more deliberate. Less like something she wielded and more like something that was learning how to wield her.

Illyris stirred beneath it, not speaking, not pushing. Just present. Waiting to be acknowledged.

"This is not a warning," Amber said quietly, more to herself than to Chloe. "It's already in motion."

She turned her head then, finally looking at the witch beside her. Chloe's face had gone pale, her attention pulled far beyond the shoreline, far beyond anything Amber could see. The bond between mother and daughter was not something Amber had ever pretended to understand. But she could feel it strain now, the way one feels a bridge tremble before it fails.

Her jaw tightened.

The demon realm pressed faintly at the edge of her awareness, not calling yet, but no longer silent. She had delayed that door for as long as she could. She had told herself there would be a right moment, a cleaner need, a justification that felt less like surrender.

That moment was gone.

Amber did not say it aloud. She did not need to. The Queen did not announce decisions that had already been made by the shape of the world itself. She took a slow breath she did not require and let the fire settle deeper into her bones.

***

Chloe Tudor, O'ahu, Night

Chloe felt Zaraquel before she understood what had changed. The bond did not snap. That would have been easier. It thinned instead, stretched into something fragile and unreliable, like thread drawn too fine to hold weight much longer.

Chloe's breath caught painfully in her chest as the realization hit, sharp and undeniable. He had reached her.

It was the kind of reach that made resistance feel like harm to everyone else instead of defiance.

Her magic responded instinctively, flaring once before she could rein it in. The ground beneath her feet warmed in answer, mana stirring uneasily as if unsure which authority it was meant to obey. Chloe forced it back, jaw clenched, hands curling at her sides.

"No," she whispered.

The Avenging Angel role had always depended on distance. On Zaraquel being able to stand apart from consequence long enough to judge it. Chloe felt that space collapsing now, not because Zaraquel had chosen wrong, but because exhaustion had eaten at her and allowed her to make the choice.

If she refuses, Chloe thought, and the truth arrived fully formed, merciless and precise, *they will still take her.* Just not as she is.

Her stomach twisted violently.

This was not the kind of prophecy witches prepared for. There was no spell to counter inevitability. No ward against love used as leverage.

Chloe had sworn, generations ago, never to repeat Elizabeth Hexham's mistake. She would never confuse survival with obedience or believe that compliance could be called protection.

And yet here it was.

Neutrality had been her last defense. That illusion burned away in her chest, leaving something colder and far more dangerous behind.

"We don't have time anymore," Chloe said aloud, her voice steady despite the ache tearing through her. "If we hesitate now, we become part of it."

Amber did not argue. She didn't need to. The Queen already knew what this meant.

Chloe turned slightly toward her, not seeking permission, not asking for reassurance. Just acknowledging alignment.

"I won't wait for agreement," Chloe continued. "Not from the covens. Not from the old laws. Not from anyone who still believes delay is mercy."

Her magic shifted as she spoke, no longer contained neatly within her skin. It bled outward, thin and sharp, testing the edges of something she had never dared to cross before.

The line did not resist her.

That frightened her more than opposition ever could.

Chloe closed her eyes briefly and felt the truth settle fully into place.

This was no longer about stopping the Tall Dark Man. It was about deciding how much of her daughter would be left when the world was finished taking its due.

CHAPTER 27

THE LINE THAT HOLDS

Marcus, Oʻahu, Before Dawn

The Order did not resist his leaving. He felt the pull of magic aligning with the decision he had already made, and that was how he knew the choice had already been accepted. No wards tightened. No bells sounded. The wolves did not stir from their resting places, though Sabre lifted his head once, eyes tracking Marcus across the threshold, then rose without command to follow.

There were no goodbyes. There never were for positions like this.

He crossed the boundary between spaces and let the distance collapse. Vampire speed had always been violence disguised as movement. Tonight, it was restraint sharpened into precision.

He did not tear through the world. He moved through it cleanly, folding air and dark around himself until the ocean rose beneath him and the islands resolved out of the night like memory returning to bone.

Hawaii did not welcome him. It did not reject him either. The land recognized the choice. That was all.

Marcus slowed as his boots touched stone, breath steady, senses wide and controlled. He could feel the heat rising from the ground. Pele stirred somewhere deep, not restless, not angry, but awake with the kind of awareness that measured rather than reacted.

Sabre landed beside him without sound, massive body settling into stillness at Marcus's flank, head low, eyes alert. The bond between them had not changed. That alone anchored him more than anything else could have.

Voices carried ahead. Not raised. Not chanting. A gathering that understood silence as structure rather than absence. Marcus did not step into it. He stopped at the edge of the space where stone met open ground and waited, because this was not his place to interrupt.

Kawika stood at the center, barefoot, spine straight, his family ringed loosely around him. The god's figure loomed beyond them, carved and patient, receiving without reaction. Marcus watched without judgment. He understood the shape of what was being done. Not power taken, but responsibility accepted. The land held its breath and did not object.

Amber stood just beyond the circle. Marcus did not look at her immediately. He did not need to. Her fire pressed against his awareness the way gravity pressed against muscle, present, undeniable, yet controlled by will rather than impulse. It had changed, deepened, less forgiving than it had once been. He felt the edge of it register him and hold without striking.

Malakai stood near her, not touching, not retreating. Present in the way wolves were present when territory no longer mattered. Marcus felt the echo of recognition there too, clean and unsentimental.

Philip was farther back, posture deceptively relaxed, eyes sharp with the kind of attention forged by centuries of war and survival. Marcus felt the Serpent's awareness brush against him once through Philip and withdraw, unsettled.

None of them spoke.

The ritual ended without signal. The family loosened, breath returning in small increments, and the land eased just enough to be noticed by those who knew how to listen.

That was when Marcus stepped forward.

He stopped beside Amber, a measured distance away, Sabre settling at his other side without instruction. The wolf did not bare his teeth. He did not bow his head. He simply stayed silent.

Marcus felt eyes turn toward him. He did not meet them all. He did not need to. His presence was enough. He had not come to claim ground. He had come to stand where it mattered.

"This is where it turns," he said quietly.

The words were not prophecy. They were simple acknowledgment and acceptance.

Amber inclined her head once. "It already has."

No one challenged him. No one welcomed him.

The sky above them began to pale, not brightening, just loosening at the edges, dawn pressing against the night without permission to enter yet. Marcus felt the weight of it settle deeper into his bones. He remained where he was. Not as a king, not as a savior, not even as a man seeking forgiveness, but only as the line that would hold. That line was something he accepted that there was no going back.

***

Chloe Tudor, Oʻahu, Before Dawn

Chloe felt the gathering before she fully registered it, the pressure in the air easing the way it always did after something irrevocable had been accepted by the land. The night had loosened, just barely, dawn pressing at its edges without being allowed in yet.

She stood where she had been standing for most of it, just beyond the circle, hands loose at her sides, power drawn inward and tight. Amber was near her. Not touching, but close enough to be felt and secure.

Her witch power gave her a sense of foreboding, but she wasn't looking for Marcus. Her attention was on the ground, on the way the warmth beneath her feet had shifted, on the subtle recalibration of mana that told her the island had acknowledged something it did not intend to interfere with.

It was only when the ritual was released, when people's breath returned in small, careful increments, that she lifted her gaze.

She saw him.

He stood at the edge of the area, exactly where someone would stand who did not intend to be welcomed. He was unmoved by the eyes that had turned toward him and then away again. Sabre was at his side, massive and silent, the wolf's presence so steady it hurt to look at.

For a heartbeat, Chloe's mind offered her the comfort of familiarity. Marcus looked like Marcus, with his dark hair and controlled posture, that same contained stillness that had always fooled people into underestimating him.

Then the comfort fell apart.

It wasn't something she could name immediately. There was no visible wound, no overt change she could point to. It was absence, the way rooms felt after furniture had been removed and your body still expected to bump into it. Marcus occupied the area differently now. He wasn't leaning toward anything. He wasn't reaching, even unconsciously. He simply stood.

Chloe didn't move.

She watched the way no one approached him. The way Amber acknowledged him without stepping closer. The way Malakai stayed where he was. The way Philip observed from a distance that suggested recognition without invitation.

This wasn't avoidance. It was instinct.

People gave dangerous things room. People gave immovable things room.

Her chest tightened, and only then did she let herself reach.

She didn't push. She didn't demand. She touched the bond the way she always had, carefully, intimately, trusting that it would meet her halfway.

It answered.

The connection didn't recoil. It didn't break. It simply flattened, like a presence without warmth, awareness without pull. Marcus was there in the same way the horizon was there; real, undeniable, unreachable. No hunger. No ache. No echo of the domestic, human mess they had built together.

Chloe sucked in a breath that stung as it passed her throat.

This is what he did, she thought.

Amber shifted slightly beside her, close enough now that Chloe could feel her heat without being touched. The Queen didn't speak. She didn't explain. She didn't soften what Chloe was seeing. She stood witness and nothing more.

Chloe hated her for that and loved her for it in equal measure.

She stepped forward. Not fast, not dramatic, but just enough to cross the invisible line between watcher and participant. The ground beneath her feet warmed in response, mana stirring uneasily and then settling again, as if recognizing that whatever authority Chloe carried still belonged to her, even if the thing she wanted most did not.

Marcus turned before she reached him.

Their eyes met.

For a moment, Chloe had the irrational urge to laugh. To say something small and stupid. To ask if he'd eaten. To complain about the humidity. The words crowded her mouth and died there, useless.

Marcus opened his mouth first.

"Chloe," he said.

Her name sounded the same. That was the problem. It landed between them and failed to bridge the space it used to cross so easily.

Chloe felt the finality of it settle in her bones, heavy and precise. She stopped a few feet from him. The bond remained still. The wolf did not move.

The dawn did not arrive.

Chloe understood then, with a clarity that hurt worse than rage ever could, that whatever came next, whatever she chose to say or do, would not restore what had been altered. This was not a moment she could negotiate her way out of. Neutrality had already collapsed behind her.

She said nothing.

And in that silence, the world finished changing.

Philip II of Macedon, Oʻahu,
Before Dawn

Philip had watched men become legends in the span of a single hour. He had watched others become cautions without ever drawing a blade. This moment was neither. It was quieter than victory and heavier than defeat, and that was how he knew it mattered.

The ritual ended without anyone calling it finished. The family ring loosened the way a fist loosens after it has already decided not to strike. Breath returned in small increments. The land eased just enough to be noticed by those who listened to it.

Philip listened.

You did not survive kingship by ignoring the ground under your feet.

Marcus stood at the edge of it all like a boundary that had learned to take human shape. No crown. Sabre at his side, massive and still, a sentinel without ceremony. Philip felt the Serpent under his own skin react the way it reacted to cliffs and storms: restless, then wary, then quiet. It did not like what it could not dominate.

Chloe approached Marcus slowly, the way a woman approaches a husband she has walked toward a thousand times and still fails to recognize at the last step. Philip did not need the bond to tell him it had changed.

Amber remained near Chloe without touching her. That was restraint, not coldness. Queens did not reach for what they could not afford to break.

Malakai held his position near Amber, present in the way wolves were present when territory no longer mattered.

Philip's gaze swept the gathering and cataloged posture, distance, silence. None of it was accidental. Instinct had arranged them around Marcus the way water arranged itself around stone.

Marcus turned before Chloe reached him. Their eyes met. Philip saw Chloe's shoulders tighten as if her body remembered warmth that no longer lived where it should.

Marcus said her name once.

It sounded normal.

That was the cruelty of it.

Philip's pulse did not quicken. His body did not need to panic anymore. Panic was for mortals who believed outcomes still depended on pleading.

He watched Chloe stop a few feet from Marcus and understood, with clarity, that no sentence spoken here would return what had been altered. The thing between them had not died. It had been repurposed.

Philip shifted his stance, stepping forward just enough so that the others could feel him entering the moment rather than hovering outside it. Heads turned. Silence tightened. Even the aunties at the edge of the gathering went still, as if the island itself had asked them to listen.

Philip looked at Marcus, then at Chloe, then at Amber. He did not soften his face. Softness created hope, and hope could become a weapon. He had spent a lifetime learning the cost of false hope.

"He has crossed," Philip said quietly.

No one answered.

Philip had seen too many wars begin because people refused to name what had already happened.

Chloe did not look away from Marcus. Her hands were loose at her sides, but Philip saw the tension in her fingers, the effort it took not to reach him the way she used to. That restraint told Philip exactly how much she loved him, and exactly what she feared she would find if she touched the bond too hard.

Philip kept his voice steady.

"Not into power. Not into dominion. Into position."

Amber's eyes narrowed slightly, not in disagreement but in calculation. Malakai's gaze flicked once toward Marcus, then back to the horizon, as if already measuring what would come next.

Philip's throat tightened, surprising him. Emotion had never been his weakness. Sentiment had been. There was a difference.

He did not let sentiment in.

He spoke anyway, and what came out was not confession and not comfort. It was record.

"I was offered that choice once," Philip said. "Not by gods. Not by prophecy. By consequence."

His jaw flexed once.

"I did not take it."

The words landed harder than any boast could have. Kings confessed rarely. When they did, it was never for absolution.

Philip's gaze returned to Marcus.

"He did."

Chloe's breath hitched, small and involuntary, and she pressed her lips together as if swallowing sound itself.

Philip did not pity her. Pity was useless. He respected her because she was still standing.

He turned his head slightly, addressing the shape of the gathering without making any one person responsible for holding it.

"If you expect him to be thanked," Philip said, "you will fail him. If you expect him to be forgiven, you will break yourselves trying."

The Serpent under Philip's skin stirred, as if the word *forgiven* offended it. Philip kept his hands still. He did not indulge the curse with movement.

"This," he said, nodding once toward Marcus without making him a spectacle, "is not heroism. This is structure."

Philip let the silence hold for a breath.

"The Tall Dark Man will adapt," Philip continued. "He always does. He will not attack this directly."

Philip's eyes moved to Amber then, the Queen whose fire carried islands now.

"He will attack what you love. He will force choices that make you hate yourselves for surviving."

Amber's expression did not shift, but Philip felt the air around her tighten, attention sharpening into readiness.

Chloe finally looked away from Marcus for the first time and met Philip's eyes. There was no gratitude there.

There was something worse.

Understanding.

Philip nodded once, acknowledging it.

Then he spoke the last part, the part that mattered for what came next.

"The battle ahead will not be won by strength," Philip said. "It will be won by purpose."

His voice lowered, not secretive but solemn.

"It will reveal everything involving bloodlines and covenants. Lies that wore holiness. It will show every creature what they truly serve when fear strips away their stories."

He glanced toward the horizon where dawn pressed thin and reluctant against the night.

"And it will be decisive," he added. "Not because you will want it to be. Because the world cannot hold this many prophecies open at once without tearing."

No one spoke. Even the birds stayed quiet.

Philip felt, in that silence, the strange shape of loss settle over the group. Not loss of life, but loss of expectation. The childish belief that sacrifices purchase peace. The illusion that doing the right thing earns safety.

He took one step back, letting the moment return to Marcus and Chloe without Philip standing between them.

He had said what needed saying.

Kings did not linger where their words could become a shield people hid behind.

Barb Jones writes supernatural thrillers rooted in prophecy, legacy, and the inevitability of consequence. She is the author of the Blood Prophecy saga, a series that examines power not as fantasy, but as inheritance.

Born in Hawaii and shaped by an oral storytelling tradition, she merges ancient myth with modern psychological conflict, building worlds where faith, bloodline, and ambition collide.

Through her writing and her work with Immortal Cravings, she remains committed to stories that leave readers changed and aware the war continues.

The Blood Prophecy Saga

Queen's Destiny

Queen's Enemy

Queen's Ascension

Rise of the Hunter

Fate of an Angel

The Heaven and Hell Series

Son of Asmodeus

Hell Hounds

Standalone Novels

The Devil Inside

Henry and Anne